Pennsylvania Love Song

A Family Story

NANCY HAYES KILGORE

BROWN POSEY PRESS

an imprint of Sunbury Press, Inc.
Mechanicsburg, PA USA

an imprint of Sunbury Press, Inc.
Mechanicsburg, PA USA

For information about special discounts for bulk purchases, please contact Sunbury Press Orders Dept. at (855) 338-8359 or orders@sunburypress.com.

To request one of our authors for speaking engagements or book signings, please contact Sunbury Press Publicity Dept. at publicity@sunburypress.com.

FIRST BROWN POSEY PRESS EDITION: September 2025

Set in Adobe Garamond Pro | Interior design by Crystal Devine | Cover by Lynn Andreozzi | Edited by Sarah Peachey.

Publisher's Cataloging-in-Publication Data
Names: Kilgore, Nancy Hayes, author.
Title: Pennsylvania love song : a family story / Nancy Hayes Kilgore.
Description: First trade paperback edition. | Mechanicsburg, PA : Brown Posey Press, 2025.
Summary: It's 1910, the dawn of the suffrage movement. Young Florence, a suffragist and musician, fights tuberculosis and struggles to choose between two suitors. In the 1940s, Flossie, the daughter she never knew, faces similar choices. Should she wait for her fiancé, who is incommunicado near Pearl Harbor, or accept the proposal of the kindly young doctor?
Identifiers: ISBN : 979-8-88819-320-4 (paperback).
Subjects: FICTION / Biographical & Autofiction | FICTION / Historical / 20th Century / General | FICTION / Romance / Historical / 20th Century.

Designed in the USA
0 1 1 2 3 5 8 13 21 34 55

For the Love of Books!

For all the descendants of
Florence Rodkey, Ernest Craighead, and
Elizabeth Whitmarsh

Prologue

OVER THE RIVER

Pittsburgh, Pennsylvania, Thanksgiving 1955

"George, slow down."

"Flossie, I don't know how you put up with this every day."

My brothers and I—ten, eight, and six—squeal and tumble in the back seat of the "woody" station wagon. Daddy's at the wheel, his temper about to boil, as Mommy's reprimands come weak and ineffectual.

In the back seat, big brother Andy takes a potshot at me; I shout and kick while K.C., the youngest, laughs.

Struggling to reclaim her authority, Mommy begins to sing, belting out the same song she sings every Thanksgiving: *Over the river and through the woods, to Grandmother's house we go.* I stop kicking and sing along, as loud as I can, to drown out my brother's teasing.

Andy tries to tickle me, something he knows I hate, and I fend him off, shouting louder. "*Over the river . . .*" Daddy joins in the song, and now the family is no longer in a station wagon driving through Pittsburgh, a soot-blackened city, its three mighty rivers churning with industry. We are in a sleigh, bundled in capes and muffs, gliding through a snow-covered forest, the two chestnut horses jumping over a babbling brook. Just like the picture in our storybook.

Outside the car window, gloomy clouds drift above the steel mill smokestacks, and the mighty Ohio River heaves and surges on this cloudy day.

The river has always been there, intrinsic in the landscape of our lives. We see it from our house on the hill, we watch the trains, the towboats, and the barges whose distant horns and whistles punctuate our soundscape. In summer we children roam its shady banks. We wade in the creek, stepping through deep green light to dig in the mud, we overturn rocks to see what's underneath, we catch salamanders and swing on grapevines. We trek to the edge of the woods, where the river flows muddy gray beneath the clouds or silver in the sun. Massive barges, iron giants, glide along the rolling waters, and on the far bank, steel mills blow their whistles and exhale a smoky haze from tall chimneys.

In the car, my mother and I belt it out: *"Over the river and through the woods."* This is our Thanksgiving song. Of course, we aren't going to go over this river, just follow it for a while.

Where does the river go? The river connects the here to the there, the now to the then. Across the river of time, the still point of then and now, I am taken back, carried by the flowing of days and years, to grandmother's house.

We turn off the highway into an old suburb of hills and leafy streets lined with Victorian homes and dark red brick houses built in the 1930s. This is Edgewood, where high on a hill sits my mother's childhood home, "the old house," and for us kids, *grandmother's house* of the song. This is where my mother grew up, raised by her grandmother, Nancy/Nannie Fulton Craighead, who died a month before I was born. And here is where our grandparents live.

We bump along the cobblestones on Lacrosse Street until the car rumbles up the rough brick driveway. This tall, gray Victorian poking up above the trees on a steep hill. Grandmother's house. We children jump out of the car and race into the kitchen.

All moss green and calico, the kitchen is warm with smells of roasting turkey, corn pudding, and cranberry sauce. Grandmommy stands at the table chopping celery as Grandaddy comes into the room, blue eyes sparkling behind rimless glasses, grinning a silly grandfather grin. He breaks out into our favorite rhyme:

Andy, Andy, Bo-bandy,
Bonanna-fanna fo-fandy

Fee fi mo-mandy
Andy!

Nancy, Nancy Bo-bancy,
Bonanna-fanna-fo-fancy,
Fee fi mo-mancy
Nancy!

Casey, Casey, Bo-bacey
Bonanna-fanna-fo-facey
Fee fi mo-macey
Casey!

We laugh, delighted to hear the rhyme for the hundredth time, too young to roll our eyes as Grandmommy does.

Now we dive into our grandmother's house routine.

First on the agenda is to run through the dining room, past the heavy old sideboard and the table set with white linen, china, and crystal, then into the living room, past the horsehair sofa and the coal stove, and up the wide stairs to the second floor. I peer into Aunt Sallie's room, bright and sunny, with two windows overlooking the valley and a luxurious Victorian bed strewn with rumpled bedsheets and elegant clothes. All evidence of Sallie's existence in a different realm, an independent and grown-up life, the life of a stylish, artistic young woman, the young woman I aspire to be one day.

"Shush!" I hush the boys. I'm standing in the hall at the glass-doored cabinet that houses Grandmommy's doll collection. Well-used baby dolls with china heads and stuffed bodies, grown-up dolls from India and Holland and Mexico, intricate costumes with embroidery and ribbons in faded satin, silk, and cotton. Little dresses, hats, saris, miniature wooden shoes, sombreros, a treasure chest of textures and colors. After dinner, Grandmommy will come up and unlock the cabinet so I can touch the dolls and hold them. K.C., standing behind me, is curious, and I tell him this is not for boys. I can run and race and compete with my brothers, but some things are just for girls. If only I had a sister, like my cousins

Ginner and Cori, Uncle Roddy's daughters. When they come to visit, we share the wonder of the doll cabinet.

And now, another race. Who can get to the banister first? Who can slide down the fastest? The wide mahogany banister, polished by generations of children's bottoms, a perfect sliding board.

We start at the landing, where the stairway turns a corner. I pause, and there it is. The portrait. A sepia photograph of a young woman in profile. A white dress, a great pile of hair, a downward gaze. An expression of contemplation or, perhaps, wistfulness.

This is our *other* grandmother. Grandaddy's first wife. The grandmother we know is down in the kitchen making dinner, but here is another grandmother, unknown and mysterious.

This old-fashioned young woman in the sepia photo wears a white lace dress, her head in profile, her features pale and delicate, her thick hair piled up in a pompadour. This ancient photo has always been here, on this wall, on this landing. Like the banister and the doll cabinet, the portrait abides, a timeless part of the household.

The woman in the photo is refined, elusive. A mystery. Who is she, really? Is this my real grandmother?

By the time I'm a teenager, I'll know that this grandmother died a day after my mother was born. That she'd had tuberculosis, and she died of "ether pneumonia" after childbirth.

I don't know much else about this Florence, whom my mother was named after. I've heard snatches of stories and witnessed my grandfather's tears when her name came up. In my mother's version, Florence was a star, a vision of perfection, a woman of brilliance and beauty and grace, a musician who could charm the whole world. The unspoken wistfulness in my mother's voice seems to say, *I could never be like her.*

Perhaps, I think, *I* am like her, my first grandmother. Maybe the genes have skipped a generation. Not like my mother, whose body sweats and who has periods and babies, and lives an ordinary life in the ordinary world. I will be more like this grandmother—ethereal, talented, beautiful. I can rise above harsh realities and adolescent humiliations because I have within me my grandmother's qualities, her power and grace. When I am defeated or rejected, discouraged or depressed, I can picture this portrait in my mind. My grandmother's essence. She picks me up, she inspires me, she leads me on to my own independent life.

♪

In later life I come to a new understanding. The ancestors are real, their lives as urgent and sensual and thoughtful as mine. I am somehow connected to them, walking this earth, smelling the verdant forest or the desert sage, feeling the same things, thinking the same thoughts, gesturing with the same gestures, and laughing the same laugh.

After the tragic death of this grandmother, my grandfather's young wife, he saved everything—all of her letters, her photographs, her journals, every ticket to every play, concert, or event they attended.

In my older years, I sort through this hodgepodge, and I discover the letters. A trove of letters from my grandmother Florence, spanning ten years—from her childhood home in Mahaffey, Pennsylvania, to her sister's home in Chicago, to a ranch in New Mexico, and then to a tuberculosis sanatorium in the Pennsylvania mountains.

What I discover in the letters is both more and less than my image of the chestnut-haired muse who occupies that pedestal in my brain.

Not a saint or a star, but a very real young woman, Florence was vibrant, passionate, full of laughter and tears, sprightly, willful, arrogant, sarcastic, hopeful, and hopeless. And doomed by her weak lungs to die young.

From my grandmother's letters, I began to extract a story. Bits and pieces came together, and I had the urge to write them down, to create a larger narrative that could span her young adult life in all its joys and tribulations. And what about my mother at that same age? What was her life like?

I decided to write both of their stories—a novel.

The next day I got to work.

chapter 1

WON'T YOU COME HOME, BILL BAILEY

Mahaffey, Pennsylvania, 1910

"Won't you come home, Bill Bailey? Won't you come home?" Florence sings and strums her mandolin. Swaying on the porch swing, plunking and picking, and from the kitchen comes a refrain of women's voices: *"Won't you come home, Bill Bailey?"*

Everyone is home. It's the last day of summer. The green vines, lush and vivid, climb the arbor beside her, their purple grapes ripe for picking. The humidity of the last weeks has evaporated, and the clouds have disappeared into blue sky. Florence lays down the mandolin and pushes the swing back with her foot. She plucks a grape from the vine, popping it into her mouth, then extracting the seeds with her fingers. She flicks the seeds onto the grass and picks another grape, then tosses it to her brother, Bert.

Bert, sitting at her feet on the porch steps, catches the grape and makes a face imitating old Mr. McCracken, the neighbor who has just peered at them from the sidewalk.

Florence laughs and chokes on a grape skin.

In the kitchen behind her, Mama is fixing the picnic lunch with Florence's sisters. "The cucumbers *beside* the radishes," Edith commands in her clear voice. Edith, the eldest of eight, takes charge of organizing everything, as usual, and Mama, thankful for the help, complies.

Florence picks another grape and bites into it, holding a hand under her chin to protect her white dress. She sighs, gazing out across the grass and through the trees to the street. "We'll all be gone soon. You to Ann Arbor, me to Pittsburgh, Edith to Chicago . . . It's just not the same anymore."

This is her home, this big old farmhouse on East Main Street, the house of six sisters and one brother, the home where they've played and laughed and sung. Yes, Florence loves them all, but she has to wait hours to use the one bathroom, and then they shout that she's taking too long. And at the dressing table, she *has* to be slow and deliberate because her hair is so thick and heavy, but does Florence get any sympathy?

"Bull!" she shouts and throws two grapes onto the ground.

Her sister Ida, who has just come out the door onto the porch and is dumping a basin of water off the side, looks up with a raised eyebrow.

♪

In a few days Florence will go back to her job teaching music at the Boyd School in Pittsburgh, and she can't wait. In Pittsburgh there are concerts and plays, a group of jolly and intelligent young people, and many new things to discover.

Vivacious. Adventurous. These are the hallmarks of Florence's personality. Some of her sisters tease her for being temperamental, but she would prefer "high-spirited." Edith is a teacher in Chicago, and Bert will go back to his graduate studies in Michigan. Who would guess that this lithe young man with the mellow expression is a serious college student studying economics? He wants to be a professor, no less. This is just Bert, beloved only son among six sisters, and one year older than Florence.

Bert's slow smile spreads across his face. "We all have to do something useful in the world."

"I know. *The Rodkeys are not made of money,*" Florence says, quoting Papa.

She glances toward the red barn behind the house. The doors are open, and the nose of Papa's farm truck protrudes like a bulldog. Loud bangs, metal on metal, ring through the air. "I wish he would stop all that banging and come to the picnic."

"I think he's trying to get a wheel off. And he has to repair the seat where the mice chewed into it. You know how important that truck is."

"Yes." Florence sighs and picks up the mandolin again. She plucks a few strings as she gazes out into the clear sky. Their father, Robert Rodkey, has a farm just outside of town. Papa seems to spend all his time working on the land, but he encourages his children to go to college. He will support them, he says, but when they are out of school, they are on their own.

Like her siblings, Florence has flourished in rural life, playing in the fields, splashing in the creeks, and helping with the animals. But music is her great love, and after she graduated from music school, she was only too glad to leave the small town and find new adventure in Pittsburgh. She teaches music and dreams of being a concert pianist someday.

Bert turns toward her. "Are you excited about going back to the big city?"

"Oh," she exclaims. "I can't wait to skidoo out of old Mahaffey. Nothing to do here, and just a few yokels to cheer me up."

They both laugh at her use of this new word, *skidoo*.

"And you'll have more boys to flirt with." Bert raises an eyebrow.

Florence winces. "I know—you are referring to the *incident*. But Sue was out when her beau showed up, and just because I entertained him a little and went for a drive with him . . ."

Bert raises both eyebrows.

"I know, Mama was furious. She said I had no business to make trouble between those two." Sue, four years older than Florence, is her favorite sister and best pal, and Florence never thought she could threaten Sue's courtship until Mama accused her of flirting. Maybe she does flirt sometimes, but she resents being typecast like this. "My motives were good anyway. I tried to act in a sisterly manner, but I won't soon again. I don't get any credit for it."

Bert rolls his eyes. "And everyone has to have a job, Mama says—you girls until you get married."

"*If* we get married. So far, I haven't found anyone I'd want to spend my life with."

The boys have been around all summer, and Florence prides herself on getting the most attention, even from the Pittsburgh boys like Ernest, her friend Mary's brother. Ernest gives Florence mooning looks. But he's too young for her, only twenty to her twenty-two.

"Thank goodness," Florence says, "Mary and Ernest are coming for the picnic. They'll liven things up." Ernest makes her laugh, with his riddles and limericks, and she likes to tease him. He *is* a good friend, and they've had some fun times with the Pittsburgh crowd. Like her, Ernest loves the theater and always knows about the good productions in town.

The screen door bangs open as Edith, Ida, and Sue, followed by all the other sisters, their white dresses billowing, stream out onto the lawn, their arms laden with trays and platters, pitchers and glasses. Ida, the second-oldest sister, virtually towers over Edith, the shorter one, though the two oldest sisters otherwise look very much alike, with their soft brown hair pulled back in a bun and the same habit of tilting their heads when considering something. Now Ida straightens her back and raises an eyebrow at Florence. "A lady of leisure," she quips in her starchy voice.

"Well, it was awfully crowded in there," Florence says, "and nobody asked me to help." Everyone pampers her because she's had a little cough lately. Everyone except Ida, who accuses her of faking it. Probably she's jealous of the attention Florence gets.

Sue, carrying a tray with two enormous loaves of bread, suppresses a giggle as she passes, and winks at Florence.

Florence stands and follows the sisters out to the picnic spot, a grassy clearing beyond the shed.

Edith snaps open a red-and-white checkered tablecloth and spreads it on the lawn as the other sisters lay down platters of food: three loaves of bread, fragrant and fresh from the oven, sliced beef, and savory ham. A buttery, brown sugar aroma from the ham wafts into the air, along with the mayonnaise-y smell of the deviled eggs. Ida places a plate of cucumbers, radishes, sliced tomatoes, and lettuce in the center of the cloth—crisp greens and juicy reds—and Sue adds watermelon, grapes, and peaches.

Bert gazes at the spread, applauds the sisters, and sits on one edge of the cloth beside Ida, who gives a small "harrumph." Ida is the tallest of the sisters and considers herself second-in-command after Edith. Florence starts to sit, then springs back to her feet. "But what about Mary and Ernest?" she pleads. "They're not here yet." Mary and Ernest Craighead, her good friends from Pittsburgh.

Just then, a rattle and a squeaking of brakes sound from the driveway. Florence drops the knives and forks she's been arranging and rushes across the lawn. "Mary!" she calls, running to hug her friend stepping down from a shiny red Model T. Mary's brother, Ernest, steps out from the driver's side. A tall, thin young man with stiff hair that stands up like a bush on his head, he straightens and grins at Florence.

"Look at you!" Florence shouts. "A man with a motorcar!" She knows how proud Ernest is to be one of the first people in Pittsburgh to drive a car powered by a motor, even though it belongs to his father.

His light blue eyes twinkle. "Would you like to try it out? Go for a jaunt?"

"Oh, yes! After the picnic! Papa has a motor car, but it's not a fancy machine like this."

Mary unwraps her veil and takes off her wide-brimmed hat before patting the dust off her dress. "But what a ride!" she says. "I feel like a milkshake." Mary is so mild-mannered that even when she's frowning at Ernest, it's a gentle frown, and soon her expression returns to a serene smile. She smooths her dark hair around the loose topknot. The pompadour hairstyle is all the rage now, but Mary's hair is so fine that on her, the hair flattens into a loose pie shape rather than the full abundance of Florence's chestnut mane.

"I couldn't go at the snail's pace Mary wanted, or we'd never get here," Ernest says. "Anyway, the bumps are part of the fun."

"I know—you just couldn't hold back," Florence teases. "A young man with twenty-five horses at his command!"

Ernest blushes as he often does when Florence addresses him. He's too young, but he seems to have a crush on her, and she likes the attention. And, of course, when she gets married—*if* she gets married—she wants someone more settled, more established. Ernest wants to go to journalism school, for heaven's sake.

Florence leads the two siblings across the lawn to the picnic spot, where Bert and the other sisters, draped picturesquely in their flowing white dresses, are already sitting around the cloth. Behind them, above the trees, the ridge of Boone Mountain shimmers in a blue haze as Florence, Mary, and Ernest sit on the edges of the cloth.

Edith and Ida pass the picnic foods around, Bert says a brief blessing, and quiet falls as everyone starts to eat.

Bert takes a bite and looks up. "Ida, that was the best deviled egg I've ever had!"

Ida's stern face softens, and her lips curl up at the corners as she yields a tiny smile. Bert knows how to butter her up, that's for sure.

"Bert's a good egg." Ernest grins.

Edith chuckles and Florence rolls her eyes. "Oh, that was terrible," she moans. The moan sputters into a cough, and she turns her head away as Edith reaches over to pat her on the back. Florence shakes off the hand. Sometimes Edith's mothering becomes too much.

Everyone knows Edith is the smartest one. She doesn't have much fashion sense, though, with her hair in that old-fashioned bun, the style from ten years ago.

Edith turns to Ernest. "Tell us about the goings-on in Pittsburgh."

Ernest frowns and rubs his hair. "Did you hear about the workers' strike at McKees Rocks?"

Edith sighs. "Ah. It's hard to believe what those people have endured."

"But to strike?" Ida raises her voice. "That is surely not the way to be heard. Why can't they sit down and talk about it?" Ida wants everything to be orderly. As second-oldest, she takes on the role of the moralist, the mother hen corralling her chicks to walk the straight path.

Bert shakes his head. "I read that if someone gets hurt by a machine, the foreman will kick him aside, maimed or dead, and order another man to take his place."

The weight of these words descends on the festive group, a heavy load that squashes them into silence.

"And they have no guaranteed wage," says Edith. "The bosses can pay whatever they feel like."

"That strike was long overdue," Florence exclaims. She looks back toward the house and lowers her voice. "Sue and I went to hear Eugene Debs in Greensburg."

"That rabble-rouser." Ida sniffs.

Mary, sitting quietly beside Ernest, hasn't said much, probably overwhelmed by the noisy Rodkey siblings. But now, as she chews a crunchy carrot, she nods in agreement with Ida.

Florence looks at Mary in surprise, then turns to the group. "Oh no!" she exclaims. "He's a genius. And so eloquent. I'd vote for him *if I could.*" She looks pointedly at Ernest. The sisters exchange looks. All of them except Ida are in favor of the women's vote.

Ida clears her throat. "Well, thank goodness he didn't get elected. We don't need to become another Russia, with Bolsheviks racing around starting revolutions."

"That couldn't happen here," says Bert. "We don't have a czar running the country, and the economy would never survive a socialist takeover."

"But we need to treat the workers fairly," Florence protests. "And Ernest agrees with me, don't you, comrade?"

Ernest smiles and raises a fist as they both recall a lively debate about this daring new idea of socialism. Ernest, as usual, took the more conservative side but ultimately agreed with her. Since then, she's been calling him "comrade," partly as a tease, partly because he remains a true friend even as she flits back and forth in her romantic liaisons.

Ida puts down her fork and harumphs. "You sound like a Bolshevik yourself, Miss Flibbertigibbet!"

Florence jumps up, suppressing a cough, and holds out her hand to Ernest. "Let's take a ride," she says and starts to bound away toward the driveway.

As she begins to skip, she hears Edith's authoritative voice. "Florence needs to stop all this rushing about. I don't like the sound of that cough."

♪

Florence sits in the passenger seat of the shiny red roadster and ties a veil around her wide-brimmed hat to keep off the dust while Ernest adjusts something on the dashboard. He turns the key in the ignition and then runs around to the front to crank the handle. Once the engine splutters, he runs back, vaults into the driver's seat, and they are on the way. Florence holds her hat and waves to the family, a queen in her carriage. The noise of the motorcar breaks through the silence of the day as they pull out of the drive and putter along Main Street. Neighbors stop and wave, and Florence gaily waves back.

"Thank you for backing me up about the workers, comrade," Florence says.

"Anything for a flibbertigibbet." Ernest smiles and winks.

Florence throws back her head and laughs, and soon they are both laughing and exchanging quips and one-liners. It's like a song. *We each sing our part in counterpoint and harmony with each other.*

The car speeds up, and Florence bounces up and down with each rut and runnel, gripping the door handle. "Ooh," she shrieks. *But I'm not afraid—that was just a descant to our song.*

Ernest grins at her and the car goes faster. "At least the weather is dry today," Ernest shouts over the engine noise, "so we won't get stuck in the mud. That's not something you want to experience."

Bumpety-bump along the rutted road, onto Market Street, and across the bridge. On the River Road, they thump over even bigger ruts and potholes as Florence bounces up and down and laughs. "Crazy!" she shouts.

But then she starts to cough. Her chest heaves and the coughs keep coming, like sandpaper on her throat, unbidden and out of control. She bends down, holding her chest. Ernest pulls the car over and stops. He jumps over the door from the driver's seat, runs around to her side, and lays a hand on her shoulder. "Oh, I'm sorry," he says, "it was too fast for you." His face has transformed into a worried frown, and he rubs his bushy hair.

"No, it was fun," Florence gasps. "It's just the dust." Her breathing slows down and the coughing stops.

Ernest makes a move closer, as if to hold her, but then pulls back, not sure of his status.

Florence smiles as her heart warms to her young friend. "You are the most gentlemanly of all gentlemen. And my best comrade." *But not a suitor.*

She takes the handkerchief he holds out and covers her nose and mouth as they drive, much more slowly, back home.

chapter 2

I CAN DREAM, CAN'T I?

Pittsburgh, Pennsylvania, 1941

The trolley screeches around the corner and clanks to a stop.

"Flossie! Wait!"

A young man waves and calls from across the street. Hand on fedora, tie flying, Hammie sprints along the train platform, racing toward the intersection.

The trolley is waiting, the door open, the driver staring at Flossie.

She clutches her purse and squints toward the intersection. "Hammie," she calls, though he probably can't hear her. "I have to get to work."

The driver shifts into gear and the conductor leans out. "Are you coming, miss?"

Flossie turns to look again. Hammie's blond head bobs as he runs across the street, hat in hand. *He'll never get here before the trolley leaves.*

She steps onto the trolley, on her way to her first-ever real job. She's had it for a month now, and heaven forbid she should be late. Mrs. Doak, her boss, is very strict about punctuality.

Flossie settles into a seat beside the window. Outside, Hammie has just reached the trolley, and she waves as he fades into the distance. What could he want? He's never looked so panicked. Well, whatever it is, he can catch her later. Or she'll call him. Yes, she'll call him after work.

Today is clear and sunny, something to treasure in Pittsburgh, where the air is so often clogged with smoke from the steel mills. The humidity of summer has dissipated, and maple trees gleam red and yellow in the crisp autumn air. Even Braddock Avenue, with its cracked sidewalks and makeshift buildings, looks cheery today. Flossie smooths down the lap of her new dress, a shirtwaist in Black Watch plaid that she made from a McCall's pattern, and crosses her legs, admiring her fake alligator heels. She adjusts her new hat, green to match the green of the dress, with a bow and a jaunty brim. Today the world is her oyster. She hums the tune to one of her favorite Andrews Sisters songs, *I Can Dream, Can't I?*

The conductor, a tall man with a big nose, appears beside her, and she fishes a dime out of her purse and gives it to him. He smiles and tips his hat. "Very pretty, miss." Is he talking about the song or her? Well, it doesn't matter.

Flossie is a working girl now, living the carefree life she dreamed of in college, with parties and friends and beaus, including her old friend Hammie, who is planning to go to engineering school. Hammie considers himself her beau, but she's not sure. A social butterfly, her father calls her. There is a war going on in Europe, but it's so far away, she tries not to think about it.

The trolley turns off Braddock onto Forbes Avenue and swings around through Frick Park, a green expanse of rolling hills and graceful trees, an oasis in the stark city. Flossie breathes in the smell of trees and fresh-cut grass until the trolley emerges again into a glaring mishmash of soot-covered buildings and busy streets. But now her shoulders tense. Hammie is practically her best friend, along with Helen and Kaegy, and he has the most easygoing personality of anyone. Why was he shouting and running?

When the hospital comes into view, she rings the bell and smiles at the conductor as she disembarks. Magee Women's Hospital, an imposing brick building in three sections, like a triptych facing inward, is a Pittsburgh landmark.

This past spring, Flossie graduated from Carnegie Tech, where she majored in costume design.

Frivolous choice, Daddy scoffed, when we've just come out of the Depression. He threatened not to pay for her education. She'd never get a job, he said, but she insisted that she could work as a costume designer, and maybe, she thought, she could be an actress, too. In college she was in the theater club and had a grand time playing Mrs. Webb in *Our Town.*

In the end her father acquiesced, as he always does, since Flossie reminds him so much of her mother, Florence, the love of his life. Florence loved pretty clothes, too, and, like Flossie, had a busy social life with lots of friends.

But when Flossie graduated, there were no jobs for costume designers in Pittsburgh, and, while most of her friends were walking down the aisle, she still wasn't even engaged. Marriage is the ultimate goal for young women, and she assumes she'll get married, too—she wants to get married. But not yet. She loves to sew, loves the colors and the feel of the fabrics in her fingers, the fine wool, the soft shine of silk. The adventure of setting out the pattern paper, measuring, and cutting thrills her. Flossie delighted in all aspects of her design classes in college. Maybe she could do that for a couple of years before marriage.

But when Flossie was offered this job in the hospital gift shop, Elizabeth, her stepmother, nodded in approval. A bird in hand, she said.

Flossie gazes across the wide lawn at the hospital, and a familiar feeling arises—a flutter that starts in her gut and leaps to her chest.

This is the hospital where she was born. But it's also where her mother died. Whenever she sees the building, the fluttering feeling comes, along with a composite image—a photograph of a young woman smiling and twirling a parasol, and then Daddy's tearful face. Daddy doesn't talk about his first wife, but any time her name comes up, his eyes glisten with tears. She must have been a great beauty, an accomplished musician, a goddess on a pedestal—too perfect for words. But what was she really like?

This fluttering feeling, so automatic and deep-rooted, rises through her chest and throat. Flossie has roots here, in this hospital that connects her to her mother and in this city to a long line of ancestors, an endless flow of life and death, the generations of this family rooted in Pittsburgh.

Funny how a building can make you feel so many different things. Things that include pride, because now she is an employee, involved with this building in a new way.

Flossie swings her purse and marches across the glistening lawn past hydrangea blossoms nodding in the morning sun and wafting their fresh scent into the air.

At the door she adjusts her hat and steps inside. Mrs. Doak, her boss, stands in front of the gift shop entrance. Mrs. Doak is tall and thin, with fierce brown eyes and a gray bun that never seems to stay in place.

"Good morning, Flossie." Mrs. Doak's penetrating gaze transforms into a radiant smile. "Just get the operator to call if you need me." Mrs. Doak hurries out the door, pointing toward the switchboard operator in the next room.

Flossie scrutinizes the ceramic figurines and flower holders on the shelves. Really, Mrs. Doak is efficient, but she doesn't know how to create an eye-catching display. Flossie begins to rearrange them.

She straightens up the chewing gum and candy racks. The tins of hard candies, more elegant-looking than the candy bars, go on the counter in front. Behind them on the rack are the Jujubes, licorice twists, Lifesavers, and, of course, the chocolates. The Clark Bars, Flossie's favorite, in their bright orange and blue wrappers, need to be easily accessible for a quick snack. The chocolate cigarettes (a big hit with the children) beneath them look almost real. In the cooler the red roses should go in the center, not squished behind the pots of mums, and each bouquet needs a little space around it to breathe.

"Hello." Just inside the door, a man in a dapper three-piece suit accompanies a little girl in pigtails and a yellow smocked dress.

The girl beams. "We have a new baby," she proclaims, then scoots to hide behind her father.

The smile freezes on Flossie's face and her shoulders slump. She was a new baby here, too. Her arrival didn't herald such celebration, though. It was tinged with tragedy.

But that was a long time ago. *Chin up, Flossie,* she tells herself and claps her hands. "Congratulations!" she says. "Would you like something for the mommy or for the baby?" Flossie reaches behind the counter and holds up a baby rattle.

The father shakes his head. "I think we already have one of those. And we can't spend much."

Well, nobody has "much" to spend these days.

"Maybe something for Judy here," he says as the little girl peeks from behind his leg.

Flossie bends down to Judy, whose bright eyes open wide. "Ooh, I have something special for you." She opens a drawer and pulls out a paper book. "Voilà! A paper doll book!" The cover features a picture of a nurse in uniform with her tools arrayed around her: a stethoscope, thermometer, a peaked nurse's hat, and even a medicine bottle, all in vivid colors and ready to cut out and attach to the figure.

Judy jumps up and down, and her father pulls out his wallet.

At the end of the day, when Mrs. Doak comes in, Flossie is busy charming another customer into buying a pot of mums along with a get-well card. Mrs. Doak stands watching for a few moments, and when the customer leaves, she opens the cash register and counts the cash before locking it up.

Flossie picks up her purse and puts on her hat. "Well, goodbye, Mrs. Doak."

"Just a minute, Flossie." The older woman hands her a letter. "This is for your Aunt Mary."

Aunt Mary is Mrs. Doak's friend, and it is through her that Flossie has this job. Aunt Mary, her father's sister, is the same age as her own mother, Florence, would have been, and they had been friends as well as sisters-in-law.

Aunt Mary is elegant and gracious, and Flossie wants to be just like her. She and Mrs. Doak are both active in the Pittsburgh Woman's Club, a group devoted to charity. They collect toys for the blind children at Christmas, find jobs for the unemployed, plant trees for soil conservation, and, of course, go to lots of teas and social occasions.

Flossie is beginning to admire Mrs. Doak, too. Mrs. Doak, whose manner is hard where Aunt Mary's is soft, rules the gift shop, the hospital volunteers, and, it seems, a lot of other hospital operations. A formidable woman with strong principles about good works and charity and a presence that brokers no opposition, she also has a surprising sense of humor. Flossie likes to be in charge herself, and in Mrs. Doak, she's found a role model. Mrs. Doak proves that a woman can be an executive.

Flossie tucks the letter into her purse. Fine stationery paper engraved with Mrs. Doak's name, addressed to *Mrs. James Brinton* in a firm hand. What could Mrs. Doak be writing to Aunt Mary? Is it about Flossie?

Flossie steps lightly out of the hospital door, alligator heels clicking, and, instead of going to the trolley stop for home, walks around the building to the Fifth Avenue trolley stop. She is earning her own money now, and she has time to do a little shopping downtown before dinner.

Maybe she'll buy some two-tone heels with brogue stitching, like the ones she saw in *Vogue*. Or she could get a pair of the new swing-dancing heels with the ankle strap. She might even buy both!

She sighs. *Who am I kidding?* She barely has enough money for an ice cream cone at Isaly's. *But I can dream, can't I?* And she can window shop.

Flossie strolls along Fifth Avenue, gazing in the store window. Maybe she can find a *Vogue* pattern like that and make it herself. She glances at her watch. Whoops. *I'd better skedaddle home and call Hammie. He was running like the devil, his expression frantic. What could it be?*

chapter 3

THE BELLE OF CHICAGO

Chicago, Illinois, 1910

The train jolts to a stop and Florence opens her eyes.

"Chicago!" roars the conductor.

Outside the window: a vast underground space. Light from domed skylights sheds a misty glow on the warren of tracks and walkways as people rush to and fro. Train wheels screech, engines start up with hoots and blasts of steam, and people shout. How will she ever find Edith in this crowd? Or how will Edith find her?

Florence stands to brush ash and soot off her coat. Coal seeps through the train windows no matter how tight they are closed.

Whyever did they think this trip would be good for her? She's been coughing more on this journey in the last two days than she had been at home in Mahaffey.

The picnic was only two weeks ago, but it feels like the distant past. After her coughing fit, Edith took charge and called the doctor. Pneumonia, he declared.

"But—" Florence began.

No questions were allowed. Florence must get away from Pennsylvania's damp climate and Pittsburgh's smoke.

"She'll come to Chicago with me," Edith said.

"No," Doctor Miller declared. "Tuberculosis is spreading like wildfire. Florence needs a drier climate."

Ida, who was heading back to her teaching job in Arizona, wrote to the district head of education, Mr. Reed. Despite her crusty manner, Ida is loyal to the family, committed to her sisters, and highly efficient. A week later, Florence was appointed schoolmarm at a ranch in New Mexico.

Into the wild west, she thought. Wild Indians, wild cowboys, and wild animals.

On the way she would stay with Edith in Chicago for a week. *Civilization!* she cheered to herself. Art museums, Broadway shows, and even opera.

Edith, fifteen years older, has been like a mother to Florence. When Florence was born, the seventh of eight children, Mama needed all the help she could get, so Edith, the eldest, who had already tended the other sisters and one brother, stepped in, and little Florence soon became "her" baby.

Florence still has mixed feelings about that. When she was little, Edith could be bossy, and Florence would cry and run to Mama to smooth things over. But she knows that Edith really loves "her" girl.

Edith took it upon herself to see that Florence received a good education in music, and she still wants her to go to college. Florence, though, isn't interested in college. She's too interested, she admits to herself, in boys and having fun. She also loves her music. She earned her diploma at the Altoona School of Music, and she plays the piano and sings in the church choir. Mr. Reed said the ranch family in New Mexico was thrilled that Florence could teach the daughters music as well as English and arithmetic.

♪

Florence steps onto the station platform into the smells of smoke, burnt ham, and stale coffee, people pushing and shoving.

She covers her mouth and nose with a handkerchief. At the far end of the grand hall, through the smoke and fog, she sees an exit door. But even if a porter carried her trunk, she couldn't possibly make her way through all these people. Her chest gurgles and she bends over and coughs again, taking shallow breaths to squelch the cough as tears run down her cheeks.

A faint animal smell rises just in front of her. She straightens up and looks into a magnificent fur coat, golden brown and gleaming, and a woman smiling at her. "Oh!" Florence gasps, reaching out to touch the fur, then pulling her hand back.

"Don't worry, darlin'. It won't bite," the woman says in a rich low voice. Her blond hair is pulled up in some new kind of pompadour, topped by an enormous hat piled high with silk flowers, making her look about ten feet tall. She smiles with full lips painted a deep red. "Are you lost?" She thrusts out her hand to take Florence's arm and steer her through the crowd.

Florence, shocked out of coughing, stammers, "I—I'm looking for my sister." Should she go with this stylish woman? Tall and poised, like a lioness on the savannah, the woman radiates fierce confidence.

Just then a small figure in black elbows her way through the crowd toward her. There's no mistaking that air of authority. "Oh, there she is!" says Florence. Thank heavens. Who knows where she would have gone with the fur-bedecked lady?

"Florence, dear!" Edith exclaims as she bustles up and takes her in her arms.

"Aah," Florence sighs. Edith smells like Lily of the Valley, the same toilet water their mother uses. Florence wraps her arms around her sister and sighs. Her body jerks into a sob as, in her mind's eye, she and Mama stand in the garden on a fresh spring morning, picking peas off the vine.

How long before she can go home?

Edith looks around and taps her foot. "Now where is the porter? We must get you out of here."

The fur-clad woman melts back into the crowd as Edith mutters, "Painted hussy."

"Oh, but I love the color!" Florence protests. "People at home think makeup is immoral, but isn't it different here in Chicago? Look around, Edith. Everyone is wearing makeup!"

"Well, I'm not."

Florence wouldn't mind trying out some lipstick or rouge to brighten up. Her complexion has become so pale since she's had this cough. And Edith is thirty-seven after all, way behind the times. Here in Chicago, young women like Florence are already wearing the new styles: shorter dresses, more makeup, more color! *Haven't we all had enough black?*

They step out of the station into bright sunshine. And thank goodness, no smoke. But with all this traffic, there are still fumes in the air, so what started as a deep breath becomes a shallow one. Her chest is tight, and it feels like she can't get enough oxygen.

Edith, with her usual efficiency, steps into the street and hails a horse-drawn hansom cab. The porter lifts Florence's trunk into the bed, and they climb onto the seats. Then the cab plunges into the most traffic Florence has ever seen. Horse-drawn buggies, hansom cabs, and motor cars compete with people on bicycles and others walking. People saunter across the broad streets without looking, seemingly unaware of the traffic. Horns blare and shouts ring out, and a motor car crisscrosses in front of their taxi. But it's a sunny day and the air is clear, a nice surprise after Pittsburgh.

The driver urges the horse into a trot as they turn a corner and drive onto a bridge over the river.

"But what is that smell?" Florence cries as she grabs her handkerchief and covers her nose.

"Oh," Edith says, "they're dredging the river again, and I guess they've dredged up some of the sewage." She lowers her voice. "There's a place downriver called Bubbly Creek, where they discard the remains from the slaughterhouse."

Florence risks a glance down at the murky river and cringes. "Rotting carcasses! This is worse than Pittsburgh!"

But as they drive away from the river, the smell is gone, and they glide through a long avenue lined with stately old trees and flowering shrubs in the center island. The level parkland seems to stretch for miles, so different from Pittsburgh, where all the streets, and even the parks, are on hills.

When they arrive at Edith's apartment, Florence sits on the horsehair sofa, not very comfortable, but as familiar as the one at home. The apartment is in an elegant building of stone and brick on a wide avenue lined with elm trees. Thankfully, it's quiet. A peaceful, proper neighborhood.

Edith has dinner almost ready—lamb chops, green beans, and potatoes, Florence's favorite meal—at the little dining room table. After they eat, the sisters sit in the parlor. A silk-shaded lamp on the pianoforte and a multicolored Tiffany lamp on the table cast a warm glow on their faces.

Edith brings Florence a wool shawl and drapes it over her lap, then sits in the rocking chair. She smiles at her sister, with an expression of loving care and curiosity. Edith has both an openness to new experience or knowledge and an ability to make sense of it. A combination of benevolence and practicality that makes you feel completely accepted and at the same time challenged to do your best. "If you're feeling up to it," she says, "we're invited to a dinner tomorrow night."

"Oh." Florence pushes her hair back. She's removed the pins from her pompadour, and now her chestnut hair falls in heavy tresses around her face. "What kind of dinner?"

Edith smiles. "I think you'll like it. It's in a grand home on Astor Street. Raymond Barnes is a prominent lawyer, and his wife, Chloe, is a patron of our high school. She invited me."

Florence throws up her hands. "A grand dinner! But I have nothing to wear!"

Edith flashes a mischievous grin. "Well, I have a surprise for you."

♪

The next day they take the trolley to the biggest and fanciest department store in Chicago. Twelve stories high and occupying a whole city block, Marshall Fields is even more elegant than Florence imagined: an open rotunda surrounded by tiers of balconies, marble arches, and Grecian columns.

Edith points up to a majestic, domed ceiling made of multicolored glass. "Tiffany," she says.

They walk past a lavish array of glass cases displaying jewelry, watches, and perfumes, then take the elevator to the seventh floor.

In a noisy but luxurious tearoom, they sit beside a marble pool with a fountain trickling. Around them all the other tables are occupied by women in white dresses and brimmed hats, daytime hats banded by velvet rather than adorned with feathers and flowers. (*Maybe my ostrich feather is a bit too much here.*) The women chat and laugh, and no one looks at the new arrivals.

When the waiter arrives, Edith orders for both of them—mock turtle soup and *bouchée à la reine*, a puff pastry filled with crab and mushroom sauce.

"This *is* a surprise!" Florence shouts to be heard above the din. "What a treat, and so much grander than anything in Pittsburgh. But the prices, Edith. Your budget!"

"Well, I have something to celebrate. Something besides having my dear sister here with me." She pauses.

"You're getting married!"

Edith laughs. "No, I'm not ready for that and perhaps never will be."

"But aren't we all supposed to get married?" *Oops,* Florence thinks, *of course Edith isn't getting married. She's thirty-seven!*

"I got a promotion," Edith says, ignoring the question, her eyes shining with pride. "You are looking at the new principal of Lake View High School."

"Oh, dilly!" says Florence. "My sister, a school principal! Now you don't even *have* to get married. I wish I had that choice. But on a music teacher's salary . . ." Papa made it clear that all the daughters should get married, and soon. Florence is twenty-two already, and time is running out. Mama doesn't openly dispute him, but they all know she's proud of her daughters' teaching careers: Edith in Chicago, Ida in Arizona, and soon Florence in New Mexico.

Edith straightens and gives Florence her strictest teacher look. "We'll have to talk about that. You *will* go to college and then you'll have other choices."

Florence sighs. They've had this conversation before.

"But now the surprise," says Edith.

Florence looks up from her plate and speaks through a mouthful of crab and mushroom puff pastry. "Isn't this it?"

"Not yet."

When they finish, Edith pays the bill and stands. "Come with me." She leads Florence through a maze of rooms, one more extravagant than the next, and finally to the dress department. From high shelves all around the room, a rainbow of colored fabrics flows. "We're getting you a new gown."

Florence gasps as she takes in the richness—blues, greens, reds, purples, golds, silvers—in velvets, brocades, and silks, like a scene from *Arabian Nights.* "Oh, Edith," she murmurs, "you spoil me."

"We don't have time to order one, but they have some lovely ready-made dresses here." Edith leads her to a table, mounded with folded silks, and then to a rack of dresses.

Florence tries on several gowns, all of which she "adores," but one is "dazzling," they agree. A dreamy blue silk with a lace overskirt and an embroidered lace overlay at the neck and sleeves. Perfect for an elegant dinner party.

chapter 4

TAKE THE A TRAIN

Pittsburgh, Pennsylvania, 1941

Home is the Victorian house in Edgewood, where her grandmother has lived since she got married in 1855. High on a hill, 159 Lacrosse Street, with its tall windows and weathered gray siding, overlooks the city's skyscrapers and smoke and the three rivers that come together at the point. Built by Flossie's grandfather, this house where her father grew up, as did she and Roddy, is a landmark in the Craighead family. Aunt Mary and Uncle Gordy, her father's sister and brother, both live with their families on Lacrosse Street, too, farther down the street, but "one-five-nine," as everyone refers to it, still rises like a beacon, the heart of the family.

Flossie walks up Lacrosse, a hefty uphill hike. When she comes to a steep bank of ivy and underbrush, she scrambles up—up the shortcut, picking her way over rutted, lop-sided concrete slabs that serve as steps and are almost hidden by the vines and overgrowth. As usual, she teeters on her heels and, as usual, wonders, *Why didn't I go up the driveway? And why do I always have this same thought at this same spot?* She stops to take off her shoes.

At the top of the steps, Flossie walks up the sloping lawn, the grass soft beneath her stockinged feet. In the dark entrance hall, she throws her hat and gloves on the old oak coat stand and her purse on the built-in bench, then slips back into her heels. Glancing in the mirror, she smooths her long brown hair, cut and carefully pin-curled like Katherine Hepburn's.

Just the other day someone told her she looked like the actress. *I could be an actress*, she thinks, hurrying through the dark narrow hallway.

The phone sits in a nook at the end of the hall. Flossie snatches the receiver, ready to give the operator Hammie's number.

"Well, they were having a sale on silk stockings at Horne's," a scratchy voice drawls, "so I decided to just scurry on over there before they were all gone. I can at least afford a pair for me and one for Mildred. But when I got off the streetcar, there was such a crowd. And guess who I saw?" Old Mrs. Campbell is on the party line and will go on forever. Flossie sighs, hangs up the phone, and goes into the kitchen. She'll try again after dinner.

Flossie's stepmother, Elizabeth, a short buxom woman who walks with a limp, turns around from the oven. She raises her eyebrows. "Dinner is ready," she says in a soft voice and tactfully doesn't mention that Flossie is late. Elizabeth hands her a bowl of mashed potatoes and picks up a platter of pork chops, and Flossie follows her into the dining room.

"You're late!" bellows Roddy. "And I'm starving." Roddy, twenty-three, is two years older than Flossie, but he's still in college. Or rather, back in college. Roddy has a history of staying out late with his friends and breaking the rules. Their father's refrain, "You'll never amount to anything," seems to follow him everywhere.

But lately Roddy has settled back into school and is studying math and accounting.

Flossie suspects Daddy is now thinking Roddy *will* amount to something, but he'd never say it out loud. Their father doesn't want his son to get cocky or lazy.

"I'm hungry too!" seven-year-old Sallie says, fiddling with a pigtail. Sallie is tall for her age and has long golden-brown hair braided into two pigtails. Like her mother, Elizabeth, Sallie is quiet and thoughtful but not shy when she has an opinion.

"First the blessing," says Nannie, giving Sallie a disapproving look. Tall and thin with gray-flecked dark hair, Nannie, Daddy's mother, is the executive in this family, and she rules the roost. Her husband, Flossie's grandfather, died when Flossie was a baby, and now Nannie sees no reason to cede her position as head of household to her son or any daughters-in-law. Daddy can be imperious, too, and sometimes Nannie and Daddy clash wills, but luckily Elizabeth is gracious about this pecking order.

Tradition holds that the oldest male says grace, and at Nannie's words, with a glance at her son at the head of the table, all eyes close and heads bow. Nannie has decreed that everyone stay silent for a few minutes before the prayer.

In the sudden quiet, Flossie breathes a sigh of relief. She used to resent this practice of forced silence, but now it feels good, like a respite. Evening sun streaks in from the tall windows, making the glass and silverware sparkle and burnishing the faces. A moment of peace. This, being together around the table, this is the feeling of peace, and of family.

Daddy lowers his voice as he says the prayer: *Bless, O Lord, this food to our use and us to thy service. In Jesus's name, Amen.*

Now everyone speaks at once:

"Did you hear . . ."

"Hammie's coming for . . ."

"Here, kitty, kitty . . ."

Daddy serves from the platters and bowls in front of him: pork chops, mashed potatoes, beets, and peas.

"No beets, please, Daddy," says Sallie.

"You'll eat everything set before you." Daddy heaps a large spoonful of boiled beets beside the mashed potatoes and pork chop on Sallie's plate and hands it to her.

Sallie makes a face, screwing up her nose, and Nannie wags a finger at her. "Remember the starving Armenians. And take that pigtail out of your mouth."

Sallie sinks back in her chair with a pout, and Elizabeth raises her eyebrows at her, a finger to her lips. Roddy and Flossie exchange a look. They both think Elizabeth spoils Sallie.

Sallie came into their lives when Roddy was fifteen and Flossie was thirteen, and her birth changed everything. The two older siblings finally had to admit that Elizabeth was a real mother in this family. Even though Elizabeth was loving and gentle, Roddy and Flossie felt pushed aside, secondary, because Sallie came first with her. Feeling left out, though, strengthened the bond between them.

Flossie soon forgets this habitual resentment as she and Roddy laugh and talk. "Hammie's teaching me the Lindy Hop," she says, "and we're going to the Crawford Grill."

Nannie frowns. "Proper young ladies do not go gallivanting to speak-easies at night with colored people."

"But Nannie," Roddy shouts. "The Crawford Grill is the best place in Pittsburgh for jazz and swing! Everyone's going!" He looks at Flossie. "And did you hear who's coming?"

"Who?" she says through a mouthful of mashed potatoes.

"The Duke!"

Sallie's eyes open wide. "A real duke?"

"Yes, ma'am!" Roddy laughs. "And he's the *king* too, the king of jazz."

"Oh, Roddy, you have to take me," Flossie trills.

"No nightclubs for you, young lady." Her father has a thin face, pointed nose, and pale blue eyes that can twinkle with glee or turn cold and hard as they are now.

"But Daddy, I'm not a girl anymore. I'm a working woman, and I can make my own decisions about where I go." Flossie looks pleadingly at Elizabeth, the family peacemaker. "And besides, this is a once-in-a-lifetime opportunity. Duke Ellington! In Pittsburgh!"

Elizabeth looks at her with sympathy. "Well—"

"Not while she's living in my house," Daddy says with finality, and Nannie nods in agreement.

Flossie's shoulders sink, and she looks across the table at Roddy.

Roddy winks at her, and now she knows they will somehow manage to go to the club. Though he still teases her, Roddy has always been protective of his little sister. They both inherited the *joie de vivre* of their biological mother and sometimes feel constricted in the somber Craighead household ruled by their paternal grandmother.

To change the subject, Elizabeth says, "I read in the *Post-Gazette* that the Germans attacked England again. It's terrible what's happening over there. Maybe it's time for us to help them out."

Daddy frowns. "That war is none of our business. The Depression is over, thank goodness, and we need to concentrate on America."

"Yes, that's just what Lindbergh said," Nannie adds. "Did you hear his speech?" Nannie knows full well they all heard Charles Lindbergh speaking on the radio just the other night. "America first."

Roddy frowns. "But Lindbergh is an isolationist," he says, his voice rising in intensity. "At school they're saying we should join in and give a hand to the Brits. We can't let the Nazis take over Europe."

"Heavens, no," Elizabeth answers in her mild voice. "That Hitler is a weasel. I wouldn't trust him to bring in the groceries."

Flossie laughs. Elizabeth was an English teacher before she married Daddy, and she has a way of stating things with dry humor.

"President Roosevelt has said we won't go to war," says Nannie, "and a very sensible thing that is. We don't need to send our boys to die in another war in Europe." Almost tearful, she looks at Roddy. "Your Uncle Gordy was stuck in a cold, muddy trench, and luckily he survived, but the horrors were unspeakable." Nannie always talked about the fearful times when her youngest and favorite child, Gordy, was sent to the Great War in Europe. Flossie's father was posted only briefly to the National Guard at Fort Indiantown Gap, a unit that stayed in Pennsylvania to defend the home front.

Flossie sighs. "That war is an ocean away. Can't we talk about something else?"

♪

After dinner, Sallie scoots away to find her new kitten while Roddy and Flossie take their usual route to the piano in the parlor. With its heavy Victorian furniture, all from their grandmother's era, when the family had more money, the parlor has a dark feel. But now, at the end of the day, tall western windows bring in bands of sun that stripe the worn Persian rugs with light and warmth.

Flossie sits at the piano and begins to play and sing "Don't Fence Me In." Like her mother, she's a pianist, and the music makes Flossie feel a connection to her. Daddy kept all of Florence's sheet music in the piano bench, and Flossie has learned some of her favorites. Especially when she plays Elgar's "Salut d'Amour," she almost feels, with the melancholy sweetness of the tune, that her mother is here, inside of her. Her mother's love is like a melody that runs within her.

Now, though, instead of the Mozart and Bach her mother favored, Flossie prefers the popular songs of the day: "I'll Never Smile Again," "Chattanooga Choo Choo," "Red Sails in the Sunset." She launches into "Don't Sit Under the Apple Tree," one of her favorites—*with nobody else but me.* Does she feel this way about Hammie? Not really, but she and Roddy sing out with zest as she plays, Flossie on stage, the bandleader.

She misses a few notes. So what? She skips over the mistakes and nobody minds.

When the song ends, Flossie riffles through the sheet music. "I'll try a new one," she says, and then begins Duke Ellington's "Take the A Train."

Roddy taps his feet as he belts out, trying to imitate the jazz recording he heard at a friend's house.

Elizabeth limps into the room, using her cane as she does at the end of the day, when her leg is weaker from the polio she had as a child. She stops and points back toward the door.

Behind Elizabeth appears the blond and tousled figure of Hammie. Flossie stops playing. My goodness, she forgot to phone him. She rushes over, still bouncing to the beat, to greet her beau. Is Hammie her beau? Well, one of several beaus—the young men from college and her high school class in Edgewood. Flossie hasn't thought of him in a romantic way (*or have I?*), but Hammie is a dear friend, maybe as close as she and her best friend Kaegy. They've played tennis, sung in the glee club, acted in school plays, and had a lot of fun together. There is no one she'd rather dance and laugh with than Hammie.

"Hi, Hammie. What did you want this morning?"

Hammie, tall and big-shouldered, blushes and shuffles his feet. He points to the hallway, and she follows him out. From the parlor come the stumbling notes of the song as Roddy attempts to pick it up.

Flossie looks up at Hammie. "Is it something bad?"

"Well, maybe, maybe not," he says and sighs, his eyes downcast. "I got drafted."

"Oh, no!" Flossie exclaims. "They just announced the draft the other day. How could it happen so fast?"

"Just lucky, I guess." He shifts from one foot to the other. "And, you know, Flossie, maybe it's time to—" He fumbles in his jacket pocket.

Flossie knows where he's going with this. She's always had fun dancing and flirting with Hammie, and he is as handsome as a movie star. But marriage? She does want to get married; it's what everyone does, after all, unless they want to be an old maid living off their relatives.

And Flossie is fond of Hammie. He's practically her best friend, and they've known each other since childhood. But shouldn't there be something more? A spark or a flash or a drum roll when she's with him?

Well, but there *is* a spark, sort of, with Hammie. In so many ways he's her perfect match . . . those tennis games during summer vacation were pure fun. Flossie is a good athlete, and though Hammie taught her the game, she got so good at it that she beat him almost every time. Luckily, he was a good sport about it. They share so many memories: laughing and strolling along Maple Avenue, the smell of summer sunshine through the trees, ice-cold Cokes from the soda fountain.

And the dazzling final dance at college when she wore her Ginger Rogers swing dress. During the slow dance, Flossie and Hammie suddenly stopped, stunned by a voice—the smoothest, most magnificent baritone voice they'd ever heard—crooning, low and deep. Who was it? They couldn't see. They inched their way through the crowd to the front, and there he was, a skinny little guy in a baggy suit, so insignificant-looking but with the voice of a giant—Frank Sinatra.

That kind of experience bonds people for a lifetime.

Flossie and Hammie danced again, and they were so synchronized, it was almost like they were one being. Everyone stopped and clapped, and she and Hammie took a bow.

♪

In the dark hallway, with Roddy's enthusiastic voice and piano strains of a halting "Take the A Train," Hammie fumbles in his pocket and pulls out a little box. Dark red velvet. He hands it to Flossie.

"Oh!" She catches her breath as she opens the box. "A diamond ring! An engagement ring?"

Hammie nods. He's going into the army. What does this mean? Flossie has managed to avoid thinking about war, but now the image from a newsreel—German soldiers with guns—pops into her mind like a muffled scream.

She squashes down that image as she slips the ring onto her finger. A perfect fit. Three small diamonds flank a bigger one in the middle, and it sparkles like a star. She holds up her hand and twirls around like Lana Turner in *Tap Dance*. "Engaged!"

Hammie chuckles. "I guess that's a yes."

He reaches out and kisses her on the lips. His are soft and warm, and she feels comforted.

Flossie steps back. What did she just agree to? *Am I engaged? To Hammie? Do I really want to get married? Or do I just like the ring and the idea of being engaged? Or did I accept because I feel sorry for him and want to give him something to hope for when he goes into the army?* She puts the ring back in the velvet box, slips it into her pocket, and turns around. "But I just don't know, Hammie."

"You don't know? If you want to get married?" Hammie's hopeful face is now crestfallen.

"No, I *do* want to. But maybe I'm not ready. Maybe *we're* not ready. With you going into the army and all." Flossie gives a helpless shrug and Hammie is silent. "Let's go back and sing."

That night, as she climbs the stairs, Flossie stops on the landing. A sepia photograph of her mother hangs prominently in the center of the landing wall. A beautiful woman in profile, with an abundance of hair bound up in a puffy pompadour. *What should I do?* Flossie asks her mother. *Should I marry Hammie? I'm not ready. I don't want to settle down yet. But will this be my only chance?* Why couldn't she have had a real mother, like everyone else?

In her room she sits at her dressing table, winding sections of hair around rags to make pin curls, the velvet box beside her, the letter for Aunt Mary off to the side. She takes out the ring and turns it round and round. She swore Hammie to secrecy until they are both sure. *But what am I so scared of? Everyone thinks Hammie is a perfect catch. And I always thought we would get married.* She swallows and her throat clenches. She places the ring on the dressing table, in the center of her lipsticks and face powder, bobby pins and curler rags. She studies her face in the mirror, wipes away a smudge of lipstick, and smiles.

A white lace dress, a veil, the church at twilight, the organ playing, and her cousin Helen, maid of honor, smiling at her from the altar, dressed in blue. No, Helen in lilac, with Sallie beside her in pink ruffles.

For some reason Hammie is not in this picture.

chapter 5

EINE KLEINE NACHTMUSIK

Chicago, Illinois, 1910

Edith and Florence step from the hansom cab onto the sidewalk outside of a massive edifice three stories high in brick and stone, with tall windows fronted by wrought-iron balconies.

Edith smiles. "This is the Barnes house."

Florence gasps. At the top of the building, a pilaster balustrade rims the rooftop. "It's a castle!"

"Probably as big."

At the door a butler takes their cloaks and directs them into a vast room with a fireplace at one end and floor-to-ceiling windows lining one side. The windows look out on a lawn dotted with bare trees and tall hemlocks, their boughs swooping to the ground.

A fire blazes in the fireplace, and above the mantel a white-haired man from the previous century scowls out from a huge portrait. Electric chandeliers shed a warm light on the walnut-paneled walls as people gathered in small groups around the room stop talking and stare at the sisters. Florence blushes and fingers her evening purse.

"Dear Edith." An elegant gray-haired woman has come up beside them. She touches Edith's shoulder.

"Chloe, this is my sister, Florence," says Edith. "Florence, Mrs. Barnes."

Mrs. Barnes is a tall woman with a slight stoop in a shimmering, green velvet gown. "Welcome, Florence." She smiles. "I understand you are a pianist. Perhaps you'll play for us after dinner?"

"Oh, ah, yes, of course," Florence stammers and, when Mrs. Barnes turns her head, Florence raises her eyebrows at Edith. She is used to performing but didn't expect it here.

Edith nods, pats her hand, and addresses Mrs. Barnes. "Yes, everyone studied music in our family, but Florence is the musician." Mrs. Barnes nods, then glides away to another group, and Edith whispers, "Your Chicago debut!"

A cough threatens to emerge from Florence's congested chest, and she exhales to suppress it.

Across the room stands a small group of men, natty and sophisticated in their silk-bordered evening jackets and sleek trousers, holding drinks and cigarettes and shouting over each other.

One of them is not talking, however. Turned away from the group, he stares at Florence. He catches her eye and smiles, but she looks away quickly. Then suddenly he is at her side, a tall, handsome gentleman, smooth in his evening suit, with slicked-back hair, a pencil mustache, and deep brown eyes.

"Good evening, ladies." He bows. "Phillip Landers. Can I get you a drink?" He smiles at Florence again, a warm and friendly smile.

"Thank you," says Edith. "Red wine for me and lemonade for my sister."

Phillip turns on his heel and makes his way across the room.

Florence bends down to Edith's ear. "I can speak for myself, Edith," she hisses. "And you don't have to worry about me drinking alcohol. I am following doctor's orders to a T."

When Phillip returns, he hands them their drinks with a playful grin. "And here we have the fair damsels from Pennsylvania?"

"Yes," Edith says, "Florence and Edith Rodkey."

"Well, I must congratulate you."

"Congratulate us?" Florence puzzles.

"Yes, your team beat our team."

"Oh, the World Series," says Edith, turning to Florence. "The Philadelphia Athletics beat the Chicago Cubs."

"Oh? Oh, yes, but we're not from Philadelphia. Closer to Pittsburgh."

She won't mention Mahaffey, as he's probably never heard of it.

Florence is not the least bit interested in baseball and knows nothing about it, but she is charmed by this man's smile and his melodious bass voice. "Do you sing?" she asks.

He laughs. "Only at church."

She giggles and almost chokes on her lemonade, stifling another cough. Phillip Landers couldn't be more different from the Mahaffey boys.

He tells them he is a construction lawyer, and he lives nearby.

"Then you must be quite busy with all the new buildings in Chicago," Edith says.

"Yes, I suppose so."

He's a *lawyer* and he lives on *Astor Street*, Florence thinks. With a man like this, she wouldn't *have* to struggle on a schoolteacher's salary. Not that she wants to get married, she reminds herself.

When dinner is announced, Phillip guides Florence to the dining room and seats her beside him with a bow. "Miss Rodkey."

"Oh, just Florence, please."

"And please call me Zib," he says. "It's what all my friends say."

"Zib. Where does that nickname come from?"

"When I was a basketball player in high school, my buddies started calling me that. Easier than 'Phillip,' I guess. And it stuck."

Dinner consists of five courses: oysters, a cream soup, a lovely poached fish, asparagus, salad, a perfect strawberry Charlotte for dessert, and a different wine with every course. Florence eyes the wine with longing but maintains her discipline and desists. She has no trouble eating almost everything in this luxurious atmosphere.

After dinner, basking in Zib's admiring gaze, and with a nod from Mrs. Barnes, she decides to play something light, "Eine Kleine Nachtmusik." Simple and festive, she's known it since she was a girl, and it flows from her hands like magic. Everyone applauds.

♪

The next day, at Edith's insistence, Florence spends most of her time propped up with pillows, quilts, and a featherbed on the horsehair sofa, gazing into the coal fire. When Edith comes into the room, Florence sighs. "Phillip Landers! Did you see how much attention he paid me? He must be one of the most eligible bachelors in Chicago."

Edith raises an eyebrow in a look of skepticism.

"Well, I know you all think of me as a flirt, but that was just having fun with the hometown boys. This could be the real thing."

After lunch there's a knock at the door, and a delivery boy presents a package for Florence. A box tied with a huge, red velvet ribbon.

She opens the box and gasps at an array of chocolates, with a large chocolate soldier resting in the center. She reads aloud the embossed card: *"Miss Florence Rodkey is invited to accompany Mr. Phillip Landers to the operetta,* The Chocolate Soldier.*"* With a note at the bottom: *I hope you'll come with me tomorrow. Zib.*

"Tomorrow?" exclaims Edith. "So soon!"

"I told him I'm only here for a week. And besides, Edith, an operetta straight from New York! I've heard it's marvelous."

Edith raises an eyebrow. "Well, as long as you rest today—*all* day."

But what to wear? They pick out one of Edith's gowns that would normally be too small for Florence but now fits her because, as Edith points out in a disapproving tone, Florence has lost weight since the summer. It's scarlet silk georgette and "elegant!" Florence exclaims.

Phillip arrives in a fancy carriage, and they drive along the wide avenues of upper-class Chicago to the Garrick Theater, another colossal Chicago edifice.

As they make their way to seats in the orchestra section, several people greet Phillip, and when he introduces her, Florence smiles graciously, a star bestowing her favors.

The Chocolate Soldier is a light-hearted love story that makes Florence laugh, but the music, in her opinion, is not wonderful. Phillip compliments her on her lovely smile and makes a few comments about the play. But it's obvious he doesn't know much about theater, and she feels a sudden wave of nostalgia for Ernest and Pittsburgh. But, of course, Ernest is just her friend and comrade.

In the next few days, Phillip sends her flowers and more candy, "*Chicago's Best Candy*," the box proclaims, and they go out to dinner, again to a fancy restaurant, and then to another play, *The Bachelor Belles*, a big hit, he tells her.

On the journey home from the second play, a light drizzle surrounds the carriage, and the streetlights glow in a misty corona. The carriage bumps along to the muffled clopping of the horse's hoofbeats. Streetlights blink on and off, glimmering in the carriage's dark interior, a fairy-tale setting. Cinderella leaving the ball with Prince Charming.

Fairy tale. Hah! Florence thinks as she twists the glove in her hand. Her mood has plunged.

Oblivious, Zib smiles at her. "What did you think of the play?

Florence lets out a huff. "The costumes were jolly, but I thought the story was dismal. The bachelor belles were fluffy-headed flirts, and all they wanted was to get married!"

He frowns. "But isn't that what all women want?"

She straightens in her most authoritative schoolteacher pose. "Perhaps, but we want more than that. We need to be taken seriously. And for a start, women need to be equal citizens under the law."

"Do you mean suffrage? Are you one of those?"

She raises her eyebrows. "Why not?" This is raising her ire, but is she shooting herself in the foot?

His smile mutates into a wince.

"Are you not in favor of women's suffrage?"

"Not in favor of these wild women marching around the streets with signs," he says with a snort.

She snorts inwardly. Maybe he's not the perfect man.

His face suddenly softens into a smile, and he winks at her. "But if anyone deserves a say in the country's matters, it's you." He looks out through the steamy window, then back at her. "Florence, you are the most delightful creature I've met in years."

Creature?

"Oh!" she sinks back on the seat, a lump of fear in her chest. *Isn't he exactly what I wanted? A charming man with a good income. But he's not in favor of women's suffrage! And wasn't that "creature" comment condescending?*

Ernest has never looked down on her.

But Phillip Landers is what anyone would call a good catch.

♪

At breakfast Florence puts down her coffee cup and smiles. "I might be falling in love, Edith."

"Again?" Edith smiles as they both remember a few times Florence has said that before.

"But Phillip is handsome and successful, not like old Tommy Schweizer in old Mahaffey. *And* he might ask me to marry him."

"My dear, you hardly know him! You just met him last week."

"I know, but just think, I'd never have to work again! I wouldn't have to scrimp and save every penny."

"Are you in love with him?"

"Well . . . I don't want to be an old maid."

Edith frowns.

"Oh, I didn't mean—*You* have a career, Edith, and a good income. All I have is a lowly schoolteacher's salary. But I'll go to New Mexico and then see if he's still interested." *And if I'm still interested.*

The next day Edith takes Florence on another trolley ride, this time to a different part of the city. People stroll along a street lined with little stores, and when the trolley clangs to a stop, the sisters get off in front of a large shop with a big sign over the door, BAKERY. Beneath the sign, three women in tailored jackets and skirts hold up a signboard that almost conceals the bakery window: VOTES FOR WOMEN.

Florence claps her hands. "Oh! Brava! Brava!"

Inside, another three women sit at a small table. "Please join us," one woman says, pointing to a petition in front of her. Florence peers at the long list of signatures, mostly women's but even some men's names.

"That's exactly why we came," Edith says as she bends over and takes a pen.

On the wall behind the women, a huge sign reads, UNIVERSAL SUFFRAGE

"Oh, yes," Florence exclaims. "I completely agree."

"In some states," a serious-looking young woman declaims, "the vote is ratified already, but we need a national law that allows *all* of us a say. If we have to obey the laws, we should be able to vote on them!"

"And make them!" says Edith.

The sisters sign the petition. *Here's something to write to Ernest about,* Florence thinks. He'll be as excited as she is.

chapter 6

SENTIMENTAL JOURNEY

Pittsburgh, Pennsylvania, 1941

"Sallie, did you go to the bathroom?"

"I don't have to go, Daddy."

"Go anyway. There won't be a bathroom there."

Sallie harumphs and runs up the stairs two at a time.

Flossie sighs. This happens every time they go out the door. Daddy orders everyone to use the bathroom, even Elizabeth.

"And, Flossie, put on another pair of shoes, for goodness' sake," he says. "You can't walk through the cemetery in high heels."

"These aren't really high," she protests, but shrugs and runs back up to her room. On her bed are strewn clothes she already considered for today's outing: a dress, a skirt and blouse, and her new belt. She gathers them and puts them in the wardrobe, then examines herself in the full-length cheval mirror, smoothing her long, dark curls. She admires the wide-legged pants she'd just finished making, the short-sleeved sweater blouse, and a dashing little scarf at the neck. A Joan Crawford look, very chic right now. The platform shoes go with it, but she slips them off and puts on her Keds, not stylish at all. You can't argue with Daddy and his rules.

Flossie walks to the stairs as Sallie grins and slides down the banister, pigtails flopping. "Beat you!" she calls and runs to the kitchen. Flossie considers the banister, polished to a dark gleam from so many children sliding on it. *Well, I've got my pants on, so why not?* She throws a leg over and coasts down to the front hall, hitting the newel post with a hard bump on her behind. An undignified relapse into childhood, but no one saw.

The day has turned warm, unseasonable for late October, and Ernest has rallied the family for an outing to his favorite place, the Homewood Cemetery. They pile into the old gray Ford, Nannie in front, Elizabeth, Flossie, and Sallie in the back. Roddy, out with his friends, has escaped this outing.

The Homewood Cemetery, like much of Pittsburgh, is situated on hilly terrain. In the summer, elms, maples, and oaks shade the sloping lawns; now, in the end-of-autumn light, their spindly limbs quiver black against a gray sky.

The family gets out of the car and starts the trek up the hill to the Craighead plot. As they walk past a larger-than-life stone angel, its massive wings emerging from the slab of a tomb, Flossie's arms prickle with goose bumps. Death, a human-like figure, frozen in cold stone.

Ernest declaims, pointing out dates and names as he hurries everyone toward the Craighead plot, while Elizabeth, always a good sport, lopes along behind with her cane, and Sallie runs back and forth, leaping over the lower gravestones. Nannie, not to be pushed by her bossy son, comes last at her own slow pace, and Flossie weaves in and out of the headstones, pausing to read inscriptions. Some of the stones mark names she's familiar with. Eleanor Hamilton—Hammie's grandmother—and here are some Mellons and Carnegies, prominent Pittsburgh names, though these must be the more distant members of these families. The stones are small and not in the more impressive family plots.

"We'll take a detour here." Ernest consults his cemetery map. "Now, come up this hill to see the Fricks." He says it as if they were visiting the family in their home. He likes to claim familiarity with the Pittsburgh notables.

Sallie races ahead, Flossie follows her father, and Nannie and Elizabeth trudge behind them up the hill, its grass still green in late October. At the summit they stop at the Frick family section, a large rectangular stone monument overlooking smaller headstones.

"Henry Clay Frick was one of the first Pittsburgh industrialists," Ernest declaims in a proud voice. "He started the steel business here."

A gust of wind blows dry leaves around the graves, and Elizabeth rolls her eyes.

This, Flossie knows, means Elizabeth has an opinion. "What is it?" Flossie asks.

Elizabeth straightens, her cane propped in front of her, and blots her forehead with a handkerchief. "That man wasn't very popular in Pittsburgh."

"Why not?"

"He caused the Johnstown Flood." She pauses dramatically. "Two thousand people died."

"Oh!" Flossie says as everyone, even Sallie, falls silent.

"Well, we don't know if he actually caused it," Ernest says.

Nannie, with a fierce look in her brown eyes, glares at Ernest. "He certainly did," she says. "Frick's negligence caused the dam to break. Up there, living the sporting life, while the flood waters took out Johnstown. It was like an Old Testament plague."

They stand in silence, looking at the grave.

Henry Clay Frick
December 18, 1849
December 2, 1919
Father

"All life must end," says Nannie. "And our task is to make the best of it. Not to take from others but to help them in Christian love. Thank goodness for people like Elizabeth Barton. She organized the rescue and recovery for Johnstown."

After a silence, Ernest pauses and rubs his chin. "But *Mrs.* Frick was a lovely lady."

"Did you know her, Daddy?" Flossie asks.

"Yes indeed. She was in the historical society with me."

"But why are those gravestones lying down?" Sallie points to the horizontal slabs, flat marble with curving headstones like headboards.

"It's just to make it look like the people are sleeping," Elizabeth says.

They troop back down the hill to the less grand Craighead site, where several ordinary-looking stones are lined up amid open spaces for subsequent graves. "There's your grandfather," Ernest announces to Flossie and Sallie with a glance at Nannie. He points at one of the older gravestones inscribed in blackened script.

Franklin Craighead
1842–1920

"This is a pretty one!" Sallie skips over to a marble stone engraved with a wreath of roses and ivy.

Florence Rodkey Craighead
1887–1918

Ernest stands still and silent, his eyes filling with tears.
"That's my mother," says Flossie.
Elizabeth, her stepmother, stands quietly behind Daddy.
"She was so young," Nannie sighs.

♪

Flossie stands in the doorway of her father's study and waits for him to turn around. He loads a piece of onion skin paper into his brand new 1939 Royal typewriter and resumes typing. Around him, neatly arranged on the colossal mahogany desk, sit stacks of typewriter paper sorted into piles according to dates and family names, and on the floor, musty-smelling boxes of letters and books, all in an order only he understands.

For ten years, he's been sitting at this enormous desk in this dark room, writing a book. *The Fulton Family of Westmoreland County, Pennsylvania,* chronicles the lives of almost two thousand descendants of Abraham Fulton, the aptly named patriarch who came to Pennsylvania from Northern Ireland in 1772.

Flossie watches as her father types in another name and a number. He is proud of the system he invented for designating each of the descendant's places in the family tree. Every person has a number. Descendants of Abraham's first child start with a one, his second with a two, and subsequent generations add numbers in a similar order. Ernest, who descended from the first child of Abraham's third child, is number 31222.

Daddy pauses from typing and gazes out the grimy little window to the backyard where Sallie, in her winter coat, is swinging on the swing hung from the old elm tree. Sallie is happiest playing by herself or with her dog, Apollo. A quiet child, so different from Flossie, who never stops talking, according to Nannie. Daddy says Flossie is a lot like her mother. So, Flossie tries, even when she's sad inside, to be cheerful, to smile, to be lively.

Daddy still hasn't noticed her. Maybe she shouldn't be spying on him like this, but she knows that, as he dwells on the past, he is also dwelling on *her*. Her mother, his first wife. He is such a packrat that he probably has all kinds of things—letters and papers and souvenirs. Flossie has seen some of the photos and heard stories about her mother's music and her marching in the suffrage parade, but there is still so much he *hasn't* said about her. Doesn't Flossie have a right to know? To see some of those things?

Daddy sighs and picks up the cedar box. It's been sitting on his desk forever, but he never talks about what's inside it.

He caresses the box, and a woody balsamic scent fills the air.

"Daddy!" Flossie steps into the study, jolting him out of his reverie.

"Flossie, how many times have I told you to knock?"

"I know, but this is important." She glances at the cedar box he's holding. "I'm going Christmas shopping for Hammie. Do you think it will get all the way to Hawaii?" Might as well start with something easy.

"Yes, but it will probably take a long time."

She stands quiet. The cedar box is still in his hands. She knows it has something to do with her mother.

"What else do you want?"

"What's in that box?"

Daddy is silent.

Flossie waits.

"This was your mother's box. She would sit at her dressing table, brushing her hair and looking through it. She had an abundance of chestnut-colored hair. She was quite beautiful, you know."

"I know." She's heard this before.

"That was in the bedroom of our first apartment. Our own first home."

Flossie blinks. This is something she's never heard before. "You had an apartment? Where was it?"

"Down on Hawthorne Avenue."

"And after she died, you brought Roddy and me here to live with Nannie and Grandaddy?"

Ernest winces. He doesn't like to hear the word "die." But it's been twenty-two years, after all. He gazes out the window to the sky above the old elm tree. "In here, Florence kept theater tickets, souvenirs, trinkets, and her yellow sash. Sometimes she would take it out. It had VOTES FOR WOMEN printed on it."

"Yes, I've seen it in the scrapbook."

"She wore it in the big suffragist parade in Pittsburgh in 1914. It was the first integrated suffragist event. She was so proud of that. She never failed to tell people. Colored and white women marching together."

"But what's in the box now?"

"I keep her letters here."

"Could I see them?" To read her mother's own words in her own handwriting—that would be wonderful. It would be almost like finding her, connecting with her, daughter to mother. And after all this time . . .

It's not that Flossie has complaints about Elizabeth and Nannie. They do their best. Even though Nannie can be overly strict sometimes, and Elizabeth, who is kind and gentle, doesn't stand up to Nannie. Or Daddy. Besides, Elizabeth has Sallie, who is clearly favored.

Flossie peers past her father and through the little window. It's starting to rain and a misty cloud blurs the sight of Sallie and Apollo. *Girl on swing with dog*, Flossie thinks, a scene from an old-fashioned storybook. Sallie's life is so cozy, so complete, while there's always been this hole in Flossie's, the place where her own mother should be. A mother who loves her own child the best.

Ernest has retracted into himself like a turtle, into a silent stillness.

"Maybe just one letter?" Flossie says.

Ernest turns to look out the window again. "Someday."

♪

On the landing, Flossie stops and looks at the portrait. *You are the only one who knows about my engagement to Hammie. What would you say?*

I do want to get married, and have a little house with a yard and two sweet children. My children will be like Roddy and me, going to parties, laughing and dancing. Well, not with Roddy's incessant teasing and definitely not with Roddy's drinking and staying out all night. My children will have me, a real *mother.*

But will Hammie be a good husband? A good father?

Flossie pauses, twisting a lock of hair round and round her finger, while from the parlor comes the sound of the piano and Nannie singing a hymn. Nannie is almost eighty, but she still has a clear soprano voice. "*Shall we gather at the river, where bright angel feet have trod . . .*"

Nannie always seems to know the right thing to do. Maybe Flossie can ask her about getting married. Nannie is always softer and happier with music.

Flossie skips down the stairs and into the dark parlor with its heavy mahogany tables and old-fashioned furniture. Nannie sings and plays with such heart; the song seems to bring light into the room. It was Nannie, after all, who taught music to Flossie and Roddy.

Flossie stands behind Nannie and joins in, singing the alto part. "*Yes, we'll gather at the river, the beautiful, the beautiful river . . .*"

When the song ends, they both smile and feel the afterglow of the music.

After a suitable pause, Flossie speaks up. "Nannie, can I talk to you?"

"Of course, dear." Nannie turns around on the piano bench. "What is on your mind?" Nannie truly is beautiful, with her fine, chiseled features and her silver hair pulled back in a bun. And when she smiles, she radiates love.

"I'm thinking about getting married."

"Married? Now?" Nannie's back straightens and the soft smile transforms into a stiff frown. "To whom?"

Flossie sits and shrinks into the chair. "Well," her voice trembling, "Hammie?"

"Hammie Hamilton? He's just a boy. And you're just a girl. Much too young to get married."

"Nannie, I'm twenty-two! And so is Hammie. Most of our friends are already married!"

"Well, that's fine for other families. But no one in this family gets married until they are at least twenty-five."

"Twenty-*five?* I'll be an old maid by then." How could Flossie think Nannie would help her with this decision? It just makes her want to elope.

"I was twenty-eight when I married your grandfather. And your mother was almost thirty when she and your father married." She turns her gaze to the windows and the gloomy sky. "No. Absolutely not."

Flossie feels a tear forming and she clenches her fist. *I will not cry . . .*

"Besides," Nannie says, "it looks like our dithering president is leading us into war. You are not to even think about marriage now!" She turns back to the piano and picks up the hymnal.

Nannie is so opinionated, and on top of that she thinks Flossie needs her permission to get married! *I am twenty-two. I don't need her permission.*

Flossie stomps out of the room. There's no point in talking with Nannie.

chapter 7

THE NIGHT TRAIN

Chihuahuan Desert, New Mexico, 1910

Two thousand miles from home, night has fallen. With all the jostling and lurching, the engine rumbling and the train whistle blasting, Florence hasn't fallen asleep yet. But just as she starts to drift off, the whole train thuds to a stop with a knock so hard it jolts her to a sitting position.

From the corridor come the sounds of scurrying feet, knocks on doors, and shouts of "Everybody up!"

"What?" Florence cries. "What happened?"

"Train wreck," the conductor calls from behind her door. "Everyone out."

"But what do you mean?" She peers out her window into the dark. "We're in the middle of the desert!"

"Sorry, lady, that's the order."

"In my nightdress?"

"Oh, you have time to change. But make haste and gather your things."

To go into the desert? She's never set foot in the desert, that black, empty space out there, with wolves and javelinas and whatever other wild animals roam about, snapping their jaws in the dark.

Why couldn't she have stayed in Pittsburgh this year? Gone back to the apartment on Coal Street with Mary and seen the children with their eager faces in her classroom? Gone to a play with Mary and Ernest, laughed with the others? Florence pounds the pillow. She wasn't *that* sick, and when the train reached Ohio, the cough had subsided. Well, it did come back by the time she reached Chicago, but that was only because of the smoke and coal dust.

And now she *is* keen to discover the west, an exotic and foreign country—cowboys and Indians, deserts and mountains. Who knows what adventures await.

She peels off her nightgown, hastily pulls on her dress and shoes, and opens the door.

"We're boarding another train," the conductor says with a sympathetic smile. "Just ahead of the wreck."

A train wreck. Wait till she tells Ernest. He thinks she's traveling in luxury out here, with conductors and waiters dressed in white coats serving Champagne. Now he'll find out how adventurous she is. She will forge her way ahead, trek through the desert. She starts throwing everything into the trunk. She was so tired last night she didn't put anything away, but at least that makes it easier to stuff it all in now.

She peers out above the window shade; dark eyes stare in, and she jumps.

"Who are those people?" she shouts as she throws on her dress.

"Mexicans," a man's voice says from the corridor.

Mexicans? Florence has never seen a Mexican. Are they dangerous? Will they rob her?

"They're here to help," the voice calls again.

But those piercing dark eyes.

Florence shakes out her skirt. She stands up straight and goes out to the corridor. *I can be bold*, she thinks, *and this is an adventure.*

"But who will bring our trunks?" she calls to anyone who might hear.

"Don't you worry, miss. We'll get everything." The conductor, a short, chubby man, appears from behind her. "You just make your way on out there, now. Just follow the people."

She grips her valise and steps down from the train onto the sand and into the dark. Not completely dark, as distant mountain silhouettes emerge black against an indigo sky. And the smell—clean and earthy with a tang of sage.

But where are the other passengers? Far ahead of her, no doubt. She stumbles, trips, and almost falls, trying to catch up.

A sudden gust of wind whips up the sand, thrashing her dress up and across, obscuring everything.

A young man emerges from the darkness and extends his arm.

"Oh!" Florence starts. He's almost as dark as the night. He must be one of the Mexicans. The conductor said they were here to help, and this man seems polite. *Well, this is the only help on offer, and it's not easy walking on the sand with these heels.* She takes his arm.

As abruptly as it started, the wind dies down, and the distant mountain range becomes a majestic citadel under a halo of glittering stars. She breathes in. "Aah."

The young man, who she now sees is quite handsome, smiles. "The most magnificent sky in the world."

She nods. "Not like home."

But perhaps now this is home.

chapter 8

A NEW KIND OF LOVE

Pittsburgh, Pennsylvania, 1941

Flossie looks up from the letter she's writing. From the window seat she can see down the hillside to the line of six poplar trees. Tall and narrow, their branches bare and spindly now, they were planted by Flossie's grandfather, Franklin Craighead, who built this house, and they each have a name. She scans her eyes across them, silently reciting their names in her well-worn ritual: Franklin, Nancy, Ernest, Mary, Sophie, Gordy—her grandparents, father, aunts, and uncle. The Craighead ancestors, standing there like guardians, marking the edge of the property, protecting and shaping the borders of Flossie's life.

The family trees. Her father tends the trees as if they really are people. He feeds them and prunes them, and when one or the other looks to be declining, losing branches or not growing like the others, he worries and frets, muttering about Sophie dwindling or Gordy falling behind. And then Nannie wrings her hands, as if the trees are not just symbols but have some real connection to the people, as if the essence of the people is somehow imbued in the trees. Sometimes Flossie wonders why no one planted trees for her generation—her mother, her brother, and herself. Maybe a dogwood tree for her, a magnolia for her mother, and something flashy for Roddy, like a flowering cherry that screeches out bright colors for a brief time.

But most of the time the trees give her a sense of security, a feeling of permanence and stability, something akin to what her father pursues with his family history studies. A stability disrupted when her mother died.

A few yellow leaves sail off in the wind and float over the rooftops of the city, as if across the railroad tracks and all the way to Schenley Park, like pieces of the Craighead family spreading throughout Pittsburgh.

But what about the other side of her family, the Rodkeys? How do they shape her life? Daddy still hasn't allowed her to see her mother's letters. He can be awfully stubborn. Flossie clenches her fist. Wouldn't it help her to know what her mother was thinking about being engaged? About getting married?

Flossie twists the diamond ring around on her finger. She hasn't yet told the family that she's engaged, so she only wears it when she's alone. *Did I accept it only because Hammie was going into the army? Do you get engaged out of pity? Or do I really love him? He's been such a good friend all these years.*

Hammie writes to Flossie every week, and she tries to write back just as often. He was sent to basic training at Fort Indiantown Gap and then deployed to the Pacific islands. But what if America enters the war and something terrible happens to him? This threat that she has successfully ignored so far is now front and center in her mind.

She misses him. She misses the way he bounces when he walks and how he breaks into belly laughs at silly things. And how they dance together. They are such a good fit, in step and in tune with each other.

She and Hammie have been good friends since they were six years old, when Hammie's grandmother, a friend of Nannie's, brought him with her for tea one day. Hurray for a boy her own age to play with, Flossie thought, someone different than Roddy, who was eight—older and rougher. With Hammie she took turns on the swing and ran around the house playing tag, and when Roddy tried to make her taste a worm on her tongue, Hammie defended her. He tasted the worm first and then threw it away.

She bends over the letter again, trying not to write too fast, trying to keep her handwriting legible. She tells him about their crowd: who is courting whom, who has been drafted, the picnics in the mountains in Ligonier, the dancing at the "speakeasies," as Nannie calls them.

She looks up again as the last of the yellow leaves flutter away, and picks up Hammie's letter. For someone so loquacious in person, he doesn't say much in his letters. He writes "hot here" and "pretty nice weather" or "saw some nice fish," vacuous phrases that don't mean much. And he never says exactly where he is. He's probably not supposed to, and if he did, it might be censored. She's already received a couple of letters with big black cross-out marks through a couple of lines. But Hammie likes hearing about everyone from home, so she elaborates in her letters. She's still not sure about the engagement. *But if we join the war, and he has to fight* . . . The newsreels are getting scarier, with images of soldiers marching in Europe and planes dropping bombs. She clutches her chest and swallows. Hammie will need all the love he can get.

But why has she been so hesitant about the engagement? Hammie is her best friend, and he loves her. He'll make the perfect husband. She's known Hammie almost all her life. He's a deep-rooted part of her, almost like the family trees. She takes a deep breath and sighs. *Yes*, she writes. *When you come home, we can get married.*

She finishes with *Love, Flossie*, and a red lipstick kiss under her signature.

She seals the letter, puts two airmail stamps on it, and hurries down the stairs before she changes her mind. Out through the screen door from the kitchen and across the lawn, still green in this warm October. The formal front door is on the other side, the downhill side of the house, but the kitchen door is, for all intents and purposes, the main entrance; it opens to the uphill side, the back lawn and the driveway. Flossie picks her way down the cobbled drive.

On Lacrosse Street she slips the thin envelope into the mailbox and waves to Mildred Campbell, her neighbor, who huffs as she pushes a baby buggy up the steep sidewalk across the street. *When I have a baby,* Flossie thinks, *I will not live on a steep hill like this.*

Flossie trudges back up the cobblestone driveway. Elizabeth's young cousin George is coming for dinner tonight, and she reminds herself to slow down so she doesn't perspire. She's already wearing her best blue serge dress and the bright red lipstick her father disapproves of. *But I am twenty-two, after all. And still unmarried.*

George isn't as lively as Hammie, but he is nice. And gentle. He's a doctor or will be soon. George is nine years older than Flossie, thirty-one. Is she too young for him? Is he too old for her? No, of course not. He's mature, a welcome change after some of the boys in her crowd with their silly antics. She fidgets with the bobby pin in her hair, takes it out and reinserts it to keep the Hepburn wave up and back. *But why am I thinking like this about George when I just accepted Hammie's proposal?* She slows her pace on the uneven cobblestones. *Well, I can be friendly and welcoming without becoming romantic.*

George is finishing a medical residency at Allegheny General Hospital in Pittsburgh's North Side, and Elizabeth, his only relative in Pittsburgh, has welcomed him into the family in Edgewood. Lately George has been showing up more and more often for Sunday dinner.

Flossie takes off the ring and puts it in her pocket. Her shoulders tense with guilt and she stops. She glances at the house, but no one is around. *Well, push on,* she tells herself. This murky cloud in her mind has to clear up soon.

Sunday dinner is at mid-day, following the morning church service at Edgewood Presbyterian Church. The church, perched on a triangular corner of Edgewood Avenue near the bottom of Lacrosse Street, is an imposing edifice of stone, modeled after its Scottish ancestors. Like much of Pittsburgh, its facade is blackened by soot. Perhaps daunting to a passerby, with its somber black stones sticking out like a fortress, this church is a cornerstone in Craighead family history. Since Flossie's grandfather's time, the family has come here every Sunday, and it's where Ernest met Elizabeth when Roddy and Flossie were young.

When Daddy announced the marriage plans, the siblings were outraged. It seemed so soon, even though it was twelve years after their mother died. But no one could question the suitability of a second wife who attended Edgewood Presbyterian—and was an English teacher to boot.

At the top of the driveway, Flossie takes a detour through the side garden, where daisies, marigolds, and purple asters are still blooming. She picks a bunch, then goes to the back porch, and the scent of mint greets her. "Mm," she murmurs, stooping to pick a few sprigs.

In the kitchen Elizabeth turns from taking a bowl of coleslaw out of the icebox and smiles at Flossie. Eventually, she and Roddy admitted that if they had to have a stepmother, Elizabeth was the best choice. Elizabeth, a short, buxom woman with classic beauty—high cheekbones and a straight nose, like Jean Arthur—is kind and mild-tempered, as

opposed to their father, who can be bullish and brusque. Elizabeth sometimes steps in, too, with a peaceful distraction if Nannie or Daddy get
too harsh. Flossie has learned to count on Elizabeth to back her up if she
needs it.

"Look!" Flossie holds up the mint and lays it on the table. "For the
iced tea."

"Good." Elizabeth nods and turns back to the oven.

Flossie takes a vase out of the cupboard, fills it with water, and steps
into the dining room. She arranges the flowers in the vase, stepping back
to examine and then reposition them until she's satisfied. The top drawer
of the heavy old sideboard creaks as she opens it to take out the good
silver. Late afternoon sun streams in through the high windows, streak-
ing bars of light across the table to burnish the purple and white flowers
of the centerpiece.

George can sit here, directly across from me. Flossie lays down the last
salad fork and turns to the china cabinet. As usual, Elizabeth has polished
the silverware, and it gleams in the sunlight. The china was a wedding
gift for her mother, and it's only used for Sunday dinner. Flossie pauses.
Elizabeth has never said anything about it, but what does she think about
using the china of her husband's first wife?

Flossie rearranges George's butter plate. George doesn't laugh uproar-
iously like Hammie, but when Flossie laughs, which is often, his face
breaks into a sweet smile. Over the past few months, he's become less shy
and, thanks to Elizabeth, seems to feel at home here.

♪

When everyone is seated at the table and the blessing has been said,
Ernest doles out the ham with baked beans, brown bread, and coleslaw,
and the room falls silent as everyone begins to eat.

Roddy is the first to speak. "How are things at the hospital, Doc?" he
addresses George. "Save any lives this week?"

Flossie frowns at Roddy. "That's not something to take lightly."

"That's okay," George says. "But I'm not in the emergency room
anymore. Now I'm in obstetrics." He takes a dinner roll and passes the
dish to Sallie. "But it's a lot of work, and it's nice to get away. I've been
learning to play golf."

"Hotsy totsy!" Roddy exclaims, leaning forward with a big smile. "I'm gonna do that someday, too, but for that you need some big clams."

Nannie puts down her fork. "Clams to play golf?"

Roddy and Flossie laugh, and George explains that "clams" means money.

Nannie draws herself up into her straightest posture and, with a stern expression, says, "In this house we do not use slang at the dinner table, Rodkey Craighead."

Everyone goes silent.

Nannie looks around the table and the corner of her mouth twitches. "Unless you're really *blotto, buster.*"

Roddy and Flossie break out into belly laughs, and Roddy claps his hands. "*Two* slang words in one sentence, Nannie! Hurrah!"

Nannie presses her mouth closed to suppress the smile that shows in her eyes. With her gray hair pulled back in a bun and her pale blue eyes behind rimless glasses, she looks a lot like Daddy. For both Daddy and Nannie, order is tantamount. Everything has its time and place, and the rhythms of the days and nights help to anchor us in the world. Dinner at six, bedtime at nine, kneeling at the bedside for prayers before bed, and so on. But they both know how to laugh and make a joke, a quality that softens the strictness and makes them both, at times, endearing.

"What's slang?" asks Sallie.

♪

After dinner, Sallie scoots away to find Ruthie, her cat, and Ernest retires to his study. George turns to Flossie. "Would you like to go out for ice cream?"

"Oh." She's taken aback, but in a good way, and she blushes. "But we've just had dessert! And I have to do the dishes." Nannie smiles down at her empty plate. It's important not to appear too eager, but Flossie is smiling on the inside.

"Well, how about a ride to Schenley Park," he counters, "after the dishes?"

"I'd love it."

George offers to help with the dishes and tries to send Elizabeth out of the kitchen, but she shoos him away. "Much faster if we do it."

Flossie and Elizabeth finish the dishes, and Flossie throws down her dish towel. "Okay, let's go!" she shouts and storms through the kitchen door that closes with a bang. George stands from his seat on the porch glider, and they walk across the lawn to the car. George beams as he pats the hood of his shiny new Buick and opens the door for her. The car bounces down the steep driveway to the street.

"So luxurious!" Flossie gushes as she settles into the plush upholstery. "And it's so much nicer to see the sights this way instead of from the trolley." The car turns onto Forbes Avenue, and they cruise past the Pittsburgh landmarks—the Frick mansion, ornate and austere on a hill above the street, the Carnegie Museum, massive in blackened stone, and the glass-domed Phipps Conservatory, where you can see tropical flowers at any time of year.

Everything is beautiful today: the sweet-smelling air, the scent of the car leather, George's sensitive hands on the big steering wheel. Flossie grins and he gives her one of his loving smiles. It *is* there, a real spark between them, and she knows he feels it, too.

Around the bend past the Carnegie Museum and Phipps Conservatory, they coast from a gray and brown city of stone into a shady green landscape of grassy hills and tall trees. Schenley Park. George pulls the car over and stops on the side of the road. "Okay to stop here?"

Flossie smiles. "How did you know? This is my favorite place in the park!" She jumps out and they stroll along a winding path under the trees. They climb a shallow slope and step under the bright canopy of a maple tree with leaves just starting to turn yellow.

Walking side by side, their hands brush briefly. *Will he take my hand?* she wonders. *He's a little shy—maybe I should take the initiative.* She reaches out, then pulls back. Should she encourage him? She doesn't want to look too pushy. And anyway, she's engaged to Hammie, isn't she?

This is the first time Flossie has been alone with George, and it's so different from walking with Hammie. George has a grace and a peaceful quality, striding on his long legs, whereas Hammie is all movement and exclamation. Walking beside George, she has a sudden insight. It's like his gentleness is a counterpoint to her lively energy, as if they are together in a dance or a song, he the bass, she the alto.

Flossie stops and faces him. Enough fantasizing. She wants to tell him her news. Might as well blurt it out. "Mrs. Doak is retiring," she says.

"Who's Mrs. Doak?"

"She's my boss at the gift shop. And I'm going to be in charge!"

♪

The day Flossie got Mrs. Doak's letter for Aunt Mary was the same day Hammie proposed. She sat at her dressing table, trying on the ring and taking it off and wondering. Could she marry Hammie? Should she wait for him? Her shoulders hunched, her eyebrows squeezed together, and she focused on the letter. She was too worked up to go to bed.

Flossie grabbed the letter and flew out of the house, skipping down the hill to Aunt Mary's home, a small brick Tudor. Flossie rushed to the back door.

Aunt Mary's kitchen, a cozy room wallpapered in blue, backs up against the hillside, and is dark, but her aunt's presence always seems to lighten the atmosphere, her graceful calm a mainstay for Flossie.

Through the screen door she spied her aunt in her customary dress of pastel blue, washing dishes.

"Come in, Flossie." Aunt Mary smiled and wiped her hands on a dish towel. "To what do I owe the honor?"

Flossie had two important things on her mind—the ring and the letter. If she could tell anyone about the "engagement," it would be Aunt Mary, but her aunt would probably disapprove of Flossie's having accepted the ring when she wasn't sure about the marriage.

Instead, she handed Aunt Mary the letter and plopped herself down at the kitchen table.

"What's this?" Mary stood, looking at the letter with just her name on the front. No address or postmark. "From Mrs. Doak?"

"I just have to know if it's about me," Flossie said, taking a chocolate cookie from a plate on the table. Aunt Mary made the most delicious baked goods.

Mary sat across from Flossie, still pondering the letter, while Flossie took a big bite of the cookie, trying not to prod.

Mary lifted her coffee cup and examined the envelope in her hand,

Flossie clasped her hands together. "Please, Aunt Mary, could you open the letter?"

Mary opened the letter, and as she read, a slow smile crossed her face. "Well?"

"She's inviting me to lunch."

"Oh." Flossie bowed her head, covering her eyes with her hands.

"And—" Mary's smile turned mischievous. "She's retiring from the gift shop. And promoting you to manager."

Flossie skipped home all the way up the steep hill.

The next day at the gift shop, Mrs. Doak had just finished instructing a volunteer on how to present a rosebud at a patient's bedside. She turned and smiled at Flossie. "Such a good idea of yours."

Flossie smiled, then couldn't help blurting out, "Aunt Mary told me about the letter."

"Oh, yes, I wasn't going to tell you yet. You've done a good job here, and you know it's time for me to retire. I think you can manage on your own."

Flossie beamed at the praise and listened as her role model elaborated on the responsibilities of the manager. Of course, she would miss the woman's strong and forceful presence. It was almost as if Mrs. Doak herself *was* the shop. But Flossie was eager to practice being that presence herself.

♪

George stops and faces Flossie. "In charge of what?"

"The whole gift shop!"

He raises his eyebrows. "I'm sure you'll be good at it."

George is right. She is good at being in charge, and it's a role she likes. "And I'm making some innovations, too. I had the idea of getting people to donate a single rose in a bud vase for people who don't get visitors. The hospital loved it, and they even put an article about it in the *Post-Gazette* with my picture."

George nods and gives her a look of admiration. "You're a charitable woman. And an entrepreneur."

"An entrepreneur?" Flossie casts her eyes up to the sky. This is a new thought. "Maybe I am. Maybe it runs in the family. You know, Daddy has his real estate business, and his father, my Grandfather Craighead, owned a lamp shop in Pittsburgh."

I could start a business, Flossie thinks. In her mind's eye she sees fabrics—rich brown and green woolens, plaids with a nubby weave for a suit. The suit would have a peplum edge to the jacket, very feminine. And dresses. A long, silk gown in baby blue, a bright red cocktail dress in satin with a deep V neck . . . She can just see them in the window of that little shop on Fifth Avenue in Shadyside . . .

"You look like you're off in the clouds," George says with an amused smile.

"Oh, yes! I'm thinking I could design dresses, like I did in college! And sell them!"

"Of course you could."

On the way home they pass a tall, Art Deco building in pale beige brick, standing alone, a futuristic edifice reaching into the sky.

"Oh, let's stop at Isaly's," Flossie burbles. Everyone knows that Isaly's has the best ice cream in Pittsburgh, and this odd lone building is a Pittsburgh icon.

They sit at a little round table, dwarfed in this high room. Blond brick on all sides extends to the twenty-foot ceiling. Only two other customers occupy this cavernous room: an old woman and a large young man, apparently her son, sitting in the back. The little tables in this vast space look like doll furniture and the people like dolls in a dollhouse

Flossie orders a peppermint cone, her favorite. Isaly's molds the ice cream into an upside-down cone shape, their own invention, and George has a Klondike, another signature Isaly's creation.

Flossie licks the pink ice cream and bites into a crunchy peppermint candy, glancing up at George. "I guess you're almost done with your residency? Do you have plans for your new practice?"

George straightens up in his chair and grins. "I bought a little building in Ambridge."

"Ambridge?" She swallows a big chunk of ice cream. "That's the town with all the steel mills?"

"Yes. Ambridge, short for American Bridge. It's north and west up the Ohio River. And Bethlehem Steel is there, too. I've been out there and talked to the manager at the mill. And it looks like I might become their mill doctor for a while."

"In the steel mill?" Flossie shudders. "I've heard of so many injuries at those mills."

"Well, that's why they need a doctor. But it's only part-time, and the rest of the time I'll be starting my practice."

She places her hand on her heart and gazes at him with admiration. "You are dedicating your life to helping people. It's what Nannie always tells us to do with our lives. As Christians, our highest purpose should be to help others."

George blushes. "Well—"

"And it means you'll be staying in Pittsburgh?"

"For a long time, I think." He hesitates. Flossie has an urge to jump in and fill in the silence, but she stays quiet as he coughs and takes her hand.

He smiles. Here they are, together, sitting at a fairy-tale table in this lofty room with the high cold walls, a world of gleaming brick, clanking ice cream scoopers, peppermint ice cream and Klondikes—a world that has suddenly become a magical place, a bubble enveloping them.

The magic is a warmth and a glow inside Flossie, and she wants to stay in this moment forever.

But what about Hammie?

chapter 9

LA CUCARACHA

Clovis, New Mexico, October, 1910

Florence sits beside the driver, a quiet Mexican man named Manuel, as the wagon bumps along the arid land, dry and hard like a washboard. She'd gotten settled on the new train as it wheezed and whistled and enveloped her in smoke through the Texas panhandle and the New Mexican plains and finally arrived in Clovis. The Clovis train station resembles a little shack in the wilderness. When she alighted, the only person besides her on the platform was this inscrutable man in a sombrero who knew her name. "Senorita Rodkey, El Rancho Yeso," he said, pointing to the cart and horse.

The horse trots at a steady pace as the cart thuds and jolts, bouncing her up and down. Manuel doesn't move or look around.

In the distance, a tabletop of rock thrusts up from the flat plain.

Florence points to the outcropping. "What's that?"

Manuel turns his head toward her with a tiny grin, not looking her in the eye. "Mesa," he says. "Mesa Yeso."

"Mesa Yeso," she repeats in a singsong voice. It sounds like a children's song. El Yeso is the name of the ranch, so a mesa must be what they call that flat-topped hill. She hums a little tune to herself.

Suddenly Manuel lifts his head and starts to sing. In a beautiful tenor, he belts out a cheerful, bouncy song that seems to have many verses. "*La cucaracha, la cucaracha . . .*"

Florence strains to understand, but her French doesn't help her much with the Spanish. She does recognize one word, though: *Pancho Villa.*

Manuel's song goes on and on for at least five minutes, and when he stops, he is silent again, staring ahead.

"What does it mean?" she asks.

His eyes shift toward her, but his head doesn't move.

"Is it about Pancho Villa? I recognize that name." It's the only Mexican name she knows. But she can't remember anything about him.

Manuel shrugs. He's so still, sitting there beside her, staring ahead. She can't tell if he's sullen or shy. Such a sudden change from the lyrical, swinging song he just finished. "*La cucaracha*," he says finally, "means little insect."

"Pancho Villa and a little insect?"

A brief smile passes over his face and then he's silent again. She'll have to ask someone at the ranch.

They ascend a gradual rise and descend again, and before them, in the middle of the vast, flat land, squats a one-story house. In the distance, just outside an endless fence, sits a small windmill and two tents, and spread out beyond the fence, hundreds of gray specks. Sheep.

The little house has a wraparound veranda, and a lone cottonwood tree, windblown and meager, leans away from a corner.

Is this it? "Where is the ranch house?" Florence asks.

Manuel raises an arm and gestures at the squat building.

Her chest sinks. That? Just a little structure with one small tree on a wide open plain, so lonely looking? What has she gotten herself into? Mr. Reed, the state education supervisor, told Ida that this was a respectable and well-known ranch. In a letter to her, he'd *implied*, though he hadn't said, that these people were wealthy.

Florence had imagined something large and elegant, like a southern plantation surrounded by gracious trees. In Pennsylvania, all the houses she knows have trees and greenery. But, she remembers, this land is a desert, and its dry climate is exactly why she's come. She takes a deep breath and realizes that she *can* breathe more easily here. The wind whooshes and sways the top of the cottonwood, and she lifts her face to the sky. A new land, and she *will* be well. She is well already! She has an urge to jump off the wagon and skip. But she restrains herself. The new schoolmarm should be dignified.

They pull up in front of the house. Under the veranda, the door opens. A small, thin woman steps out onto the steps. "Miss Rodkey?" she calls.

"Yes," Florence smiles tentatively, and Manuel helps her down from the wagon. He takes down her trunk.

The woman extends her hand. "I'm Mrs. DeGraftenreid," she says, her weathered face crinkling into a smile.

Florence takes the outstretched hand, and Mrs. DeGraftenreid shakes it vigorously. Behind her on the veranda appear two girls. These must be Florence's pupils. The taller one smiles shyly. She's wearing a fringed leather skirt, cowboy boots with spurs, and a man's shirt, and her light brown hair is pulled back in a messy arrangement. The younger girl, in a conventional but worn brown dress, stares with hostile eyes at Florence.

"Here are Mildred and Ethel," says their mother. "Come in. Come in!"

As Manuel lugs her trunk up onto the porch, Florence follows Mrs. DeGraftenreid into a large room with a long pine table in the middle and a kitchen at one end. The walls are lined with polished wood, making the room warm and brown. Smells of cooking meat waft from the kitchen, and Florence's stomach rumbles. She ate on the train but managed only half of a dried-out sandwich.

Mrs. DeGraftenreid leads her past the table into a little passageway with one door on the right and one on the left. She opens the left-hand door. "This is the school room," she says, smiling with pride. In the room three small desks face a blackboard, and in the corner sits a bed.

Florence stops, shocked again after seeing the house. "Is that—" She points to the bed, a small iron bedstead, the mattress covered with a red, white, and blue quilt.

"Yes, that is for you."

Silence.

Is this really where she will sleep? In the school room? The bed is against one side, and at the front of the room, a large blackboard hangs on the wall. *Chalk dust*, she thinks. *Edith said chalk dust can injure the breathing apparatus.*

"Well, I'll leave you to your unpacking. I must see to supper," says Mrs. DeGraftenreid as she bustles out of the room, closing the door behind her.

Florence goes to the window and looks out. The distant mesa, just a bump, really, is the only thing that breaks the monotony of the landscape. She sighs. *Bereft*, she thinks. *I have a terrible disease, and now I'm an exile in the desert.*

But just as she begins to sink into maudlin self-pity, something changes outside the window. Sudden bands of clouds, as long as the horizon, travel across the sky. The sky darkens, and the clouds turn a lurid pink, shot through with ribbons of scarlet and blue. Below them the mesa glows in such a vivid copper-orange that the whole earth shimmers with radiance. Florence takes a deep breath and is amazed again. *I can breathe without coughing.* She feels her body imbued with something beautiful, and now the despair of a few minutes ago morphs into something like ecstasy. Such simple things—the beauty of the land and an easy breath—change her emotions so quickly, from one extreme to the other. It must be a sign, a forecast that, despite this room and the chalk dust, she will heal and thrive in this place.

When she comes out to the main room for supper, the long table is fully occupied. Mrs. DeGraftenreid sits at one end, the two girls on one side, and two young men across from them.

At the head of the table a hearty-looking man, Mr. DeGraftenreid, no doubt, stands to greet her. His tall form fills the space with a proprietary manner, but his voice is soft as he speaks. "Welcome to El Yeso, Miss Rodkey."

"Thank you."

Mr. DeGraftenreid sits down immediately and, after saying a lengthy blessing, spoons the beef stew into large bowls and passes them around. In the center of the table sits a warm, fragrant plate of cornbread.

Florence sits beside Ethel, the ten-year-old. Ethel is small and thin like her mother, with a snub nose and pale skin and hair. She looks as drab as her brown dress. As if in answer to Florence's thoughts, Ethel scowls at her.

Mr. DeGraftenreid clears his throat. "How was your journey, Miss Rodkey? You came from Illinois, where your sister is?"

"Yes, it was a long ride," she says, then smiles. "But I met some jolly people on the train who kept me amused."

The master of the house frowns and glances at his wife.

Was that the wrong thing to say? Is he wondering what kind of woman they hired, sight unseen?

"*We* can show you some jolly amusement!" says one of the ranch hands.

Mrs. DeGraftenreid frowns. "Now—"

The short young man smiles a mischievous smile. He has curly blond hair, bleached eyebrows, and a red face. He and the young man beside him, tall and dark, must be the boys who stay in the tents out beside the corral.

There is no sign of Manuel. Florence had seen a stream of smoke near one of the tents. Manuel must cook his own dinner out there.

"He means the roping and the rodeo tricks," says Mildred, her wide smile revealing a gap in her front teeth. "Have you ever seen those, Miss Rodkey?"

"No!"

"I can show you."

"Mildred rides bareback on the bucking bronco," says Mr. DeGraftenreid with quiet pride.

"My, my," Florence says. "That sounds quite daring."

The two cowboys exchange a smile. "And Millie can shoot like Annie Oakley!" the tall one brags.

Mildred blushes and sinks in her chair. "Annie Oakley!" she says with her head down. "I wish I seen her."

Florence raises an eyebrow. There's something to work on right away: grammar.

chapter 10

HOME ON THE RANGE

El Yeso Ranch, New Mexico, 1910

Clang! Clang! Clang! Florence sits up in bed. Is there a fire? No, it's cowbells. She still hasn't got used to that sound. She gets out of bed, shivering and hopping until she throws on her coat and some thick wool socks, and goes to the window.

The morning swells as the mesa lightens into gray against a naked sky. Outside the window, a herd of cows with the cowpunchers, Nash and Bailey. They ride past her window, making their horses buck and rear as they shout, "Whee haw!" Nash, tall and dark, sees Florence and tips his black Stetson hat.

She laughs and waves.

Now that she's been here a month, she's getting used to her routine: up at six, breakfast at six-thirty, then she has a (glorious) hour and a half to herself. She straightens her room, reads the newspaper, practices the piano (a good piano, a Steinway, although it needs to be tuned) for half an hour, then begins school at eight-thirty. An hour for lunch at noon, and then school until three. She then practices piano for another hour and takes a walk for her constitutional, usually two miles. And then she sits on the veranda and attends to her correspondence. She's had three letters from Phillip and also a poem, "That Double Chance," by Franklin Pierce Adams. It's a whimsical poem about Phillip's beloved Chicago Cubs, and it is funny. It's not what she meant when she said she likes poetry, but she thanked him politely in her last letter. And now here is good news: Phillip is coming for a visit.

This morning Florence steps into the main room and sits at the table, tucking into a breakfast of scrambled eggs, biscuits, ham, and coffee, taking care with the broken cream pitcher. Her appetite has picked up since being here in the desert air, and Edith would be proud. She hums that catchy tune Manuel was singing, "La Cucaracha," and as she takes another bite of ham, the cowpunchers come in, whooping, laughing, and slapping one another, pulling out their chairs and arranging their chaps as they sit. How can two young men make so much noise?

"Good morning," she says in her most dignified voice. One feels a bit compelled to instill some civilization here.

Bailey, the fair-haired boy, looks at Florence and blushes, his face turning a redder shade of red.

"Mornin', Tenderfoot," Nash says with a wink. Tenderfoot? Just because she was a little hesitant about riding the old horse the other day.

"Was that 'La Cucaracha' you were singing?" asks Bailey.

"Yes, I guess so. Manuel was singing it, but he wouldn't tell me what it meant. Do you know?"

Both boys laugh with loud guffaws. Nash picks up his fork. "It's about our famous outlaw, Pancho Villa. He's trying to overtake the Mexican government, and the Mexicans here think of him as their hero."

"Why is he called 'La Cucaracha?' I looked it up and it means cockroach?"

Laughing even louder, Nash says, "That's what they call his car!" The two boys smirk at each other.

Florence raises an eyebrow and shakes her head. It must be a Mexican joke.

"See ya, Tenderfoot," calls Nash as, without further ado, the boys gobble up their breakfast and stomp out the door.

Tenderfoot? Well, she'll show them. Mildred has procured a real cowgirl outfit for her, and today she'll go out and ride—really ride—one of the horses.

She adjourns to the parlor, the nicest room in the house, and begins her piano practice. Chopin's "Nocturne in E Flat." Ooh, she winces at the high C, flat as a pancake.

When she turns around, Mildred is sitting in the high-backed chair by the window. The girl smiles shyly and holds up an armful of fabric—fringe, leather, and a rough cotton fabric.

"What do you have there, Mildred?"

"For you to wear—for riding."

"Oh, wonderful! Let me see." Florence jumps up and skips across the room.

♪

When the afternoon lesson is finished, she dismisses the girls and takes off her proper white schoolmarm dress, including, thankfully, the corset and stays, and puts on the rough chamois shirt, the fringed leather skirt, and the boots with spurs. Spurs! She kicks out her heels. If Ernest could see her now.

Out behind the ranch house, Mildred, holding the reins of a docile-looking horse, is waiting. "This is Old Fred," she says.

chapter 11

LOVE IS A SONG

El Yeso Ranch, New Mexico, 1910

In the evening Florence gazes out to the horizon, over the open plain to the dazzling colors in a sunset sky. This place that has so quickly become etched into her soul. How could anyone not be deeply affected by this magic land?

So different from her city life in Pittsburgh or Chicago, places of noise and people and laughter. *Chicago*, she sighs. What is Phillip doing now? Dining in splendor? Sitting at the opera with a Chicago belle?

Music. Phillip loves music, and when she thinks of him, of living in Chicago, going to plays and concerts, riding through the enchanting parks around Astor Street, Florence feels happiness, like a song running through her. Love *is* a song, she thinks, like the Mozart she practiced this morning, the tune that has been running through her all day, "Fantasia in D Minor." Ernest loves music, too, and he always glows with happiness when she plays. Perhaps her love for Ernest is also a song. But in a different way. With Ernest she and he create the song together, point-counterpoint, as they discuss music or plays or the state of the world. She gazes at the sky as it darkens, clouds mutating from pink to purple. Oh, if only she could talk to Ernest now. She frowns. But why is she longing for Ernest instead of Phillip?

Florence picks up her pen and a piece of stationery paper. What shall she write? About the ranch, the cows, the sheep in the distance, the dry air? How to describe the feeling, the vastness, of being here?

Rancho El Yeso
October 10
Dear Ernest,

 To describe the ranch life is impossible. I simply could not do it justice, so I will send you some pictures as soon as I can. A kind youth in Clovis loaned me his Kodak and I am making merry with it, I assure you.

 I am learning to ride horseback and shoot, of course. Today I had quite an experience. I was riding Fred out for the cows, and when we (Fred & I) were about a mile from the house, I encountered a gate that had to be opened. I dismounted and then tried to lead Fred up to the gate, but he would not lead up. I thought he'd stand until I opened the gate and left the reins go. Of course, he immediately took himself off at a fast rate over the plains. I considered going back for one of the boys, but upon thinking twice, I decided I could not stand the laugh I'd be sure to get (they are so willing to laugh at a tenderfoot) that I started out after him myself.

 I got him, too. I caught the reins, prepared to mount, & got the act about half completed when he started off at a gallop. I hung on but could not use the reins until I succeeded in drawing myself into the saddle, and then tell me if I didn't jerk him in good. My foremost sensation was anger. I was awfully glad I had not been killed or had not gone back to the house. I was awfully sick for about five minutes, too, but I went on and got the cows & came on home prepared to say nothing about it.

 But alas! The boys saw the horse go off and leave me & prepared to come out to my aid. When they saw me start out after him, they stopped and watched me through the field glass. When I arrived at the ranch, I was already a heroine. The boys said they expected to see me killed when he started to gallop with me half on him. So, I have gained myself the name "Tenderfoot."

 My friend, I am in a mood for "raising Cain" tonight, and here I am tamely sitting, writing to you. Not that this is not a great joy to me, dear comrade, but some way or another I'd rather have you here to see if I couldn't make you mad. That's it. That's what I want. A fight. Not a really, truly hard one, you know, but the kind where you don't get angry. I fear I will lose all my brains if I stay here. I think up something real smart to say and no one knows what I am talking about.

Young man, my devotion to you is of a true and lasting nature, but this night air is freezing all the blood in my veins and it's a pretty severe test. If I stop suddenly, you will know that the thermometer is still dropping. I have lots more to say to you, but I guess this is as long a letter as you really deserve.

Phillip is the dearest ever to me. He sends me the loveliest things. Everything but candy. Chance for Ernest (!)

I really must close. I'm freezing.

Good night, Comrade. May this letter find you as well and as happy as it leaves me. Write soon. This letter deserves an answer.

Same,

Florence

chapter 12

A LONG WAY TO TIPPERARY

Pittsburgh, Pennsylvania, 1941

"I think I'll plant geraniums next year," Elizabeth says. "I love the pink and red together."

"So cheerful," Nannie answers, "but we must save room for Ernest's tomatoes. He had such a good crop last year, and even Cousin May raved about them." She shifts in the rocking chair, trying to find a more comfortable position. Cousin May is the oldest member of the family and also the most respected. She lives by herself in a neighboring house, and Nannie visits her often to pay her respect.

Flossie has stepped into the parlor where her stepmother and grandmother sit at their usual places in front of the big, new Philco radio, with its polished veneer and mahogany insets. One day last month Daddy brought it home, smiling secretively as he hauled the big box into the living room on a dolly. Nannie, who'd objected to her son buying a radio and made a sarcastic comment about "the new family hearth," has now become its biggest devotee. She sits closest to it, mending stockings, while Elizabeth reads a novel, *For Whom the Bell Tolls*. The house is quiet now, after the noisy dinner tonight when Roddy and Flossie roared and laughed and Roddy engaged in an endless argument about prohibition with Daddy.

Their father is a teetotaler and a non-smoker who believes that drinking is sinful and that women especially should not smoke cigarettes.

"There'll be no alcohol in this house," he says, as if he hasn't said that a hundred times before. In this he and Nannie are in agreement. Nannie is so adamant about temperance that sometimes Flossie suspects that her Grandfather Craighead was a heavy drinker. Of course, Roddy takes the opposite position from Daddy and points out the harmful effects of prohibition, with bootlegging and the rise of the Mafia.

Nannie looks at the clock. "It's time," she calls, her rich voice reverberating throughout the house. Nannie has a lovely voice, unlike Daddy, who can't carry a tune. Flossie thinks this is what endeared Nannie to her mother. "Ah, but Florence was a songbird," Nannie says, as if excusing some unspoken fault in her first daughter-in-law.

Elizabeth puts down the magazine and turns the radio's dial. Roddy arrives as Sallie clatters in, and they all pull up seats around the radio. It's time for *The Burns and Allen Show.*

As the orchestra starts up, Flossie begins to giggle, even before George and Gracie begin their act. The radio coming on at eight o'clock on Monday means George and Gracie, and that puts her in a laughing mood.

Gracie starts the banter. In her squeaky voice, she tells George, "I've decided to run for president."

Everyone breaks into laughter—who could imagine a woman, especially the zany Gracie, as president?

The gag goes on and evolves into others, and finally George says, "Say good night, Gracie."

"Good night, Gracie," says Gracie.

This one repeats for a few more lines. Everyone laughs again, and even Nannie giggles, even though the comedy team repeats this joke every week.

But just as Gracie is saying her last "Good night, Gracie," an outside voice breaks into the broadcast.

As if from a far distance, the voice says, "Ladies and gentlemen, the president has an announcement."

"What?" Elizabeth looks up in surprise, and Roddy and Flossie exchange a puzzled look.

"Hmph," snorts Nannie, who still disapproves of President Roosevelt even though everyone knows he pulled the country out of the Depression. In 1932, when he first ran, only Elizabeth voted for Franklin Roosevelt, although, since then, everyone in the family except Nannie has grown to admire him.

Daddy takes off his glasses and leans in toward the radio. "Quiet, everyone."

Now comes that familiar voice, measured and patrician, filtering through the tinny sound of the airwaves: "*Yesterday, December seventh, nineteen forty-one, a date which will live in infamy, the United States of America was suddenly and deliberately attacked by naval and air forces of the Empire of Japan.*"

The family sits in stunned silence as the president continues his speech. The Japanese, he says, have bombed American naval bases in the Pacific and the Hawaiian Islands.

Roddy jumps up from his seat. "What the—"

"But the Hawaiian Islands—Hammie—" Flossie clutches Nannie's hand.

"Shush!" says Elizabeth in an uncharacteristically harsh tone as the president goes on.

"*I ask that the Congress declare that since the unprovoked and dastardly attack by Japan on Sunday, December seventh, nineteen forty-one, a state of war has existed between the United States and the Japanese Empire.*"

Daddy sinks his head into his hands, and Nannie gasps.

"But what does it mean?" Flossie squeaks.

"It's war!" Roddy shouts. "The Japanese bombed Pearl Harbor, and the president has declared war!"

Elizabeth drops her head over her lap, where her open book rests. *For Whom the Bell Tolls.* She shakes her head and taps the book. "War is brutal. It's inhumane." The book cover shows a painting, murky and dark, a mountain range in black and white and the title in bold red, screaming out like an ominous warning. She sighs. "But we have to help out. The Japanese are killing our boys, and the Germans are trying to destroy Europe."

Nannie begins to weep silently, and Daddy clenches his fists. "Now we're in it for sure," he says. "Let's just hope our own boys don't go."

Roddy jumps up from his chair and shouts, "But I want to go, Daddy! Everyone's talking about it, and all the fellows at college are planning to sign up. If we aren't drafted, that is."

"Pearl Harbor!" Flossie shouts. "That's near where Hammie is!" After reading as many newspapers as she could about it, she figured he might be at Wheeler Field or Camp Malakole, both places close to Pearl Harbor. Her whole body tenses into a tight knot. Was Hammie's unit hit? Was he killed? She might not be sure about marrying him, but she doesn't want to lose him. Suddenly her eyes are wet, and she realizes that the war is no longer a distant battle she can ignore.

We are in it. The war is ours now. Hammie is there, and maybe Roddy will go. Flossie's tears flow; it's as if her life is now one big red wound, like the titles on Elizabeth's book cover.

Silence.

Daddy's head drops again, and he nods. "Pearl Harbor."

Another silent pause.

Roddy stands and walks to the door. "That does it. I'm signing up."

As Roddy leaves, from the radio comes a sweet and melancholy tenor voice, singing "It's a Long Way to Tipperary." The song everybody knows, the soldiers' song from the Great War. Flossie's tears come again, and Nannie pulls a handkerchief out of her sleeve and weeps along.

♪

In the following days and weeks, everybody is at sixes and sevens. When Daddy comes home from work, he is either overbearing, ordering everyone about, or he retreats to his upstairs office.

Elizabeth goes on a cleaning spree, washing curtains and rugs that are usually never washed until spring. Roddy develops a false jollity that gets on Flossie's nerves. Nannie walks into rooms and turns around, forgetting what she's doing. Sometimes she just sits in her rocker, staring out the window.

Flossie goes to her window seat and picks up the pile of Hammie's letters. Hammie has been writing, but no letters have come for almost a month. Was he in one of the places that was struck? Has he been wounded? Killed? Yesterday, she called Hammie's parents, and she even called the draft board. There is no record of him or his division, at least that they're telling his family. No one knows.

Is it her fault Hammie disappeared? Because she was attracted to George? Did she somehow cause it because she stopped thinking of him and focused on another man? She knows this is superstition, but she can't help it.

It's the middle of the day, and she always says her prayers at bedtime, but now she goes to the bed and kneels. *Please, God, keep Hammie safe.*

Back at her dressing table she opens the red velvet box and puts the ring on, holding up her hand and wiggling her finger. Three delicate diamonds arranged around a larger one in the center, just stunning. She twists the ring around on her finger. She has to admit it looks just right on her, but her feelings keep circling. Should she wait for Hammie? Wouldn't that be the right thing to do? Maybe if she wears it backward, no one will know she's engaged. Well, that doesn't make sense. And anyway, maybe she doesn't want to be engaged to Hammie. But how could she tell him so when he's about to fight a war who-knows-where? She takes off the ring and puts it back in the box. She clenches her fist. Why couldn't she have a mother to talk to like everyone else?

Flossie has to know more about her mother. What was her engagement to Daddy like? Did she have any second thoughts? Those letters in the cedar box were from before they were married, so she must have talked about their engagement.

chapter 13

SALUT D'AMOUR

El Yeso Ranch, New Mexico, 1910

Florence lifts her hands with a flourish and drops them onto the keys for the final chord of Elgar's "Salut d'Amour," a quiet tune of sweet longing. She's learned to skip the flat high C so she doesn't have to cringe.

Mrs. DeGraftenried, who told Florence to call her "Mrs. DeG," wipes her eyes as everyone claps, and Florence makes a dramatic bow while the boys hoot. She is the center of attention tonight, and she loves it. Everyone is gathered round the piano: Mr. and Mrs. DeG, Mildred and Ethel, Nash and Bailey, and Mrs. DeG's brother, Ike. Florence has played a little Mozart, a little Bach, lively melodies chasing and following one another, then ended with the bittersweet Elgar.

The ranch life is a busy one, and she, too, has established a brisk pace in this new land—lessons, meals with the family and cowboys, writing letters, and sparring with Phillip.

How did she get herself into this adversarial place with Phillip? In one letter she told him about all the male attention she's getting here, just to tease him a little, like she does with Ernest, who responds in kind. But Phillip wrote back that he "was not pleased" with her companions at the ranch. He wants her to stop flirting with these "ill-bred ruffians" and every other man she encounters. Well, he can come for a visit, she wrote, and then she'll flirt with *him*.

Now, standing in the back of the room, Mrs. DeG's brother, Ike Blanton, claps and whistles. Tall and broad-shouldered, with sun-bleached curls and a smile to write home about (but not to Phillip, obviously,) he's been coming around more often lately. Ike is not a lowly cowpuncher. He's an educated man who chose life on the plains rather than, as he says, idle pursuits of his college classmates who sit in stuffy offices in Chicago.

Was that a reference to Phillip? Everyone here knows about Phillip, with all the letters and gifts he sends, and Florence has bragged about his important law practice. She knows he's winding up for a proposal, but she's managed to put him off. She's just not sure about him and really not sure she wants to get married at all.

Why is she so reluctant about Phillip? He is steady and responsible, with a good income. Would she give up that kind of life for a charming sheepherder? To live in this rough and ready world of hot sun and desert air?

Well, when the cat's away . . . why shouldn't she have fun with her admirers? Time enough to be stolid and sober when she's a married woman.

"Bravo!" Ike is still clapping. "Now how about some ragtime?" he shouts. The cowpunchers holler out their agreement.

"All right!" she says and launches into "Alexander's Ragtime Band," rallying her energy in defiance of the touch of nostalgia this brings. This is Ernest's favorite song.

Soon they are all stomping their feet and singing along, and even Mr. DeG is smiling.

Florence's face flushes as she pounds out the tune, speeding it up, going faster and faster, twirling her senses up and up into a finer atmosphere, a fiery cloud of delight above the ordinary world.

Until she stops. Her head droops over the keys.

The room becomes silent as everyone stares at Florence. She takes a deep breath and sits up. "Just a touch of fatigue," she says with a laugh.

Mrs. DeG wrings her hands but finally breaks the silence. "Now we've worn her out," she says. "To bed, to bed, everyone."

If only Florence were at home. If only she could hear Mama's soothing voice and drink a cup of hot milk. She sighs and her head sinks back down onto the piano.

Reluctantly the men shuffle out the door, Ike lingering a bit behind. "Don't forget tomorrow, Miss Rodkey!" he calls as he closes the door.

"What's tomorrow?" Mrs. DeG asks.

Florence sits up and smiles. "He's promised me a ride in the joy buggy—whatever that is."

Mrs. DeG rolls her eyes. "Oh, Ike and his joy buggy."

♪

The next day is a Saturday, so no lessons, and Florence sleeps in until six-thirty. After breakfast she sits in a rocking chair on the veranda. November mornings in the desert, she's discovered, are colder than chilly, and she huddles in her coat as the sun rises. The sky over the horizon transforms from a deep, dark blue, to purple, to shrieking red. And suddenly a rounded sliver of gold peeks up behind the distant mountain range, slowly lifting itself into a giant yellow disc, a dignified god rising to bless the land.

The low clouds turn pink as daylight illuminates the plain, and the sound of a clanking motor punctures the air.

Ike in his motor car thuds over the ridge. The rickety-looking vehicle stops with a bang in front of Florence, and Ike smiles like a boy with his favorite Christmas present.

Florence claps her hands. "So this is the joy buggy!"

"The sixty-horse Overland Joy Buggy here to escort you to Devil's Rendezvous." Ike tips his Stetson with a jaunty flourish.

"Oh, that sounds wicked." She laughs as he helps her into the seat. She secures a scarf around her hat and ties it under her chin as the motor starts up again with a tremendous roar.

They bump and clatter along the rutted road, the smell of gasoline infusing the air.

Suddenly Ike turns the buggy off the road and heads straight into the field.

"Where are we going?" she shouts.

"Devil's Rendezvous," he calls as he grins, steering the car into a dry arroyo and increasing the speed. She thought Devil's Rendezvous was a town, but clearly they are not heading toward a town.

An arroyo, she learned, is a ditch to gather rain. Sometimes the stormwater can descend out of nowhere and wash through the arroyo with a ferocity that will knock you over and drown you. Hopefully that won't happen now. Florence clutches the door handle. Ike grins at her as the buggy whacks itself back and forth onto the crusted sides of the ditch, barreling through the arroyo toward the mesa.

The arroyo narrows, becoming barely wider than the car, but Ike does not slow. Florence laughs in fear and holds tight to the door handle. "How will we get out of this ditch?" she calls.

Just then the car follows a turn in the track, and Ike guns the engine as they climb up a rise and onto the desert floor. The mesa looms ahead, enormous and forbidding. And there, what looked from a distance like a dark streak on the stone, is an opening in the wall, a canyon.

Ike stops the car, adjusts his hat, and steps out. "Behold!" He points to the canyon.

Ike helps Florence out of the car into the sudden silence. Florence turns and gazes toward the endless expanse of desert plain behind them. A year ago, she was walking past houses, stores, and machine shops in a city filled with smoke, noise, and horse dung, horses and carriages competing with motor cars, and then to her schoolroom of twenty boisterous children.

She pulls down her hat brim to shade her eyes. Here: boundless desert to a distant horizon. Not a single soul in sight. Two scrawny cacti in the baking sun. Sand, rocks, and stone. The fleeting scent of earth and sage. Silence punctuated only by an occasional scratch of lizard on rock, a whoosh of wind through a lone scrub oak.

They stand in silence, man and woman, rooted in this land of awe and wonder.

Perhaps here, Florence thinks, *I don't need the bustle and hurry.* She loves the silent desert, the Mexicans whose dark eyes hide feelings or opinions. Even the rowdy cowboys, from time to time, stand quiet and still, like Ike right now. It's a silence that vibrates from the endless land and sky, suffusing the people with such fullness that there's no need to talk.

It's as though she has been transported here, into this other dimension, a magic place where she can find another dimension of herself. Not only in her mind, but in her body. After only a month, she can breathe easier and has all but forgotten the cough.

Just the other day Mr. DeG took her to the doctor in Clovis, another charming man who flirted with her. But Doctor Lovelace said he, too, had a history of pneumonia, and he warned her: "You can go back east and die, or stay out here and live, like me." Then he asked if she would save a dance for him at the upcoming officers' ball. Was his dire warning sincere, or did he say it so she would stay?

Ike gestures and turns, and she follows him into the canyon. The canyon is a giant rift in the rock wall looming high above. They round a bend, and the rock face grows darker, narrowing and closing in on them. The high wall—layers of red, yellow, and sand-colored stone—loom above them on both sides.

They round another bend in the rock wall, where a faint trickle of water runs down the middle of the canyon.

Little cottonwood trees, lacy and sparse with leaves in flaming yellow and orange, perch along the stream bank. "And trees!" she says. Their soft and delicate branches bring a feeling of life into this parched land. She takes a deep, unhindered breath. "How beautiful. But why do they call it Devil's Rendezvous?"

Ike cocks his hat and looks around. "This is where the bad boys gather when they come to raid."

"Bad boys? Raids?"

"Cattle rustlers. They come from across the way." He points to the mesa.

Florence shudders. "I hope they're not coming any time soon."

"We usually know when they're around. We just caught a couple before you came. Two boys from the ranch over that-a-way," he says, gesturing to the east. "They took some calves before they were branded and thought they could get away with it." He smirks. "When we caught them, they kept claiming the calves were from *their* herd."

"How did you know they weren't?"

"We have a secret weapon, and he's called Old Abner. He knows cattle from way back. He brought the calves near our cows, and the calves soon found their own mothers."

"Oh, that was clever." There is so much to learn in this world of cattle, sheep, and cowboys. Could she stay and live in this land? Could she be a ranch woman like Mrs. DeG?

The sun is searing, and Florence steps into the shade of an overhanging ledge. She touches the canyon wall and runs her fingers over some markings, little stick figures on the rock surface. "It looks like someone carved pictures here."

Ike lifts his chest and chuckles. "Yes, that's another reason this is called Devil's Rendezvous. Old-time Indians were here, and maybe those drawings are some kind of black magic."

As the shadows lengthen, they step back into the buggy and Ike starts the engine with a roar. It bumps and rattles along the arroyo and then the road as Ike, raising an eyebrow at Florence, shouts out a story about "another tenderfoot."

Florence is laughing as they pull up in front of the ranch.

Suddenly, from the shade of the veranda, a dark figure emerges. Dressed in a black city suit and hat, the tall man with the pencil mustache stands at the edge of the porch, dark eyes glaring at the two of them.

Florence's laugh dies in her throat. "Phillip."

chapter 14

PACK UP YOUR TROUBLES

Pittsburgh, Pennsylvania, 1942

Flossie sighs as she passes the back stairs to Daddy's office. It's been over a month since she asked to see her mother's letters, but he keeps putting her off. She pulls on her galoshes and steps out the door. The snow that fell two days ago is now slushy and sooty in the sunshine, and the air is soft and warm. In the snowy yard, Sallie lies on her back, waving her arms up and down while Apollo runs round and round her.

"Sallie," Flossie calls. "It's too wet for snow angels. You'll get soaked."

"I don't care," Sallie yells, and Apollo speeds up his circuit, yipping and burrowing his nose into the snow.

On the other side of the yard, Nannie, in her old-fashioned black coat, stands in the middle of the garden like a skinny scarecrow. All around her brown stalks of old broccoli and tomato plants poke out of the snow.

"Nannie, what are you doing?"

"I'm studying the garden."

"In January?" Flossie kicks the slush and rotates her foot in a circle to clear a spot for standing.

"We are at war now," Nannie proclaims, poking her cane into the snow.

War. Flossie's eyebrows squinch together as she tries not to cry. Nannie can be so blunt. "I know we're at war," Flossie whispers, now more angry than hurt. How could anyone not know this new reality where nothing feels real anymore? No word from Hammie. Roddy threatening to enlist any minute. She squelches the sarcastic reply that is ready to surface.

Nannie raises her cane in the air. "We have to prepare. Plant more of everything."

"But we're not poor, Nannie. We have plenty of food!"

"In the last war, we ran out of everything, even vegetables."

"But this war won't last that long, surely? Our boys will beat the Japanese, and the fighting will be over in a few months."

"That's what they said the last time." Nannie turns and sloshes through the snow, counting her steps as she measures out a new section. She stops and points with her cane as she recites, "Cabbage, carrots, green beans, beets . . ."

"Beets! ee-yuw!" Sallie shouts. Apollo barks in agreement.

Since December 7, the world has become a different place. Not only has the family on Lacrosse Street been stricken with the unimaginable—*America the great, the invulnerable, has been attacked*—but on the streets of Pittsburgh, people walk around in shock or burst into unexpected tirades and weeping fits. Even at the hospital, everyone seems numb. People come into the gift shop looking tearful and buy more flowers than ever, while Mrs. Doak, in triage mode, has been super-efficient, rallying the troops.

Nannie continues her inventory, and Flossie turns to go into the house. In the kitchen, warm and cozy, she stomps her foot. A Victory Garden. Now it's real. War. She's tried so hard to push it away. But now a black cloud of despair is moving over everyone. Flossie, however, will not give in. She pounds the kitchen table and straightens her back. She will push the dark thoughts away. She doesn't have to be helpless. She'll pack up her troubles, the way she's always dealt with negative feelings, like the hurt and anger about her mother's death. And it usually works. Because then she feels better. And if she stays positive, it will help the war effort. *But what will happen to Hammie? Will the Japanese withdraw if Hitler is defeated? And what about Roddy?*

Flossie runs up the stairs, singing, "*Pack up your troubles in your old kit-bag,*" and shouting, "Smile, smile, smile." The whole world is at war, but Flossie will not be demoralized. Nannie is planning a garden, and Flossie will go skiing.

Her new ski suit lies on the bed, looking trim and gleaming despite her making the pants out of an old wool dress of Aunt Mary's. But the jacket is white satin, tailored to the waist, and in the mirror she sees a girl who could be in *Vogue*. No more knickerbockers for Flossie.

She grabs her cap and boots from the wardrobe, checks her pocket for the money she carefully counted out yesterday, and runs back down the stairs. "I'm off!" she shouts, dashing through the dining room past Elizabeth, who looks up from polishing the silver.

In the snowy yard, Nannie and Sallie hover over Sallie's sled while Apollo sits and watches. "Where are you going?" Sallie calls.

"Skiing with Helen." Flossie runs to the barn to get her skis and poles. This is a big occasion; the first time Daddy has let her take the car for any distance. Flossie is going out to the mountains in Ligonier with her cousin Helen.

Flossie starts loading her skis and poles into the back seat.

"Why can't I come, too?" Sallie wails.

Nannie bends down and tries to reason with her as Sallie shouts, "I never get to go skiing!"

"Next time," Flossie calls as she gets into the car. Really, she'd have to stay with Sallie all day and wouldn't be able to ski down the big hills. And anyway, she's done enough babysitting for Sallie. Whenever Elizabeth and Nannie go shopping or to their women's group at the church, Flossie has to watch her. And Elizabeth spoils her, so Sallie thinks she can get whatever she wants. Well, this time, she won't.

Flossie inches the car down the slippery driveway to the street and then bumps down Lacrosse over uneven bricks a hundred years old.

Helen is waiting on the sidewalk, her skis and poles propped up beside her, when Flossie pulls up to the curb. Helen's father is Uncle Gordy, and they live on Lacrosse Street, just like Aunt Mary.

"Hi!" says Helen, her glasses sparkling in the sun as she loads her equipment in the back seat and hops into the front. Helen, a cheerful soul with a laughing face, is Flossie's cousin and best friend. "Ooh, Flossie, I like your new ski clothes. Did you make them?"

"Yes, just finished yesterday."

"You'll have to lend me the pattern." Helen is wearing an old jacket and baggy pants. She's not the jealous type, but she likes to keep up with

Flossie and her fashion sense. And Helen is a seamstress, too. She makes all sorts of crafty things with leftover fabrics—potholders and dolls and aprons, and she crochets and embroiders as well.

Flossie turns the wheel, and the car coasts down Maple Avenue. "I can't wait to get away from this town. Everything in Pittsburgh is 'Enlist! Fight! Guns!' And Nannie with her Victory Garden. Like we're supposed to be thinking about war twenty-four hours a day."

"Hear, hear," says Helen.

Soon they are on the highway driving east toward the Laurel Mountains. They've come out here before with friends, but this time there is something new at the ski hill—a rope tow.

"It's hard to believe," Flossie says. "We won't have to climb back up the hill."

"I know. Just hold onto the rope and it pulls you up." Helen's eyes twinkle behind her glasses. "And there's something else. I'm not supposed to tell anyone—"

"What? What is it? Oh, I know. You're engaged!"

"No," Helen laughs as she takes off her glasses and wipes them with a Kleenex. "Well . . ." She puts her glasses back on and lowers her voice. *As if anyone could hear us.*

"My parents are thinking of buying some land near Ligonier, in Somerset. It has hills and a perfect spot for a rope tow! And they'd put up a restaurant."

"Oh, Helen, we could ski on your own hill!"

"Well, it might be just a pipe dream. They'd have to sell our house in Pittsburgh to afford it. And Nancy is still in school, so it would have to wait a few years."

"But it might really happen?"

The silhouette of the mountain range undulates across the horizon, glistening white in the sudden sunlight.

"They're thinking it will be after the war," Helen says, "whenever that is, so Sonny can help out too."

"Oh, Sonny, the golden boy," Flossie responds in a melodramatic tone. Sonny is Helen's handsome younger brother, with curly blond hair and lots of ambition. Sonny enlisted soon after Hammie was drafted.

Helen screws up her face.

Flossie frowns. "I know. That awful war. Where is he now?"

"He's stationed out of Hawaii, but we don't know where he might be now."

Flossie grips the steering wheel. "We don't know where Hammie is either, and now Roddy is threatening to enlist! Even though he's in college and doesn't have to."

Helen scowls. "Who would have thought that our country would be at war again? Just when we're ready to enjoy life, this awful thing hangs over us."

"I know. I try to forget about it, but underneath, I feel guilty that we're going skiing now. I can't imagine what it must be like to live in France, or to be sent somewhere to go out and shoot people. Or be shot at. I pray every day for Sonny and Hammie and hope Roddy doesn't go, too. Though I know he wants to." Flossie sighs. "I guess we can't get away from it."

The mood in the car shifts from bright to murky, a gray cloud engulfing them in the midst of a sunny day.

When Flossie turns the car off the highway, Laurel Mountain looms sudden and massive before them. The ski hill, with its two slopes and a trail winding down from the top, comes into view, and she finds a place to park behind two other cars on the road. The girls get out of the car, put on their hats and mittens, and take the skis and poles from the back seat. As Flossie suspected, it's just cold enough in the mountains that the snow has stayed light and fluffy. Perfect for skiing.

Helen stands, a broad smile revealing the gap in her front teeth. "Mmm, I love the smell of snow."

"Me too. So clean and fresh."

Helen sighs. "Wouldn't it be wonderful to live up here in the mountains?"

"Hmm. Yes and no. It might be lonely."

"Oh, *you* need all your friends and your parties. But me, I'd love it."

"When you move up here, I can bring the friends here. We could all ski and then have a party in your restaurant!"

"But what would Nannie think?" Helen presses her lips together, smiling mischievously.

"She'd be standing at the bottom of the hill shouting directions to everybody."

"In her long black coat." Helen's laugh comes like a hiccup, and they both laugh as they start toward the ski hill. On a flat area at the base of the hill, several people stand in a huddle and turn to see the newcomers.

"Flossie Craighead!" a young man shouts. "And another fair maiden!"

The stocky young man in a black and orange Princeton sweatshirt approaches, and Flossie chuckles. "Hi, Howard. Helen, this is Howard Schwartz; Howard, my cousin Helen."

Howard bends into a dramatic bow. "Charmed."

"Howard's dad is Daddy's best friend."

"The two most loyal Shriners," Howard says as Flossie recalls her father wearing his red velvet fez in the Syria Mosque when he takes the children to the circus. The men in the Shriners Club like to evoke an aura of mystery with their rituals and Arabic symbols, but they also do extensive charity work in Pittsburgh. "And are you two ladies ready to try the new ski lift?"

Flossie and Helen exchange a look. "Is that it?" Helen points to a long rope lying on the snow, snaking up the hill. She skis over to it. "I don't know about this."

But Howard is persuasive, and soon they are standing beside the rope, while behind them someone cranks a handle. The rope lifts and begins to roll up the hill.

"Just grab on," Howard says.

Flossie goes first, then Helen, and as the rope moves, they both fall forward onto the snow, skis and poles tangled.

After the initial shock, they giggle and then hoot with laughter.

Howard explains that they have to lean back from the rope as it pulls them. "Right hand forward, left hand behind your back to distribute the force." They try again, and soon both girls are at the top of the hill and then gliding down with delight. Helen snowplows, and Flossie tries out the parallel skiing she's been learning. She's pretty good at it. There's nothing like the feeling of gliding silently down a snow-covered hill, smelling the cool mountain air, and then going back up and doing it again.

They stop for a break to eat the sandwiches they brought, then take the rope tow and soar down the hill, again and again, getting in three times the number of runs they used to when they had to herringbone and sidestep back up.

As they pack their skis into the car, Howard approaches, looking solemn, unusual for him. "Well, this is goodbye for a while."

Flossie stops. "What do you mean?"

"I've enlisted. I'm leaving tomorrow."

"Oh no!" Another friend gone to who-knows-where. She gives Howard a hug. "Be safe now," she chirps, though on the inside, her mood is bleak. Nobody is safe now.

On the way home, Flossie watches the landscape flatten out as they drive toward Pittsburgh while Helen lies back and nods off.

The car thumps over a pothole and Helen awakens with a start. "George!" she says.

"George?"

"I'm a little bit madly in love with him."

Oh no. Is this the same George? Flossie's chest tightens. "How do you know him?"

"He's a boy from school." Helen smiles. "His nickname is Jiggs. Isn't that cute?"

Flossie exhales the breath she's been holding. A different George.

Now they're on familiar territory. Flossie tells Helen about the George she knows and they discuss the two men, Helen's "Jiggs," an outgoing guy who talks to everybody, and Flossie's George, who is quiet and shy and gives her butterflies in her chest whenever she sees him.

"Thank goodness my George is not going into the war," Flossie says. "He's a doctor, so he's needed at home." She glances at Helen. "But I'm in a bit of a dilemma. And this is *my* secret that *you* can't tell."

"Okay."

Flossie sighs. "Hammie asked me to marry him."

Helen's eyes open wide and she hesitates. "Jeepers, that's swell, Flossie?" More of a question than a statement.

Flossie winces as she stares out the window past flat white fields of snow-covered farmland. "I'm not so sure."

"But aren't you happy about it? Hammie is such a dreamboat."

"Yes, I know, and he gave me a beautiful diamond ring."

"When? I've never seen an engagement ring on your finger."

"Because I don't wear it. I'm just not sure. I always thought Hammie and I would get married someday, but that was before I met George."

♪

After dinner, when Daddy adjourns to his office, Flossie sits in the parlor with Nannie and Elizabeth. A pile of green yarn covers Nannie's lap as she knits a pair of socks to send to the soldiers overseas, and Elizabeth, too, is knitting a sweater. First Lady Eleanor Roosevelt inspired them to knit warm clothes for the soldier boys.

A fire in the grate crackles and hisses as the knitting needles click in a continual rhythm, and Flossie thumbs through *Good Housekeeping*. She turns a page and stops. Here's an article about love letters. An illustration with pink and red hearts and the title, "Valentine's Day: Love Letters." Hammie is not the type to write love letters, but how will she feel if he does write one? Her shoulders sink at the thought. *I do love him, but not like that.* Actually, she can't imagine George writing one either, but just the thought of a love letter from George is like a breath of fresh air filling her lungs and lifting her up.

Those letters from her mother to her father in the cedar box. Flossie has been thinking about them constantly, and once she even snuck into Daddy's study, but the cedar box was locked.

Are they love letters? She stands with a sudden urge to try again, to *see* those letters, to find out what her mother wrote to her father before they were married. Could they give her a clue about her own dilemma?

Flossie rushes up the stairs to Daddy's study and knocks on the door. "Come in."

She opens the door and sudden tears spring into her eyes. "Daddy, I need to know something about my mother! Can I please see those letters?"

Daddy's hand reaches to touch the cedar box. "Well, these were personal," he says, "between your mother and me."

"But it's been twenty-two years since she died." When she notices his eyes are wet, she backtracks. "Oh, I'm sorry—I didn't mean to upset you."

"No, you are right, Flossie. These are precious to me, but someday they'll be yours. I'll give you *one*." He opens the box and rifles through the pile of envelopes. "I'll find one from 1910 when she was your age."

Flossie stands mute. After all this time, he's agreeing to let her see a letter. Finally, she'll get a glimpse of who her mother was. In her own words.

Daddy plucks the envelope from the box and hands it to her.

She takes the thin envelope, feeling the fragility of the paper, and turns to go. "Thank you, Daddy."

As she runs up the front stairs, she pauses at the landing. Beside her, hanging on the wall, where it's always been, is the portrait of her mother. A young woman in profile, hair swept up in a luxurious pile, her head bowed in a pose of contemplation or melancholy. The sepia tint lends a mystery, a romantic glow to the picture.

In her room Flossie sits at the window seat, the letter in her hand, and gazes down over the city at pinpricks of light and faint outlines of buildings, headlights that blink and disappear on Braddock Avenue, and, over the river, a line of clouds that pale and blur the night sky.

Now, after all this time, she hesitates. She doesn't want to open the letter. *What is the matter with me?* She feels paralyzed, panicked. *What am I so scared of?* Maybe she doesn't want to find out that Florence Rodkey was not the way Flossie had always imagined—a perfect angel on a pedestal. She tucks the letter into her jewelry box. She'll save it for later.

chapter 15

LET ME CALL YOU SWEETHEART

El Yeso Ranch, New Mexico, 1910

It's Phillip's last night at the ranch. He and Florence sit side by side on the veranda, admiring the sunset. They've had a wonderful week. It started a little rocky, since when Phillip saw her in the joy buggy with Ike, his eyes flashed fire, and, as Ike stepped out of the buggy, Phillip raised his arm as if to strike.

Florence's chest gripped with fear, but she quickly rallied, desperately flirting and jollying him out of that black mood. The next day she took him out riding, proudly showing off her horsemanship on Old Fred, while Phillip, his dignity restored, smiled down at her from his perch on the biggest horse in the stable.

Florence picks up the mandolin she found in the parlor and starts to strum. The neck is a bit warped, and she needs to keep tuning it, but she plucks and improvises as a delicate, lazy waltz emerges. The sound of the strings harmonizes with the dramatic reds and yellows of the sky, and the song mutates into a slow version of "Let Me Call You Sweetheart." Florence hums along.

Phillip smiles contentedly as he gazes out at the glorious sky—bands of clouds with reds shading to purple at the top and a brilliant yellow flash of sun beneath. But when the song stops, he sits up in his chair as if roused from slumber and turns to face her. "Florence, I *do* want to call you sweetheart. I'm head over heels in love with you!"

"Oh." She stops strumming, puts down the mandolin, and reaches for his hand. What a perfect moment—the clean desert air, the glow of the falling sun, and the most handsome man in the world declaring his love for her. But can she say the same to him?

In another move, he reaches into his pocket and takes something out. He opens his hand to reveal a green velvet box, which he slowly opens. There, shimmering against a white silk lining, rests an enormous diamond set in a gold band. "Florence, will you marry me?"

Florence gasps. *Oh no, I'm not ready for this.* She looks around, desperately trying to think of something to change the subject.

She has to admit they've had a lot of fun. When they went out riding, she teased him for being a tenderfoot, laughing at his stumble, and he'd good-naturedly laughed at himself, too.

But this? "Oh, Phillip, this is a surprise. I . . . I just don't know. Give me a minute." She jumps up, runs into the house, and throws herself down on the bed. She can just hear Edith's disapproving voice: *You made this happen. You hardly know him, but you shamelessly encouraged him. You know quite well this is way too fast.*

Edith would probably be right, as usual. But Phillip is a real gentleman, and this is what Florence has dreamed of—a big house in Chicago with elegant furnishings, trips to the theater, art galleries, and concerts, and a dashing gentleman as a husband.

Phillip has his faults, of course—everybody does. He's not in favor of women's suffrage. But Florence is a teacher, after all, so she can educate him out of that backward opinion. Because she intends to be active in the movement.

But in conversation, Phillip can go on and on about building and development and how he will make a killing in Seattle. In fact, when he gets on the subject, it's not a conversation, it's a lecture. She feels trapped, having to sit and listen.

And Phillip can be critical. He disapproves of her flirting with the other boys and is jealous of her corresponding with Ernest. But Ernest is her best friend, and besides, he's much easier to converse with than Phillip. She can tell Ernest anything. The exchange in their letters nourishes her soul and keeps her from being so lonely out here.

But Ernest is too young, of course—*and* he's planning to go to journalism school. No big fancy house with him as a husband.

You need to stop dithering, Florence.

She goes to the window and looks at the mesa in the distance. Maybe Phillip is not the perfect choice . . .

The mesa stands stark and gray in the fading light. She holds her hand over her heart. Lurking under there, somewhere in her chest and her throat, is the hidden thing, the thing she hides from herself. A quiver of fear. Dread. What if the pneumonia comes back? What if it gets worse?

Push it down, back down into the dark cave, and come into the light.

She breathes in and out, a long, slow breath. Maybe Phillip is not the perfect choice, but no one could be. Phillip truly loves her. He always compliments her, on her looks, her intelligence, her music, and he showers her with gifts—lo, the jewelry, cards, and trinkets that now grace her tiny corner of the schoolroom.

She might never get a better offer.

Florence jumps up, runs out to the veranda, and plops down onto her seat before the doubts can reappear. "Yes! I will!"

Phillip smiles, dashing and dark, and then they kiss. A slow, sweet kiss, marred only by the feel of his bristly mustache.

But she can get used to that.

♪

It's been a week since Phillip left, and Florence hasn't revealed the ring, or her engagement, to anyone. She has kept to her routine of piano practice, lessons with the girls, meals with the family, and long walks in the evening. As she said in a letter to Ernest, "*The walk is the hardest thing I have ever done. I simply have to drive myself out. But I resolved to do it because I know I need the exercise and air, and to make resolutions and break them is weakening to the character, and thus I argue with myself when my lazy spirit urges me to stay in by the fire.*"

Florence studies her face in the mirror. Yes, she has gained color, if not weight. She has been eating more and spending lots of time outside. Besides walking, she has ridden the horse out to the mesa and even beyond it to the foothills. One time she saw a herd of pronghorn antelope, tall creatures that look so ungainly with their rack of horns, but when they run, they become as graceful as ballerinas. Ike and the boys hunt them, and Mrs. DeG makes them into a terrific roast.

November has brought cooler weather, and at night the temperature dips below freezing, so Florence piles on more blankets, but in the day-time the sun is always out, bright and invigorating.

Today Florence has been invited to take a trail ride with the "boys." Nash, the tall, dark cowpuncher, smiles, and Bailey winks at Florence as the three of them ride out. She laughs and winks back. Why not? Bedecked in her new outfit—a long leather skirt that's split like pants, a loose shirt (no stays, hurrah!), boots with spurs, and a wide-brimmed hat—she feels like a real cowgirl. She even has a holster slung jauntily around her hips with a six-shooter tucked into it. The boys are going to teach her to shoot. She'll be the Annie Oakley of El Yeso.

She and Old Fred follow Nash and Bailey out onto the plain. Tumbleweeds roll along the sand as the horses trot sedately. Fred is, for the most part, a compliant old beast, and it doesn't seem kind to use the spurs on him, so she leads with the reins. Again, she is struck by the quiet and emptiness of this land. The boys are friendly, and they make it clear that they like being with her, but today a shadow of loneliness descends.

She does love this land where she feels free and happy-go-lucky, and aside from the question of Phillip, she is a little homesick. What were Mama and the sisters doing now? Walking through a new snow, mak-ing a snowman, laughing, cooking up a hearty Pennsylvania meal like chicken, succotash, and pumpkin pie. If Florence coughed, Mama would come put her arms around her.

Is it strange that she yearns for Mama and the sisters rather than for Phillip?

♪

Tonight, Florence sits at her usual spot on the veranda with pen and paper. In Phillip's last letter, he scolded her for going out with the other boys, and maybe he's right. But if being married means not having fun with other people, maybe she's not suited for marriage. She reaches under her neckline and fingers the ring on the chain. Is she doing the right thing?

Of course she is. She won't have to work, and she can spend more time with her music and the women's suffrage campaign. And if the pneumonia comes back, who better than Philip to pay for the best treat-ment there is?

She should tell Ernest, but one thing and another gets in the way: extra lessons with the girls, a trip into Clovis to see the young, handsome Doctor Lovelace. He said she was better but could never live in the east again. Was he serious or just flirting? But she feels much better and is having fun learning to ride Western style.

After two weeks, Florence finally writes to Ernest with the news. And then, silence on his part. Every day she looks in the mail, and no letter from him. She misses him, the letters, the conversation, the jokes and teasing. She's always seen him as the younger brother she never had—someone to boss around if she feels like it, instead of always having to be the youngest with six older siblings telling *her* what to do.

Is it possible he is more than that?

Finally, after another three weeks, on the table by the front door—an envelope addressed to her in Ernest's distinctive handwriting, clear and logical, like a clerk's or secretary's.

But the letter is short, almost curt, and Ernest doesn't sound happy. He congratulates her, but his cold tone emanates from the page before he softens and falls back into the newsy tales of the Pittsburgh gang.

She can't lose Ernest. She will write back immediately, cajoling and begging if necessary.

November 1910
My dearest comrade,

Your letter was dandy, and I'm so glad you have accepted my engagement.

How good it is to have you to write to and scold if I wish. I feel perfectly free to tell you my innermost thoughts and allow you to become perfectly acquainted with me, for I know you will love me "in spite of my faults."

Went down to Fort Sumner last Saturday and I certainly had a dandy time. Everyone was lovely to me.

Met some dandy men. One married, one whom I liked particularly well. He is a Cornell man and speaks French better than I do, despite my conceit in that line. He also plays the mandolin, and I'm fairly in love with him. Of course, his wife is "way back East." And the fact of the matter is he never told me he had a wife, but I found it out. He is entirely too nice to be single.

They are getting up a dance especially in my honor for Dec. 16. And I am resurrecting all of my "glad rags" for that occasion.

That's one thing awfully nice out here. You don't need to buy new clothes. I find my old ones look better than anyone else's, so I am for once in my life perfectly content with last year's clothes.

Phillip is as dear as ever. It's a plain cinch he does not approve of my corresponding with you, so be nice, comrade.

You ask when I am to enter the matrimonial sea. Well, it largely depends upon whether I get cured this year or not. I see you smile. I am not as strong constitutionally as you think, young man, or I'd never be out in this wild hole. Dr. Lovelace told me I would never be able to live in the east again and that I could not hope to be cured by spring. And I write it down thus coolly. He asked me if I would rather be dead in in the east than alive in the West. He also volunteered to try to make Western life endurable for me if I'd allow him. Should I? I hear you say yes, of course, but that's because you hate Phillip, but don't believe that he shall ever know or shall ever suffer one pang of jealousy if I can help it.

I had a note from Dr. Lovelace today about engaging in some dances. Rather premature, isn't he? He says, "I foresee that if one dances with you, one will have to speak early, and may I plead this as an excuse for this liberty & etc."

Oh, my dear comrade, there is no place on earth I guess where one may not have a little fun. At least if there is, I've never seen it.

I am looking fine. Redder cheeks than I ever had, and I am gaining weight.

You never seem to think I'm ill and I'm glad. Continue on.

I must close. Will write more later.

Adios, amigo,

Florence

Florence starts a letter to Edith, but the pen stops in mid-air. Edith does not approve of Phillip or the marriage. And she, in her deepest, most truthful self, has to admit she, too, has doubts about Phillip. And of course, she wouldn't tell Edith about the fun she's having with the other men. But the fun is harmless, and she's discovered that if you keep moving, keep flitting and flirting, you don't have to think about what's underneath—those dark clouds of despair that threaten her horizon. If you sing and dance and move fast enough, you'll outrun it; if you make enough noise, you can silence it, bury that truth, and do what you have to do to survive.

The sun has gone down and a million stars pop up like fireflies in the boundless dark night.

chapter 16

THE SPRING GARDEN

Pittsburgh, Pennsylvania, 1942

"Peas! I *love* peas!" shouts Sallie, as she opens a pod and plops a pea into her mouth. She jumps up and down, skipping through the garden, her fluffy-haired companion jogging behind her.

"Don't eat them all," Flossie says as she puts down the hoe and exchanges a smile with Nannie. Sallie always proclaimed her *hatred* of peas until the day Flossie persuaded her to pick a plump green pod and open it along the seam. There's a treasure inside, Flossie said. Just look at those juicy green peas in a little line. Just try one. Just *one*. Now Sallie is unstoppable.

Flossie turns back to hoeing the furrows between the rows of new spinach, the tiny leaves just beginning to peek out from the soil.

The Victory Garden has been expanded to encompass the entire side yard, extending to the rim of the wooded hillside. Nannie has planned and supervised the neat rows and squares, working harder than anyone at digging up the sod, weeding and sifting the soil, and planting each precious seed.

Nannie walks across the garden now, holding up her old gingham housedress to keep it from sweeping the ground. Flossie suggested she wear a shorter dress, but Nannie rolled her eyes at that. *She needs to come out of the nineteenth century. At least she's wearing a warm-weather dress instead of that shapeless old black one.*

"Well done, Flossie!" Nannie smiles.

Flossie pulls up her shirt sleeves and adjusts her overall straps as she straightens. Now, that is *something*. Earning both praise *and* a smile from Nannie.

It's a bright, warm April day, perfect for working in the garden. Sun shines on raised rows of raw earth with lacy green carrot tops shooting up alongside sprouts of lettuce and spinach.

It's Saturday, and everyone, including Sallie, has been conscripted for garden work. Elizabeth's smile opens wide as she limps along the garden's edge, carrying a bouquet of daffodils and tulips. Sallie runs to plunge her face into the flowers and sniff, then turns toward the mail truck tottering up the driveway.

Before the mailman steps out of the truck, Sallie shouts, "A letter from Roddy!" Roddy enlisted in January, and almost the next day, he was gone. Since then, they've received one postcard—for Sallie. Every day since, Sallie has been running out to the mail truck expressing what everyone else feels but doesn't say: anxiety and hope for word from their soldier boy.

Flossie bites her lip. She hasn't heard from Hammie since before Pearl Harbor. *Where could he be? Is he still alive? And could I write to tell him the truth?* She's been seeing George, spending more and more time with him, and now she's less sure about Hammie. But how horrible to break off an engagement while he's at war.

Nannie and Elizabeth stop in their tracks and watch as Sallie grabs a pile of mail from the mailman and then drops half of it on the grass as she shuffles through it. "Nothing from Roddy," Sallie shouts as she flops down onto the grass and flicks the other mail away. "Why doesn't he write?"

Nannie's eyes glisten.

Elizabeth shakes her head. "Well, he's awful busy over there. He's fighting a war for us."

"But we're fighting, too," Sallie says, "like it says on the poster: Plant a Victory Garden: Our food is fighting!"

A sad look passes between Nannie and Elizabeth. Elizabeth purses her lips. "Let's go have lunch."

Elizabeth, followed by Flossie and Nannie, walks somberly into the kitchen. Sallie picks up the mail and skips behind, with Apollo merrily trotting at the end of the procession.

chapter 17

THE LINDY HOP

Pittsburgh, Pennsylvania, 1942

When Flossie looks up from the cash register, there is George, standing in the doorway and smiling right at her. His dark hair is combed back from a receding hairline, horn-rimmed glasses are perched on his nose, and he's wearing a sleek suit and tie.

"George!" With a bang she pushes the cash register drawer in. "Come in!"

George has come to the hospital to see a few patients, he says, and he has time for lunch if Flossie is free. Of course, she's free!

In the hospital cafeteria, they beam at each other over her egg salad sandwich and George's hot lunch of corned beef and hash browns.

George is quiet, gazing out the window like he has something on his mind. Well, he must be thinking about a patient, so Flossie launches into a story about her day. First there was the old lady who fussed around asking if they had a cookbook, a stuffed horse, a particular perfume—none of which the gift store had. She shuffled around the shop picking up everything and putting it down, and then left without buying anything. Then, there was the little boy who ran in, snatched a candy bar, and ran out before his mother dragged him back in by the collar and made him return it. And then Flossie's discovery that two of the little stuffed toys were missing after the old lady left.

She pauses and smiles. "Never a dull moment!"

George has been coming by the house more often these days, and he and Flossie sit on the porch glider and talk or take rides in his car. They've gone to the museum a few times, and once, George took her to the golf course. Flossie had never played before, and he wanted to teach her. Well, it was a fun adventure, but in the long run she's not interested in hitting a little ball around the grass.

But then she said she could teach him the Lindy Hop. And he was game. They went to the Crawford Grill, where all around them, fabulous dancers, Black and White, amazed them with their spinning and kicking and jumping, so professional-looking they could have been in a Broadway show. George and Flossie stumbled around and laughed, and Flossie imagined she was in a Fred Astaire movie.

At the "speakeasy," as Nannie called it, they could forget about the soldiers over in the South Pacific and the increasingly dour news from Europe. George isn't as limber and lithe as Hammie, but he is graceful, and, like everyone else, the couple abandoned themselves to the music: the horns and the keyboards, clarinets and saxophones, the music full of life and energy, the melodies just off the beat, not like the hymns and the 4/4 tunes Nannie played. This was the music of happiness, the music of love.

George clears his throat and smiles nervously, drawing Flossie back to the cafeteria.

Is something wrong? Flossie waits with her hands clasped together, clenching and unclenching. Finally, she has to ask. "What is it, George?"

He reaches across the table and takes her hand. "Will you marry me, Flossie?"

"Oh!" she gasps. This is what she's dreamed of, a marriage proposal, though not so abrupt and in a hospital cafeteria. Well, George is not a man of many words, especially not flowery ones.

Flossie takes a deep breath, and her spirits lift into a vision: a future with George, a place of comfort and security, the loving protection of this gentle doctor. She smiles with her whole body.

But a sudden pang cuts into her chest and into the vision. What about Hammie? All those carefree days, the singing and harmonizing, the dancing, matching step for step with her best friend, her counterpart who would skip into the future with her. Wasn't she supposed to marry *him*? And what about the ring?

But the world has changed so abruptly. Hammie enlisted and went off to Hawaii, then the country entered the war and he was deployed.

If she marries George, she will lose Hammie.

Flossie and Hammie are no longer carefree teenagers, singing and dancing and bouncing tennis balls around. Hammie is a soldier, and he hasn't written since Pearl Harbor. Is he entrenched on some beach, dodging bullets, expecting to come home and marry her? Is he still alive?

The thoughts twirl and collide in her vision—elation, anxiety, guilt—until, exhausted, she rests her head in her hands.

"Flossie?" A tender touch on her arm.

In a sudden flash, she sees clearly. She *does* want to marry George. There's a warmth and light inside her that spreads all around them and into the future, like a sweet melody. They *will* have a life together, a home, a family.

She lifts her head. "I—I, yes!

Flossie and George sit in a soft cloud, their own little world, where everything is a smile. Invisible the harsh gray walls of the cafeteria, gone the smells of overcooked chicken casserole, inaudible the clashing of trays and dishes. Their meal forgotten, they hold hands and sit in silence.

"But we'll have to wait," Flossie says. Maybe Hammie will come home on leave soon. She'd hate to tell him in a letter.

"That's fine," says George with his usual sweet expression, like a kindly uncle. But there's something inscrutable about that expression today. He clears his throat again. "But I have some other news."

Flossie's chest tightens. "Oh?" Is this going to be the other shoe?

"Well, I'll just spit it out. I enlisted in the navy."

"Oh, no." This could not be happening again.

The whole room falls silent around them. Or is it the pounding in her ears? "But you're a doctor! You don't have to go. You're needed here, stateside!"

"Well, I can't sit by and let everyone else fight the war for me. They need doctors in the military, now more than ever."

"But—" Flossie's body deflates like a balloon, and she lets her head drop again. She looks up through her eyelashes. "Will you be deployed?'

He shrugs.

This is all too much. She bites her lip to keep from crying, but a silly squeal comes out anyway. "We'll get married, and then you'll go off to war? This is awful."

"No, it will be a while, if ever, before I'm deployed. I'll train to be a flight surgeon, which will take time, and then, who knows? The war might be over."

"But you'll leave Pittsburgh."

"I'll be a lieutenant. And they have married housing for officers."

"When are you going? And where are you going?"

"In two weeks. To Pensacola, Florida. Will you come down there and marry me?"

Flossie's mouth hangs open. Maybe getting married isn't a good idea. All the husbands go off to fight and leave the wives at home to wring their hands.

chapter 18

THE DARK SIDE OF THE MOON

Mahaffey, Pennsylvania, 1910

"Young lady! Young lady!" Florence wakes to the waiter shaking her shoulder. "Your head is about to drop into your soup," he says with a worried expression but a smile in his eyes. He's a nice man, tall, with a pale handlebar mustache. He's been quite solicitous, urging her to eat and eat during the two-day train ride from Chicago to Pittsburgh. He hasn't asked, but he obviously knows she's sick.

"What?" How embarrassing. She's fallen asleep at the table. "Oh, sorry," she says, standing with all the dignity she can muster. "I'm not really hungry right now. Thank you." She makes her way back to the passenger car.

After two days on the train, with a brief stop in Chicago to see Edith (and, of course she saw Phillip, with another whirlwind of a dinner party that left her exhausted), Florence has to admit she feels weak again. She sinks into her seat and turns her eyes to the window. Outside, bright sunshine reflects off the snowy banks of the Maumee River in western Ohio.

♪

After Phillip left El Yeso, Florence continued saddling Fred and joining the boys on trail rides, where the ranch hands cheered her progress. She loved her new cowgirl look and cajoled Mr. DeG into taking a photograph of her with the cowboys so she could send it to Ernest.

As for her health, she felt wonderful, and she believed her earlier presentiment was an accurate prediction. She was cured. And maybe she could go home for Christmas.

After three months in the schoolroom, she succeeded in improving Mildred's grammar and charming Ethel out of her hostile attitude. Both of them had made good progress in English, and they'd learned a few songs on the piano.

Florence could now ride out by herself, having "learned the ropes," and one day, as she rode back from the trail, the sky turning red and orange and purple, she had that feeling again—she was well, and everything would be all right. She spurred the horse into a gallop, bouncing along on Old Fred, taking big breaths, a confirmation of her health.

Guiding Fred back into a walk, she approached the fence where Manuel stood. He opened the gate and said, "Señorita," as he tipped his hat. This was the most Manuel would say to her unless prodded, which Florence was good at. But Manuel didn't appreciate her prodding, so that day she put a check on it and left him to his solitude. The little ranch house across the plain looked warm and welcoming as the cottonwood tree sighed and soughed in a gust of wind. The air was dry and warm and smelled of sagebrush, and Florence was happy. She would go home for Christmas. Maybe even not return to El Yeso. And phooey to Doctor Lovelace.

♪

Florence slumps in her seat and stares unseeing out the window. Last night, she awoke in the middle of the night with a fever. Her whole body was hot, and her chest felt like it was being scraped by a cheese grater. Her nightdress and sheets were soaked. With all the bursts of smoke and coal dust during the day, she'd been coughing again. Of course, anybody would cough in these conditions.

But she can't slough off the pain and this feeling of frailty. Is it anger or despair? Is the pneumonia returning? Just as she's returning to the cold and damp of Pennsylvania? Or is this something worse? She's tried so hard to ignore it, but now she has to admit she is sick. Sickly.

The landscape of western Ohio is a monotonous field, flat and white for miles. *Like my life, I pretend to myself that I am happy and gay, and it feels good to be admired, but isn't that a shallow satisfaction? Maybe I am just a shallow person.*

She takes out her pen and stationery. She'll write to Sue, dear Sue, the one sister who doesn't boss and scold her.

I just hate myself. I despise myself for the qualities about me that Ernest most admires. My ability to attract men is no credit to me. And I just can't help it. I have tried oh so hard to be true to Phillip, and I have come to the conclusion that it is not in me. I am not capable of true love. Mere infatuation and that, for a mighty short time, is all I can furnish. When people come for me and I am sure of their regard, there do they straightaway cease to interest me, such a smallness of nature I do possess. And I can no more keep myself from flirting with the nice men I meet than I can stop living. It's a part of me. And I don't believe it will stop with marriage either. So, you see I am in for trouble.

When the train chugs to a stop at Mahaffey Station, Florence is the only one disembarking. Slowly she pulls herself up from the seat, an effort now, and goes to stand at the open door. Crusty white mounds of snow and dirty slush cover the train platform, and everything else is gray—the sky, the fields, the streets. She is so feeble, she needs the conductor's help stepping down onto the platform.

Papa is waiting with a smile, and he helps her up onto the buggy to sit on his right side, the side of his good ear. He gives her a hug and a searching look. "You're so pale, little Flossie. Weren't you out in that western sun, riding horses and roping the calves?" Mama and Papa have always thought of her as the sickly one, but she thought she could prove them wrong.

"I know, Papa. I did have some color, but it faded on the trip home." She leans on his shoulder, and he pats her head. Papa doesn't talk much, but she knows he loves her. He's always loved her liveliness. But now that "Little Flossie" side of her is gone, like a bright shining full moon that has disappeared and shows only its dark side.

Mama stands in the doorway as Florence lugs her carpetbag into the kitchen. "My poor dear," Mama says. "You look like a destitute waif. Sit right down here and drink." She hands her a tall glass of milk. "They say milk is the best thing for building up the strength, and now you are home, we can give you plenty."

"They didn't have milk on the train," Florence says, "though I did meet some interesting people."

"Not more young men, I hope," crows Vance, who has just come into the kitchen, tying her apron behind her back. Vance, the fourth-oldest sister, born after Sue, thinks Florence is spoiled. Of course, Vance is the jealous type. Jealous of Edith, who is so accomplished, and jealous of Florence, who she thinks plays on her status as the sickly one to get attention. Vance has started nurse's training in Philadelphia, but her spoiled little sister, it seems, doesn't merit her medical attention.

Maybe Florence does enjoy the attention, but it doesn't negate the fact that she really is sick now. She was only too happy to go out West and get away from the family, but now she's grateful to be home.

Florence sticks out her chin. "I met an interesting young man in Chicago. He's a lawyer and very complimentary. And on the train, another handsome gent insisted on buying me sweets from the dining car when he saw how tired I was." She looks up at Vance with a smirk. "The lawyer wants to come to Pittsburgh to visit." She won't mention the engagement just yet. The ring is still on the chain around her neck under her dress.

Vance snorts. "She's a hopeless flirt, Mama. You shouldn't let her out of your sight."

Mama sighs. "Right now, she needs to go to bed." She herds Florence through the hallway and up the stairs. Vance comes in from the hallway as Mama starts to help her remove her layers of dresses. "I'll do it," Vance says as she moves in and unbuttons and unhooks the stays on Florence's corset.

"At the ranch, nobody wears a corset," Florence says. "What freedom!"

Vance smiles wanly and her voice softens. "Yes, they are saying now that corsets aren't very healthy." She kisses Florence on the cheek. "I do want you to get better, little Flossie." Vance puts up a stern front, but Florence knows that underneath she does care about her little sister.

When Florence is snuggled in under three blankets on the feather-bed, Mama hovers over her with a worried frown.

"Mama, I was homesick. I think that's all it was."

Her mother sighs. "Probably stayed up too late with the boys and didn't get enough sleep. In your condition, rest is essential."

"How could I rest when I had lessons all day and had to practice my piano at night? They wanted me to give a concert, so of course I had to practice. And how could I exist without some social life?" There wasn't much of that in New Mexico, of course, except for the dance, but Ike and those nice young ranch hands would come over in the evening to flirt and listen to her play. "And I even learned to ride a horse Western style!"

Mama looks at her sharply and tucks the covers up around her. "You're getting yourself all worked up again. You can tell us about that later, but now is the time to rest."

Where are the other sisters? Ida is home from her teaching job in Arizona, and Vance from nursing school. Edith is coming home from Chicago tomorrow, but what about Sue and Marge? Sue, Florence's favorite sister, is still living at home, as is Marge, the youngest.

Florence lies back as thoughts drift and evanesce through her head like wispy clouds. The ranch . . . Phillip . . . Ernest.

"Florence! Florence!" She awakens as Sue's shouts carry through the house, with Mama trying to hush her in a lower tone.

Sue bursts into the room and sits on the bed. She unbuttons her jacket as the smells of snow and horse waft around her. She bends down and hugs Florence. "Oh, little Flossie," she cries. "How I've missed you." Sue is only five years older than Florence, but, like Papa, she calls her "Little Flossie." Florence has sometimes resented this babying, but now she relaxes into being coddled. Sue is generous to a fault and lends Florence any of her dresses. Her lively blue eyes light up. "You must tell me all about New Mexico and your many conquests."

Florence smiles and takes the hand Sue proffers. "And you me."

"There's only one for me and guess what!" She holds out her left hand to show a sparkling diamond ring.

"Oh, Sue, it's really happening?"

"Yes, and Harry is the most wonderful man in the world. We've planned a winter wedding. I'm going into Pittsburgh next week with Vance to pick out some clothes for my trousseau. And you can come, too—if you're better?"

Florence closes her eyes and turns her head on the pillow. "I would so love to come, but . . ." At this moment she can hardly turn over in bed without her chest hurting, and she barely has the energy to sit up and drink the milk Mama brought. She fingers the diamond ring on the chain beneath her nightgown. Still hidden. Clearly, she's not as much in love as Sue. Shouldn't Florence be feeling that way about Phillip? But she can't feel it. Maybe she is incapable of feeling that way about anyone. *Why am I so different from other women?*

Doctor Miller comes the next day and, without any hullabaloo, examines her lungs. "Pneumonia again," he says. "You need absolute rest, milk, and meat to build up your strength. How you weathered that trip from New Mexico, I can't guess," he says. "And *why* you did it, when you should have stayed there instead of coming back here to the wet and snow in the middle of winter—"

Florence's sigh escapes in a burble of breath. "I wanted to come home for Christmas."

Everyone comes into the room to visit her, even Papa, who gives her a kindly smile and doesn't even call her a flibbertigibbet.

In a few days she feels better.

When Doctor Miller comes again, he holds out a cloth and says, "Cough."

She looks up at him with what she thinks is her most fetching expression. "I don't feel like coughing."

But he insists, and of course, the evidence that she already knew is there—blood on the cloth.

"Mont Alto," he declares. Those two words sit in the room like a hot coal everyone is afraid to touch. Mont Alto, east of Mahaffey, in the Pennsylvania mountains, is a tuberculosis sanatorium.

"But it's the middle of winter," Florence says. "And this is pneumonia, not—" She can't say the word. The White Plague, people call it, and anyone who has it is shunned because it's so contagious. She turns and punches the pillow with a feeble punch. Now she'll be an outcast, a pariah.

"All the better to go for the cure," he says.

The cure. But does it work? There have been rumors of people supposedly "cured" who relapse and have to go back to the sanatorium. Some never come home.

Sue comes in and stands beside her bed, but Florence pulls the covers over her head and moans. From under the covers she calls, "I'll miss your wedding!" That triggers more coughing, as if to confirm her sentence, and then the tears come. Sobbing and coughing in her cocoon, while outside the covers, low voices murmur. Mama and Doctor Miller consulting, Sue piping in with bursts of angry words.

"I'm not going!" Florence shouts in a feeble voice. They can't force her to go like a prisoner in chains.

Sue, glowing with health and standing tall and beautiful in her pale blue dress, steps up to the bed and puts on her most authoritative older sister voice. "You know very well you *are* that sick. And this is your only chance."

"Aah!" a fragile scream of agony. And Florence sinks farther down under the quilts.

Florence Rodkey, c. 1913

Rodkey siblings, c. 1905. On ground: Florence, Sue, and Marge; second row: Vance and Edith; standing: Ida, Mary, and Robert (Bert)

Florence Rodkey, c. 1915

Florence, 2nd from left, on Old Fred, El Yeso Ranch, c. 1910

Mont Alto Sanatorium, early 1900s

Helen Ettinger (Ruth in the novel), friend, and Florence Rodkey, Mont Alto, c. 1911

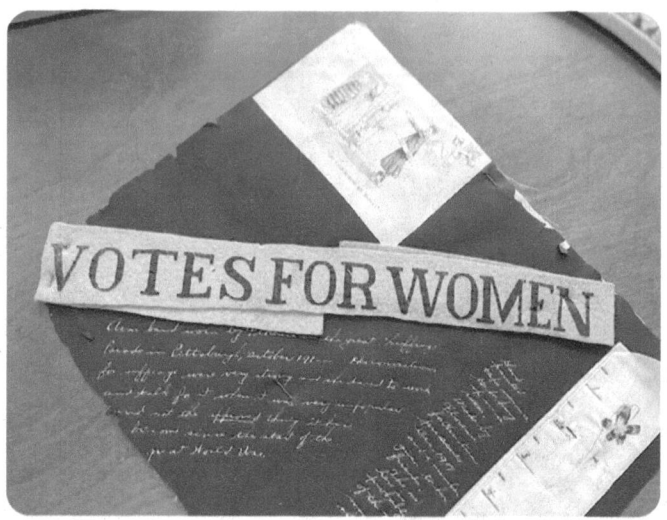

Armband from the 1914 Women Suffrage Parade, Pittsburgh, PA

Ernest and Florence Craighead, c. 1915

Florence Rodkey Craighead with Roddy, 1916

Flossie Craighead, late 1930s

Flossie Craighead & friends, c. 1941

Craighead family, c. 1942; Nannie, Roddy, Flossie, Ernest, Sallie, and Elizabeth

Nannie and Sallie Craighead, c. 1942

George Hayes & Flossie, Navy Chapel, 1942 wedding

Flossie & George, newlyweds, 1942

USS Enterprise, *WWII (similar to one George shipped out on)*

Flossie Hayes, Pensacola, Florida, 1940s. This photo was
incorporated into the book cover by designer Lynn Andreozzi.

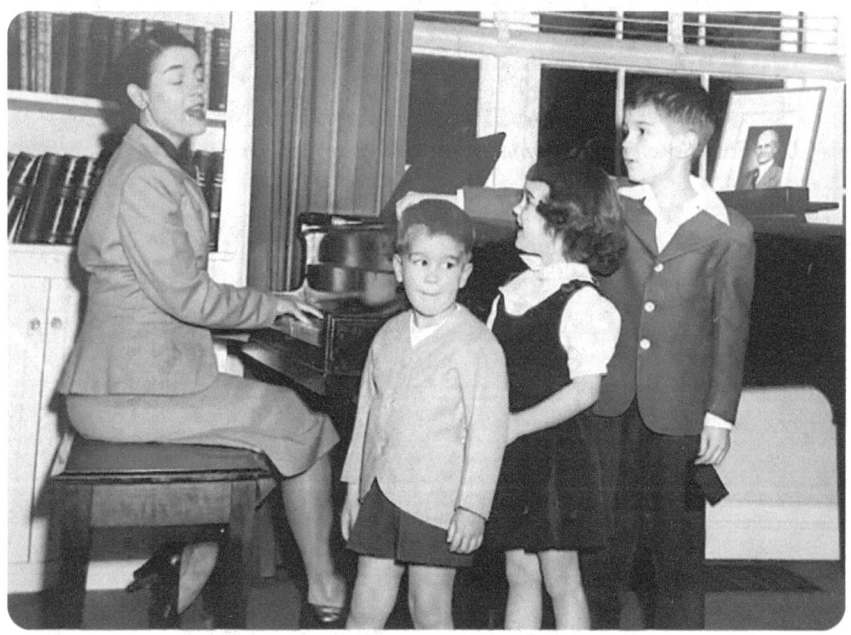

Flossie at piano with K.C., Nancy, and Andy

chapter 19

SILENT NIGHT

Mahaffey, Pennsylvania, 1910

When she wakes up on Christmas morning, Florence is ready to jump up like she always does, race little sister Marge to the bathroom—the new inside bathroom Papa is so proud of—splash her face with water, and run downstairs.

But as she starts to turn over, her chest hurts again. She tries to lift an arm, but it doesn't go up as usual. It's like a cow is lying on top of her, keeping her pressed down to the bed. How odd. It must be a dream. *Just get up, Florence.* She tries again, and now comes an excruciating pain in her chest and a wheezing cough. But surely this is all a figment of her imagination. She rolls onto her side like she always does, still ready to spring out of bed. But she only makes it halfway to a sitting position before she gets winded and has to lie down again.

Outside the window, the snow falls in big, silent flakes, covering the lawn and the street. There are no sounds of horses or wagons, no delivery men with their carts.

Silence.

She pulls up the quilt and sinks beneath it. This room is always cold in the morning, but today it's downright frigid. Hasn't anyone lit the fire yet?

"Freezing to death!" she shouts or tries to shout, though it comes out as a croaky whisper.

"What was that?" Sue sits up in the bed beside hers. "Are you awake, Florence?"

"I'm cold."

"Oh, fiddledeedee!" Ida, in her old nightgown and frayed robe, stands in the doorway, her hair hanging in a stringy mess. "Everyone's cold in the morning. Just get up and you'll feel better, Florence."

Florence buries her head under the quilt.

Sue jumps out of bed. "Ida! How can you be so cruel? How can you not see that Florence *is* ill? She can't even sit up!

Florence moans. And how can she herself believe this is happening? She, Florence, is a young woman with purpose. Full of energy. The lively one. Maybe she did play sick once to get out of cleaning the oven, and maybe she's had some setbacks, like a long and draining train journey, but she's always been strong.

Except when she *is* sick. Sometimes they call her the sickly one. She is good at denying it, but right now she has to admit she is miserable. Under the quilt she can breathe a little easier, but the wheezing comes again, and she can't stop it. Oh, how dismal. Is it even worth living with all of this?

Ida disappears into the hallway.

The wind blows against the windowpane, and Sue walks over to look out. "There's Jimmy Hoffman chasing the dog around in the snow! Oh!" she laughs. "The dog got out of the gate, and now Jimmy is stumbling out onto the street!"

Florence sinks in the bed and pulls the quilts up again. Nobody is paying her any attention. Even Sue, her strongest ally, is watching the neighbor boy fooling around, and she doesn't come over as she usually does.

Well, if everyone is ignoring her, she will, too. She'll just ignore the cough and get on with it. Really, she can't be sick. It's Christmas morning.

"Mmm," Sue murmurs. "I smell Mama's *kranzkuchen* with marzipan."

"And apricot jam," Ida roars.

Florence's very favorite. But for some reason hearing the name of her favorite treat now makes her nauseous.

Slowly she hauls herself up and makes her way to the bathroom. Little Marge, the youngest at fifteen and not so little anymore, is at the sink already, washing her face and humming "God Rest Ye Merry Gentlemen." Her long, fiery orange and yellow hair flows in a glorious mess down her back and into the sink. Florence nudges her. "I have to get in there, Marge."

"Oh, all right," Marge stamps her foot, marches away, and stands over the register, humming and giggling as her nightgown billows out in the hot air. She ignores Florence like everybody else.

Now the nausea clenches her insides and Florence leans over the sink. As her stomach erupts with a gag, last night's dinner comes tumbling out into the sink.

"What's going on?" Mama comes into the bathroom, wiping her forehead with her apron.

Florence stands at the sink, looking down.

Mama leans around her. "What's that?" she shouts. "Blood! Again! Oh, Florence!"

Mama cries, "Now we *must* follow the doctor's orders," she says. "Now we must take you straight away to—"

She doesn't have to say where. Everyone knows where. Florence limps back to the bedroom and lies back on her bed. She managed to hoodwink everyone into believing that the earlier blood was simply an aberration. She thought she could hide it, even from herself, but she has to admit it now—the blood is the proof. She has the "White Plague."

Mama and Marge follow her and stand by the bed in silence. Mama takes her hand, and Marge, her mouth open in a big O, shifts her gaze back and forth from Mama to Florence.

Later, Florence will look back on this moment as a turning point. The day she finally gives in to the truth. The day she realizes she can't fight it by denying it. The day she says the word—tuberculosis.

"All right," she sighs, "I'll go."

She writes a letter to Ernest, in fits and starts and full of self-pity. But that's who she is right now, and he'll just have to accept it.

♪

When Florence finally makes it downstairs, she lies on the horsehair sofa, wrapped in shawls and blankets, right next to the fireplace. She gazes at the candles on the tree and the beautiful glass balls that glimmer in the candlelight. Her coffee and *kranzkuchen*, barely touched, sit beside her on the little table. From the parlor come the sounds of Ida, Marge, and Sue singing "Hark the Herald Angels Sing" as Ida plays the piano. Florence clenches her fist. *She's* the one who usually plays the carols.

She bites her lip. It's not fair.

chapter 20

END OF THE LINE

Mahaffey, Pennsylvania, 1910

On the day after Christmas, Florence's trunk is packed, and she's bundled for the ride to the train station.

She sits in the front of the buggy with Papa, while Mama and Sue sit in the back. They travel the old-fashioned way, the sturdy horse trotting and pulling them along to the station over roads that would leave Papa's motor car slipping and sliding.

At the station a luggage cart is piled with trunks like a motley array of children's blocks that might topple at any moment. A porter heaves Florence's steamer trunk onto the top.

She hugs Papa, and Mama leans over for a kiss.

Mama's kind face is screwed up into a worried frown. "No staying up till all hours now."

Florence steps down onto the platform. "I know, Mama." Everyone knows the best treatment for the-word-she-still-won't-say is rest. That's what they promote at the Mont Alto Sanatorium: rest, exercise, sunshine, and nutrition. "But how long will I have to stay there?" she asks for the third time. No one has given her a straight answer.

"Only a month or two, probably," says Sue, leaning over the back seat with a reassuring smile. "I'm sure you'll be better soon. Go on now. The train is leaving."

Florence looks at the train and touches her fluttering chest. What will Mont Alto be like? A big hospital, with hundreds of sick people lying around? And she'll have to adhere to a *regimen*, they said. What does that mean? Like being in the army? And the "cure." What is that?

But first the train ride. She does love the train. From home, she usually takes it the other way, to Pittsburgh, where she can go to shows and concerts with friends, so much more interesting than what's on offer in old Mahaffey. But now she's traveling east.

A long way.

To a sanatorium.

An older woman in a Victorian coat with out-of-fashion padded shoulders and a stubby hat topped with big flowers walks across the platform. She holds the conductor's arm as she steps onto the train, while behind her, a dapper-looking man springs up the steps. These people are not from Mahaffey. Where could they be coming from? Florence can find out, do a little sleuthing on the train. This is an adventure. Her spirits lift at the thought. She can think about her destination later.

With a skip of her heart and a little wave to the family, Florence adjusts her big hat, ostrich feather bobbing in the air, and walks to the platform. The porter helps her onto the train. Now, underneath the rasping cough, there's that familiar flutter in her chest, the excitement of starting a new journey. But this time the flutter includes something else. Fear. What kind of fate is she riding toward?

She stands straight in her new traveling coat, a simple navy blue with a flowing skirt that emphasizes her slim physique. Perhaps too slim. She *has* lost weight, which is not a good sign, but hopefully she'll gain it back at the sanatorium. She swishes down the aisle to the admiring glances of several gentlemen and finds a seat by a window.

She takes off her hat and coat, settles into her seat, and watches her hometown glide by outside the window. The train crosses the Susquehanna River on the Market Street Bridge and travels beside Chest Creek. High water rushes over stones and ice, and a layer of snow like a white blanket covers the banks and fields and treetops. There are Papa's farm fields, all white and vast to the horizon, and then the woods, naked maples and elms, and snow-laden pines with bare patches underneath.

Florence leans back in her seat and closes her eyes. She had to pack for a stay of an unknown length, and everyone ran around trying to help her but mostly made chaos. When Vance came in and saw her trunk, she said, "For heaven's sake, you're not going to a dress ball." And after some arguing, Florence compromised; she took out all the elegant gowns except three of her best. She couldn't bear to leave behind the white lawn or the new brown silk that complements her chestnut hair.

She sighs. It was cold this week, and up in the mountains it will be even colder, though the weather there is unpredictable, they say. No one knows how long she'll be there, so she packed for cold weather as well as warm (the white lawn—*Horrors, to stay until spring!*). She wants to look her best, even in a hospital setting. Maybe especially in that setting, as she'll need to keep her spirits up.

The train chugs and clatters in a steady rhythm, and outside, the mountains close in around them. *Why me? Why should I be the one to get this disease?* She is young and pretty. Well, maybe a little too thin, but the boys who hover round don't think so. She is twenty-two, and it's not fair. Not fair at all. She again can't say the name of *this disease*. In fact, maybe if she doesn't say its name, it won't be true.

Around her, all the people look smug and satisfied. Is this fair? That everyone else is healthy and happy, living their lives without a care, while she has this dark secret?

Well, Florence can play the game. She can wear a hat with an ostrich feather and look beautiful and carefree. She can even act carefree. Well, maybe she *is* a little sarcastic. Maybe more than a little. But she doesn't suffer fools gladly.

Life is an adventure, and she will barrel into it like a knight on a charger, like Joan of Arc, and not be afraid. Well, she can *look* like she isn't afraid. If you pretend to be brave, you might actually *be* brave. If you pretend to be strong, you are strong.

When she opens her eyes, she feels another set of eyes focused on her. It's the dapper young man she saw getting on the train, sitting a few seats ahead of her. He's taken off his bowler hat, and his dark hair, slicked down with oil, glistens in the dim light of the train car. He sees her return his gaze and smiles, tweaking a pointy black mustache and bowing his head. She turns her head away to look out the window. There's something shifty-looking about him.

The sun is high in the sky. Almost noon. Lunch time. Florence is not hungry, but she knows she has to gain weight and strength, so she can go home sooner. She'll go to the dining car and start on her new regimen forthwith.

In the dining car, with its arched ceiling and dark wood paneling, almost all the tables are occupied. People come from all the surrounding areas—Falls Creek, Punxsutawney—to catch the Mahaffey train. Most of them are going to Harrisburg or Philadelphia. The diners look elegant and refined at the tables covered with crisp white linen and sparkling with silver and crystal. A delicate Tiffany lamp perches on each one.

Florence sashays down the aisle, with its gleaming woodwork and brass lamps in sconces, its waiters in white coats, and the smell of something delicious. A grilled salmon on someone's plate. Peas and scalloped potatoes, Parkerhouse rolls, and pats of butter in little sculpted shapes. Abundance. And she *will* eat.

Even though she isn't hungry.

She sits at the only table that's unoccupied, a table for two at the end of the car. She orders what looks to be the heartiest meal on the menu, steak with vegetables and potatoes, crusty bread, and trifle for dessert. She will start immediately on her regimen. Heaven forbid she should be here any longer than necessary.

Outside the window, the hills of Pennsylvania, bleak and white in the snow, rise behind an open vista of fields and river, interrupted now and then by little towns like Mahaffey that come and go in a flash.

The train pulls into the station at Altoona. A massive train shed and tall buildings surround the platform. She's familiar with this station since she attended music school here. Altoona is a big city compared to Mahaffey, with lots of people getting on and off the train. One woman walks by Florence's window in an enormous fur coat—chinchilla, she thinks—and a big, blousy hat with the feather curving over the side. Stunning. *I wonder if I could get one like that.* But Mama and Papa are straining to afford this sanatorium as it is, and, without her teaching job, Florence has no income.

The man with the pointy mustache sits a few tables ahead of her. He turns and smiles at her, but she looks the other way. Sometimes it's better to be alone.

This will be the biggest challenge of her life. How can she go to this sanatorium where everyone is sick? Why didn't she stay in New Mexico instead of insisting on taking that smoky train for three days to get home? She was fine in New Mexico. Well, not really fine, no matter how much she tried to ignore her condition. But it was homesickness, pure and simple, that brought her back.

She gazes at the snow-covered hills. Her stay at the sanatorium could be longer than a few months. Some people never come back.

But she will not be one of those people.

Florence has spunk. She has courage. She went to New Mexico by herself, she learned how to ride a horse, she astonished the ranch hands who were ready to laugh at her when the horse ran away. But she went after that horse and brought him back. She even jumped onto his back and rode into camp triumphant, and they applauded the greenhorn cowgirl.

The dapper man inclines his head to her as if tipping his hat. He looks a bit interesting, but really, he's rather coarse. Why has she even paid attention to him?

When everyone else went out to the church service on Christmas Day, Florence sat by the fire with Sue—a precious time with her favorite sister.

"I know I'm too flirtatious," Florence admitted, "and I know it makes people think I'm shallow. But when men admire me, I can forget the dark fear that's underneath."

"Their admiration makes you feel more alive."

"Exactly. Laughing and flirting, like a sunny blue sky, covers over the black clouds of dread, like a wash of yellow paint can hide the gloomy scene beneath it."

The man on the train starts to get up again, probably to approach her, but just then a young woman about Florence's age comes into the car. She hesitates beside Florence. Florence quickly plucks her sleeve and smiles up at her. "Won't you join me?"

The girl jumps, then sees Florence. "Oh, you startled me." She looks around again, then sits. "If you don't mind." She's wearing a white lace blouse and blue skirt. Very smart.

"Oh no, you have rescued me from a dire fate." Florence inclines her head, indicating the dapper man.

The other woman rolls her eyes. "Yes, I know Mr. Russo."

"You know him?"

"He tried to sell me a Model T automobile. 'The newest, the most marvelous invention the world has ever seen!' As if I could buy an automobile."

"He's a traveling salesman, then?"

"Yes, and more." She rolls her eyes again and extends her hand. "I'm Elsie Marshall."

"Pleased to meet you. Florence Rodkey."

Elsie orders the same meal as Florence, and they chat while they eat. The train rattles along the tracks in a comforting rhythm as they remark on the sights outside the window—a deer leaping along with two fawns, cows huddling together in a field, a lake of ice.

Elsie is on her way to Philadelphia to stay with a school friend for a week. "And where are you off to, Florence?"

Florence hesitates, her fork shaking in her hand. "To the mountains." She doesn't dare say Mont Alto. Elsie might run away from her. People are so fearful of "the White Plague" that they don't want to be anywhere near someone who might be infected. Florence takes care to lean back and away from the table so as not to breathe on her new friend. "I'm visiting friends of the family." That's a lie, but sometimes a lie is necessary.

"And won't you eat more of your steak?" Elsie says, eyeing Florence's half-eaten meal.

"I had an enormous breakfast," she lies again. It's difficult to force yourself to eat when you aren't hungry.

♪

As they walk back to their seats through the swaying train, Elsie turns to Florence. "Have you read Mary MacLane?"

"No. What is that?"

"Oh, you *must* read her. In fact, I have an extra copy, and I shall give it to you straightaway." Elsie rushes through the train cars and soon returns with a little, red volume, *The Story of Mary MacLane, by Herself.* She hands it to Florence with a salute, then walks back down the aisle to her car.

At her seat Florence opens the book. *"I have in me a quite unusual intensity of life,"* she reads. *"I have a marvelous capacity for misery and for happiness."* Florence laughs, not out of derision but from recognition. This young woman is talking about *her.*

She reads on and on, thrilling to page after page and sentence after sentence, until her head drops in exhaustion, and she's nodding off again.

The train whistle wakes her, and the conductor calls, "Newport!" Luckily, she hasn't slept through Harrisburg, where she must change trains. Outside the window, a few people stand under the overhanging hip roof of a graceful brick building.

Florence forces herself to sit up. Why is she so tired? Why does she feel frail when her real self is robust? *I am like Mary MacLane. I have within me a quite unusual intensity of life.*

The train starts up again and chugs along beside the Juniata River, bound for Harrisburg. With another whistle and a screech of brakes, it pulls into the station. Florence dons her hat and coat and makes her way through the next car to bid farewell to Elsie, who sits serenely, reading. Florence clasps Elsie's hand, and Elsie gives her a look of great sympathy. "Be well, my dear." Does Elsie perceive that Florence is not well? She thought she had hidden it quite effectively. Florence stands straighter and marches to the end of the car.

The Harrisburg station is an elegant brick building almost as big as Pittsburgh's Union Station. Inside, she sees a sign for the Mont Alto train, which is already on the platform. She rushes out, and by the time she climbs in and finds a seat, she's exhausted again.

Only two hours to Mont Alto.

When she awakens, she feels that flutter in her chest again, that combination of fear and excitement, and by the time the train stops, her whole body is tense. What is she getting herself into? Should she have refused to come? Should she have gone back to New Mexico despite the doctor and Mama? The dry western air could be a cure in itself for the-word-she-won't-say, but of course she was too weak to withstand the journey back.

The conductor marches by. "End of the line," he shouts. "Mont Alto! Everyone off."

Outside the window, several people stand on the platform looking at the train. Is someone waiting for her? She touches her hand to her heart and wipes a pesky tear from her cheek. *The end of the line.* Will this be the end of the line for her?

She scolds herself for such pessimism and repeats Sue's phrase, "Buck up, Florence."

When she emerges from the train, the sun is out again, bright and dazzling, and she squints against the glare. The train wasn't that dark, but this is like stepping into a spotlight. Sunshine like a blazing shield obstructs her sight, and she closes her eyes.

Feet shuffle around her, bags drop onto the concrete with thuds and knocks. She inhales the wool of a coat, the sour breath of someone beside her as the train whistles and the engine starts up again.

Slowly she opens her eyes and looks around. No one else on the platform. At the far edge, though, a car is parked, a roadster, red and shiny, a tall man standing beside it. He squats and fiddles with a tire, then stands and pats the hood of the car. He glances around and sees her.

The tall man strides across the platform and approaches her with a jolly smile. "Sanatorium, miss?"

"Are there any other options?" She smirks and looks around. She has a futile impulse to escape, to be anywhere but here, then sighs. "Yes."

The porter brings her trunk to the waiting car, a jaunty-looking buggy with big, narrow wheels and a canopy top.

"Stanley Steamer." The jolly man points to it and beams. "Latest edition."

"But will it run in the snow?"

"Best car for all conditions," he brags. "And besides, the snow is gone for the moment." He chuckles. "But just wait another minute. Up here, the weather changes from summer to winter and back again in the blink of an eye."

Florence steps from the bright sunshine into the passenger seat and notices someone sitting in the dark interior. He tips his bowler hat and grins. The salesman from the train. Mr. Russo.

The driver, who introduces himself as Jim Frier, starts up the car, and they take off along a snowy road. Strangely, the dapper man, so forward-seeming on the train, doesn't try to engage her, but now withdraws into himself as the car climbs the mountain roads. Florence has decided to be polite but firm with him, but now there's no need as he is turned away, staring out at the roadside. The engine noise is too loud for conversation anyway. Does he have the-word-she-won't-say? He must have deduced that she has it, too.

The car climbs a long rise, and beside the road, snow flurries dance and whirl in the wind through bare trees. It's colder here in the mountains, bleak and barren, as if the season is moving backward into winter. A journey into exile.

As the car crests the hill, a vista appears below them, a vast, open bowl lined by several large buildings and scores of small white squares laid out in a grid, resembling army barracks or tents.

"Built on a plateau in the Blue Mountains," Jim Frier calls over the engine noise. "Mont Alto is celebrated for its pure mountain air and sunshine."

"What are those tents?" Florence shouts.

"Not tents," he shouts back. "Those are the cottages. You'll be in one of those."

chapter 21

ON THE SUNNY SIDE OF THE STREET

Pensacola, Florida, 1942

Daddy lifts an arm to help Elizabeth step from the train car, and Sallie skips behind her. Flossie lugs her new green leather suitcase and matching cosmetic bag down the steep stairs and stands on the platform. A blast of air, hot and humid, envelops her in a sudden cloud. It's like being underwater.

There was no way she could have reached Hammie to tell him her news. Her latest letters had been coming back to her, and his family didn't know anything. Flossie fretted about it for a while, then decided she had to move forward with her life. Who knows when, or even if, Hammie will come back? She said yes to George, and so here she is. To begin her destiny.

For almost three days, the family rode in air-conditioned splendor, from Pennsylvania through Washington, DC, then Virginia, North Carolina, Georgia, and finally Florida. Sallie and Flossie shared one cabin in the Pullman car, and Daddy and Elizabeth the other.

When the train pulled into the Fredericksburg station, Daddy pointed out the window. "There was a famous Civil War battle near here, in Chancellorsville. Your grandfather fought there—your mother's father," he said, pointing to Flossie. "His left ear was shot off."

Flossie recalled a vague image from childhood—a jolly, smiling grandpa with a mutton chop mustache and a scar on the side of his head. "Oh, gosh, I think I remember that."

"Yes. That's why all his pictures were taken from the right side. He was only nineteen when the war started. The Confederates captured him, and he didn't get out until two years later, the end of the war."

"What about *my* grandpa, Daddy?" Sallie piped up. "Was he in the war, too?"

"Yes, your grandpa, my father, who was Flossie's grandpa, too, was in the Pennsylvania Home Guard. He defended the home front in case the Johnnies attacked Pennsylvania."

"Johnnies?" Sallie's face was pressed to the glass as if she could view the battle, although the only thing visible was the big brick station.

"They were the Confederate soldiers, the enemy, and the Union troops never knew when they might invade Pennsylvania, since we were so close to the Mason-Dixon line. Fortunately, they didn't make it that far, so your Grandfather Craighead didn't have to fight."

On the train platform in Pensacola, Daddy consults his watch and Elizabeth fans her face with a paper pamphlet as they wait, surrounded by a sea of navy uniforms. Some blue, some gray, and a few white, all the young men hurrying to and fro.

"Can I help you, miss?" A sailor in gray with a beefy red face stops beside Flossie, using a handkerchief to wipe the ribbons of sweat running down his forehead. He winks at her.

"No, thank you, I'm waiting for my fiancé," Flossie says, holding her head up high. Soon to be a navy wife, and an officer's wife to boot. And can't he see she is with her family?

"My loss," the sailor says and walks away, whistling.

But where is George? Flossie scans the crowd. Will he be wearing a uniform? And what kind?

Sallie jumps in a hopscotch pattern around Flossie, pigtails bouncing, her new gingham dress twirling. "I'm hot," she calls out.

Flossie rolls her eyes. "Then stand still, for heaven's sake."

"Flossie," comes a soft voice from behind her.

"Oh!" Flossie spins around and falls into George's arms. He's in a spiffy white uniform and a cap with a brass insignia. She lets out a breath. In his arms she feels safe and protected, a kind of comfort she didn't know she was missing. George is not only kind and gentle, but he's a doctor and a sailor, and in a few days, he'll be her *husband*. Tears spring up and they smile at each other.

"Ahoy there!" calls Daddy, who extends his hand for George to shake, while Elizabeth, with a broad smile, gives him a quick hug.

"Your bungalow is not far." George beams, then picks up Elizabeth's and Flossie's suitcases and leads them across the platform to the taxi stand.

The taxi turns onto a little street, lined with tiny bungalows and tall palm trees, and stops in front of one of the bungalows, identical to all the others except for its color, yellow.

"A palm tree!" Sallie exclaims and runs up to feel the bark.

"Watch out for falling coconuts," Daddy calls with a grin, and Sallie looks up, then runs back to the sidewalk.

"Oh, stop it," Elizabeth laughs.

"Well, sometimes they do fall," George says as he leads them up the walk. "This is your place for the week. It's not much, but it has a porch and two bedrooms. All of these bungalows were built recently to house the officers' families. This area is called Navy Point. My house—*ours*"—he winks at Flossie—"is down across the street."

Flossie blushes and looks down the road for the house she will share with George. The bungalows all look the same.

"And right on the ocean!" Elizabeth exclaims, waving an arm toward the vista across the road. Behind the bungalows, a beach forms a little bay on the calm, green water and curves to a point in the distance.

It won't be the big church wedding with the white lace dress Flossie imagined. But this is a *navy wedding*, in the navy chapel, and she has a smart new wool suit, a "victory suit," and a matching hat. No brides-maids; just the family. It will be an intimate wedding suitable for war-time. Sallie will be the flower girl. A navy wedding is adventurous and daring, something to tell her friends about. She'll be living by the beach, swimming in the warm ocean, strolling under the cottonwood trees . . . she'll be a married woman in paradise—at least while George is in flight training. After that . . . she won't think about that.

chapter 22

MOUNTAIN AIRE

Mont Alto, Pennsylvania, 1911

The car descends the drive and approaches an immense, white-framed building that resembles a resort hotel. High windows run along the front in three rows of twenty-five each. At one end, two huge screened-in porches are stacked on top of each other.

At the entrance, an elegant porch lined with white columns, a young woman in a sleek blue cape and a white nurse's cap above dark, curly hair, steps down onto the road. She smiles broadly. "Welcome to Mont Alto, Miss Rodkey."

Florence turns to look at the mustachioed man in the back seat, who still hasn't said a word. He quietly slides out the rear door of the car and disappears. The nurse, whose name tag reads "Maude," climbs into the back and takes his seat. "We will take you to the women's camp," she says.

"But"—Florence turns to indicate the disappearing man—"isn't he—"

"Oh, that's Mr. Russo," says Maude. "He's been here several times."

Mr. Russo, the vivacious salesman—though here, he's just a patient like everyone else with the same dark secret Florence has. And now, rather than repugnance, she feels sympathy. Because isn't that the way she deals with all of this? With sparkle and bounce that shows how alive she is?

The car winds through a maze of cabins, small, square buildings arranged in straight rows. Propped up on pilings with no baseboard skirting, their peaked roofs make them look like canvas tents, but on closer inspection, Florence notices the roofs are tin.

The car stops in front of one cabin, and Jim Frier and Maude jump out. Jim extends his hand to Florence. Tentatively, she steps out of the car and looks around. Across the road sits a larger square structure with no walls. A roof overhangs a veranda on all four sides of the platform, and beneath the roof, reclining chairs are lined up.

"That's the women's treatment pavilion," says Maude.

"Treatment?"

"Fresh air and sunshine. The best treatment for the lungs. Along with exercise and good food, of course."

"Not in this weather, surely?" Florence laughs.

"Oh my, yes, in every kind of weather."

With an inward groan, Florence follows Maude up the three steps into the wooden cabin. Along one wall a kerosene heater emits a faint warmth, and in the corners sit four beds neatly made with colorful quilts. Seated on the bed in the far corner, a pale girl looks up.

"Hello, Miss Adams," says Maude. "This is Miss Rodkey."

Miss Adams, a gaunt young woman, sports the same old-fashioned hairstyle as Maude's, hers sparse and blond, pulled into a tight bun. Hunched over a book, she looks up at Florence, sad eyes in a bony face.

Jim Frier brings in Florence's trunk and lays it beside one of the beds. He hastily tips his hat with a little bow and goes back outside. As she examines the room, Maude hands her a typewritten schedule. "Make yourself at home," she says and follows Jim out the door.

Florence sits on the bed. The camp cabin, one of hundreds just like it, in neat rows, the smell of pine-paneled walls and clean sheets, the air chilly despite the kerosene heater. What is she doing here in the middle of winter?

She looks up at the other girl. "I'm Florence."

"Gertrude."

"Have you been here long?"

Gertrude shrugs and bends her head down over her book again.

How should Florence respond? Should she try to draw the girl out or just ignore her? Gertrude is obviously sicker than Florence, but still, she doesn't have to be rude.

Suddenly the door bangs open and another young woman, tall and gangly, with dark, curly hair, lopes into the cottage. "Hail, comrades!" She throws off her coat and flops down on her bed.

"Comrades?" Florence brightens at the word. "Are you a socialist?"

"And proud of it."

"How wonderful. I attended a rally for Eugene Debs in Pittsburgh, and I found his ideas to be truly interesting. I had to go secretly, of course, since my parents disapprove of socialism."

The tall girl sits up. "And have you read *Das Kapital?*"

"No. But I've read some of Eugene Debs."

"You *must* read *Das Kapital.* You will see how veritably oppressed the workers are in this country. It's not only the peasants in Russia," she says with a shining fervor in her eyes. "We must abolish the dire poverty of the working classes, as Marx says."

"I quite agree." Thank goodness not everyone here is wan and frail like Gertrude. Well, everyone *is* frail, most likely, since that's why they're here, but now Florence has someone interesting to talk to. She starts unpacking, using the chest of drawers and a wardrobe beside her bed. She spreads a scallop-edged linen cloth on top of the chest and on it carefully places her toilet set: a silver hand mirror, the back and handle sculpted with wreaths and flowers, a matching silver-handled brush, and beside them a box of face powder and a tiny crystal bottle of *eau de cologne*—Lily of the Valley.

The tall girl stands behind Florence, her hair escaping her bun, intense brown eyes watching. She clears her throat. "It's lunch time," she says. "I'm Ruth, by the way."

"Florence."

Ruth and Florence put on their coats and start toward the door. Ruth looks back. "Are you coming, Gertrude?"

Gertrude, still sitting on her bed, shrugs again, and Ruth opens the door, taking Florence's arm. Their boots crunch in the snow as they walk along the road.

"Isn't Gertrude eating?" Florence asks, glancing back at the cabin.

"I don't know. She has no appetite. And she's not getting better." Ruth raises her eyebrows in sympathy.

Florence's shoulders sink. "How awful." She shudders, trying to convince herself she has an appetite.

Ruth casts a glance back at the cabin. "She *has* to eat. Maybe we can bring her something if she doesn't show up at dinner."

They walk along interconnecting paths that wind through the rows of cabins and resume the discussion of *Das Kapital*.

"It's a work of genius," says Ruth. "Everyone's talking about it in Europe. It shows how capitalism makes slaves of the workers."

"I know the workers in Pittsburgh have been ill-treated. There was a strike at the Homewood steel mill last summer, and the owners actually brought in armed men to suppress it. Some people were killed."

"I read about that. What a tragedy. And proof that the capitalist system has to go."

The dining room, high-ceilinged and outfitted with chandeliers, table linens, and real silver, feels like an elegant restaurant in a grand hotel. Waiters in uniform glide back and forth, and more than a hundred people sit at round tables amid sounds of clanking silverware and sporadic conversation.

"Like a fancy restaurant," Florence says.

"Yes," Ruth replies. "An example of capitalism. Though, I admit, it helps make people feel better. Mealtimes are sacred here."

Florence finds her assigned seat at a table for six as Ruth goes off to her own table.

"Welcome, newcomer!" shouts a dark-haired man across from her as he lifts a glass of water and tweaks his mustache. She recognizes Mr. Russo and smiles.

Florence has never been in company with other people who have the same condition. What are their stories? Are they being cured? These people don't look terribly sick. Two of the women are excessively thin, while one young man, tall and robust-looking with a rosy complexion, is eating with gusto.

"Thank you." She smiles as she sits. Immediately a waiter places a plate before her. Roast lamb, boiled potatoes, broccoli, tomatoes, and cut corn, with a roll and a slice of cherry pie in front of her place setting. It looks and smells wonderful. Maybe she will regain her appetite here. Everyone has already started eating, so Florence does the same.

They're talking about one of the doctors.

"His highness informed me that I wasn't following the regimen," complains Mr. Russo. "I said, 'How can I abide four glasses of milk a day?' It's positively uncivilized. My ancestors in Italy will be turning in their graves." He looks at the other diners who remain silent. "Wrong metaphor, I admit."

"But don't you know this is one of Dr. Trudeau's most important discoveries?" says one of the thin women. She has wispy dark hair, prominent cheekbones, and glittering brown eyes, and her small size belies a forceful presence. Florence has read of Dr. Trudeau, one of the pioneers in treating tuberculosis. He founded the first sanatorium in America at Saranac Lake in the Adirondacks and discovered the bacterium that causes the disease.

The robust man chimes in, "Yes." His ruddy color, Florence now sees, is more of a feverish flush than a healthy outdoor hue. "Trudeau insisted milk is the best cure."

"Cure! Hah!" Mr. Russo croaks. "Let's not buy into that myth."

The table falls silent again.

The other thin woman, in a bright yellow dress that makes her complexion even more sallow-looking, leans over and whispers to Florence, "We are not supposed to talk of illness here. You see where it leads."

Florence nods and works on her dinner. It really is delicious, and she finds herself enjoying it more than any other meal she's had lately, despite the pall that has fallen over the table.

"And where do you come from, pretty lady?" says Mr. Russo in an obvious attempt to change the depressing subject.

"Well, I've been working out in New Mexico, but I come from Pittsburgh."

"Ah, the smoky city. Where you have to hold a handkerchief in front of your nose. Is that true?"

"Only on some days."

"And what kind of work do you do?" asks the wispy-haired woman. They can see Florence isn't wearing a ring, so the woman doesn't ask the usual first question.

Why is she still not wearing her engagement ring? She can't forget that flash of anger in Phillip's expression when she came back to the ranch with Ike. She can't deny she was a little frightened then. And why is she still dithering about it?

She tells them about her teaching and piano concerts.

"You must play for us," says the yellow-dressed woman. "We have concerts every Sunday."

Florence nods. Although she didn't finish the whole meal, she ate most of it, and now feels better, so she will most certainly regain her strength soon.

As she savors the cherries in her pie, people get up and drift toward the doors that lead onto the porch. She looks at her schedule. *After Dinner: Veranda Rest.* She fetches her coat and follows the crowd outside, where dark night has already fallen, and oil lamps illuminate the people spread out on reclining chairs.

A nurse approaches—Maude again—and leads Florence to her assigned chair. "Fresh air and rest," she says. "Absolutely mandatory." Florence drops onto the chair and Maude drapes a heavy, fur-lined blanket over her, then hands her a strange-looking hat. Florence examines it. "What is this?"

"You'll find it very warm," Maude says.

The hat is frightful, an enormous fur and wool contraption like a stovepipe. "This will ruin my hair."

"Sorry, that's regulation. And besides, everyone wears them." She reaches over to place the hat on Florence's head.

"I'll do it." If everyone wears them, at least she won't stand out. She pulls the hat over her carefully arranged hair, knowing it will smash it down, but she is determined to follow the treatment regimen. And it *is* nice to lie back and do nothing, even though the air is positively glacial. She pulls the blanket up higher, the hat lower, and closes her eyes.

"She didn't make it," a scratchy voice says in the silence.

Florence opens her eyes; she can't see the speaker, who must be two chairs away. Is it a man or a woman? She can't tell.

"They gave up on her and let her go home."

"Home to die," says another voice.

"I've seen it more often than I care to say," an angry male voice replies.

"How often does that happen?" Florence asks into the dark. Do people just languish here and then get sent home to die?

"Oh, it's mostly the ones in the beds upstairs," he replies. "At least we get the chairs and can read in the daytime."

"And how long do we have to stay in these chairs?" she asks.

"It's on the schedule, dear," a woman's voice speaks. Florence saw "Veranda Rest" several times on the schedule but didn't realize she'd have to lie in a chair for all those hours. "Six hours in the day, two at night, and you must sleep with all the windows open in your cottage. Until they don't see any blood in your cough. Then you can take the exercise for two hours."

"Upstairs they have to stay on the porch all the time," says the man.

Presumably, the patients upstairs are more depleted than the people here. Florence has coughed up some blood, and she doesn't feel like walking around at the moment. Of course, this is temporary. It's happened before, and then she was fine.

How can she possibly lie in a chair for all those hours? She will die of boredom. Well, she could read the rest of the Mary MacLane book and Karl Marx, too.

What a gloomy place. In the dining hall there was laughter mixed with those awkward silences and all the discouraged thoughts. Is it hypocrisy or a helpful strategy? The patients have to pretend they are well and happy. Does that help them see the hopeful side of things? Or does it make people more terrified underneath?

She lies back and listens to the voices rising and falling in uneven cadences. Out there a million stars twinkle in the dark sky. Sometimes, the people fall silent, and there's a peacefulness about that. Or perhaps loneliness. Soon she hears snoring laced with coughing and gagging.

Florence sits up. Her musings are turning blue. She takes a deep breath to clear her mind. Not too deep, of course, since that would trigger another coughing episode. *Look at the stars, Florence.* Such a glorious night sky, sprinkled with lights of glory. And the Milky Way. It must be true that the air is clearer up here, because it feels like she can see every star in the galaxy.

She inhales in the mildest, slowest way, and in with the breath comes a scent. Something familiar. What is it?

Mama's kitchen garden. Like a summer afternoon at home when they all sit on the old wooden lawn chairs and drink iced tea. Or, even better, when she's in the garden with Mama. Mama is always working too hard to pay much attention to Florence, the sixth of her seven daughters. The garden is where she has Mama to herself, where they work together planting, weeding, hoeing, thinning, and, the best part, picking. Lavender, sage, comfrey, rosemary, all the herbs Florence loves to touch and smell, and then the peppermint for the iced tea. The garden is where Mama smiles at her.

She turns toward her neighbor, an older woman with a severe profile poking out of her blankets. "Is there mint down there?" Florence asks, pointing to the ground in front of the building.

"Oh my, yes!" the woman exclaims with a lilting voice that belies her appearance. "Gobs and gobs of mint. But how could you know? It's been buried in the snow for months."

"I must go and see," Florence says. She tosses off the blanket and stands quickly, walking toward the dining hall.

"No, no, Miss Rodkey." Maude rushes up and takes Florence's arm. "Veranda rest is compulsory. No exceptions."

♪

When they are finally released from the veranda, Florence goes downstairs and out the door. The ground is covered with snow, with some patches of bare grass. Beside the path, a few green sprigs poke out of the slush. No mint. The air smells clean and crisp.

"You were right about the air," Florence remarks to Ruth, who has caught up with her for the walk back. "It is pure."

"And the stars," Ruth says, gesturing overhead. "I sometimes feel I am on top of the world up here."

Ruth has been at Mont Alto for three months. She is engaged to be married back in her hometown of Gettysburg, and now she isn't so sure about that. "We delayed the wedding, because of my 'condition,'" she says, "and my beau, well . . ." She shrugs. "And anyway, I'm not sure I want to marry at all."

"This is a vital subject for me as well," Florence says. "I am engaged, too, and sometimes I feel I'm doing it because it's what women are meant for, but then I wonder, why should I do what women are expected to do?"

"And what are the benefits of marriage?" Ruth says, projecting her voice like a professor starting a lecture and speeding up in her confident stride. "Status, a family, children." Ruth notices Florence struggling for breath as she tries to keep up and slows down.

"And security of income," Florence adds. "Such worries would be relieved." Her family has never lived in dire poverty, but there were enough times when the harvest was small or even failed, when Papa became strict about money and Mama reduced everyone's meal portions. Or worse, when no one was allowed to buy any new clothes.

"I don't need that, thankfully," Ruth says. "And I don't like the idea of being secondary in my own life." Though Ruth hasn't said so directly, it's clear her family is quite wealthy. They are Quakers, and Quakers believe in women's equality. They even have women ministers.

"But children?"

"I'm not sure I want those either. When I leave here, I will go back to college at Bryn Mawr, and then I intend to devote my life to the socialist cause. *And* to women's suffrage. When would there be time for children?"

"How stirring. To think that a woman can choose her life's work like that. Ruth, you are an inspiration!" In the distance the mountain peaks poke above the mist and clouds, permanent and timeless.

Florence purses her lips. "I would like to work for women's suffrage, too, though I have always wanted children." She stops and gazes up at the heavy clouds. "My fiancé, though . . . The truth is, I am not sure I'm in love with him. He does love me, he says, and he gives me splendid gifts—flowers and candies and books. I suppose I can learn to love him in time."

"Florence!" Ruth stops and looks her straight in the eye with that same look Florence gets from Edith and Ida. "You could not be so desperate as to marry someone you don't love!"

Florence stops to face Ruth and throws both hands out wide. "And why should that be desperate? Many people marry to be taken care of. Why shouldn't I? Twenty years hence I will be twice as nice as if I still go out looking for someone I can care for when I am morally certain that person does not exist." She raises her voice, not noticing the small group of women who have gathered a few feet away from them. "I can't imagine myself a sour old maid with no attention, no home, no nothing but a lot of somebody's youngsters to teach and people's sympathy for not having been able to secure a man. Believe me, nine-tenths of the unmarried women in this world are not single because they have never had an offer of marriage but because they have refused to accept as a life companion a person they did not respect, and they have lived their youth under the delusion that somewhere in the world awaited for them their equal and mate."

Two women in the group nod in agreement, their eyes downcast.

Ruth shakes her head in disbelief, then raises her voice. "Well, maybe some of us *don't* have that delusion, and we still choose not to get married, old maid or not!"

Another woman steps closer and calls out, "Hear, hear!" Three or four others nod their heads.

Florence sees them and lowers her voice. "I didn't mean *you*, of course. You do not *have* to choose." Ruth probably doesn't know what it's like to struggle to support herself. To have a family that insists everyone works or gets married.

Ruth falls silent now, and the audience drifts away.

"Maybe I am being a bit cynical," Florence admits. "How can we change this world to where women are respected in their own right and not for who they're married to?"

"We *can*. We start with women's suffrage."

"I want to join the struggle, but it's a long uphill climb." The sky has cleared and the Milky Way fills the sky with wonder. Can she see her fate in the stars? She exhales a deep sigh. "And I don't know if I'll live that long."

Ruth falls silent and they walk back to the cottage without speaking.

chapter 23

COME ON ALONG

Mont Alto, Pennsylvania, 1911

The next day Florence has her first doctor's visit.

The clinic is in the main building, and after a delicious breakfast of sausage, eggs, broiled tomatoes, fresh bread with jam, coffee, and the omnipresent milk, she follows the directions to the other end of the building. A few people sit on benches in the hallway, and she takes her seat beside a broad woman with plump cheeks and thin, wispy hair escaping from a bun. It is unusual to see a plump woman in this place where almost everyone is thin, if not emaciated.

The woman smiles at her. "Are you new?" Her voice is unexpectedly high.

"Yes, I arrived yesterday. And you?"

"I've been here almost a year."

"A year?" Florence's chest sinks. Will she have to stay that long?

"Yes, but don't worry. You get used to it, and sometimes people don't even want to leave." She sighs. "I'm leaving tomorrow."

"Oh, how wonderful. You are cured?"

"Yes, it looks like that."

"But you don't want to leave?"

"Well, I do, and I don't. I've grown accustomed to the luxury—delightful meals I don't have to cook and all the leisure time. It's a very different story at home."

"Mrs. Weingartner?" A nurse has appeared in the hallway, and Mrs. Weingartner stands and follows her through a door. What is this woman's life like at home? A husband and children to take care of? Does she have to work, too, perhaps doing laundry for other people? Her dress is old and worn, so she probably doesn't have money for servants.

Florence squares her shoulders. She will not end up in that condition. This is even more reason to marry Phillip.

When the nurse calls Florence, she walks into a room filled with light. On the left wall, three tall windows illuminate a table arrayed with microscopes, gourd-shaped glass bottles, and canisters stacked with glass tubes. In the center of the room, a reclining examination chair awaits her.

"Good morning, Miss Rodkey." The voice from the other end of the room startles her. A handsome man in a loose white shirt and tweed trousers approaches. "I'm Dr. Black." The doctor has wavy, brown hair, a neat, yellow-brown mustache under a straight nose, and an air of quiet authority. He comes toward her and stretches out his hand to shake hers. "Please sit down." He points to the examination chair.

She sits, leaning back in the chair and spreading out her skirt.

"First, your sputum," he says and holds out a cup. This is so undignified, especially in front of such an attractive man.

She sighs and dutifully spits into the cup.

He takes the cup to the table and comes back with a thermometer. He sticks the thermometer under her tongue, looks at his watch, and when he pulls it out, frowns.

"Is it bad?" she asks.

"A bit above normal, but that's expected here. Now cough into this." He holds out a paper handkerchief.

Florence tries to cough lightly, a muffled cough that isn't really a cough.

He smiles an indulgent smile as if he knows what she's doing. "Now a real cough."

This time she really coughs, and the blood appears. "Oh! How distressful."

"That's why you're here." He raises his voice to be heard over the coughing. "We'll get rid of that and the fever as well."

"I hope so. I have great plans for my life." She'll go back to the ranch for a while and then get married. As Phillip's wife in Chicago, she'll have more time to practice the piano, and who knows? She might become a concert pianist. She'll have two children, a boy and a girl, and a nurse-maid to help out.

Dr. Black sits in a chair beside her and looks at her with eyes that emanate kindness. "A pretty girl like you—you must have quite a social life."

On the inside she trembles at the intensity of his gaze, but she forces her body to be still. "Well, yes, I suppose I do."

"Many of our patients do a great deal of socializing. It's helpful to make new friends and join in the activities."

"I have a new friend already. My cottage mate and I have much in common."

"That's good. And if you like music and dancing, we have a ball coming up."

"A ball? In a sanatorium?"

"Well, it helps to keep people cheerful, and cheer helps people get better." He smiles that beatific smile again. "I hope you'll save a dance for me."

"Of course." How could anyone refuse such charm? Apparently the doctors here socialize with the patients. She smiles. Now she's in familiar territory, and maybe being here won't be as dreary as she thought. It can't hurt to get on the good side of the doctor. And maybe more than that?

"And if you stick to the regimen, you'll be out of here in no time. Now, one more test. Hold out your arm." He scrapes at the skin, making a surface cut, then takes something out of a vial with a stick and rubs it into the open cut.

She winces. "Ouch! What's this?"

"This is the tuberculin test. Have you not had it before?"

"No."

"If your skin reacts, it will tell us you have the infection. Although the other signs indicate you have it, this is the most reliable way to diagnose."

Dr. Black takes the stick and vial to the side table. "Yes, it's positive," he says matter-of-factly.

She sighs and her mood sinks as fast as it went up. Her life is just another statistic to him.

He comes back and reads out the instructions. Florence is to drink the requisite four glasses of milk a day and continue with veranda rest until no blood shows in her cough. At that point she can join in the exercises. "Pretty simple, really," he says.

As she's leaving, Dr. Black smiles at her again. "Sometimes I meet my patients outside and we walk while we talk. Would you like that?"

"Oh." Surprised, she senses an energy, something intense and passionate, in this man. She realizes she felt it from the start. "Yes, thank you."

"Tomorrow at ten?"

"Yes." Does he do this with all the patients, or is he interested in her in a special way? Her shoulders relax. Florence feels comfortable and energized in his presence, and this gives her an excuse to get out of veranda rest. She finds herself singing under her breath, "Come on along, come on along, to Alexander's Ragtime Band," Ernest's favorite song. She hums the tune all the way back to the cabin.

♪

She awakens with the familiar flutter of fear in her chest. What will happen to her in this place? Will she get better? Or will she end up on the top floor of the veranda with all the other hopeless cases?

She shivers in the cold and pulls the blankets over her head—at least the sanatorium provides plenty of warm blankets and feather beds—and tries to go back to sleep. This feeling in her throat and chest, almost like a lifting of her heart and lungs, as if her insides would lose their anchor and float away.

Will the episodes come back? Every breath irritates her throat and makes her cough, and then her lungs feel like they've been sandpapered down to a thin sliver. She tries not to breathe, or to breathe in the smallest possible way.

Thankfully the episodes haven't happened since she's been at Mont Alto, but they're always lurking just beyond, ready to attack her again. She squeezes herself into a tight ball beneath the covers.

What if she never gets out of this place? She's heard the talk, in whispers and asides, since they are forbidden to discuss it. Of course, that makes the topic even more of a magnet and more urgent.

Yesterday, in a hushed conversation on the veranda, she overheard that someone died a few weeks ago. A young woman her age.

"Florence!" Ruth's voice, authoritative and clear like a bell, sounds from outside the covers. "Time to get up."

"It's too cold!"

"They say the cold is good for us."

"How can it be good to freeze to death!" Florence shrieks and sinks farther down on the featherbed and under the blankets.

"I'm putting on my coat!"

Oh, Florence remembers, today she will take a walk with Dr. Black! "Don't go. I'm coming!" She leaps out of bed and grabs the white lace blouse and blue serge skirt. No corset today. They don't encourage corsets here, thank goodness. This may be the fastest she's ever dressed.

"I have to do my hair first," she says, quickly brushing and winding it up into a loose pompadour.

A layer of frost crunches under their boots as they walk. Maybe this clean mountain air *is* good for her, even though it's so cold.

"The air is so pure here," Ruth remarks, as if she heard Florence's thought.

"Yes," Florence agrees, "and dry. At home we are enveloped in a blanket of humidity year-round."

"Not good for the lungs."

"It's terribly oppressive. I think that place caused my illness to begin with." Here comes that familiar black cloud of despair peeking up from the horizon of her mind. She shakes her shoulders. "Oh, enough of dreary Mahaffey. Let's see what's for breakfast!" She will not let that black cloud hide her blue sky.

The dining hall is the center of social life at Mont Alto. Here people can pretend they're in a fancy hotel, and the atmosphere seems to foster civilized conversations. It's like how she imagines a spa hotel in Europe, except for the underlying fact that everyone here is in some stage of illness.

Florence sits at her table, the faces now familiar, each one keeping up a front. The florid young man winks at her as he shovels food into his mouth. Mr. Russo smirks—his usual expression, she surmises.

She eats another big breakfast and is proud she can finish most of it. The sanatorium has its own bakery, and everyone agrees the biscuits and rolls fresh from the oven are better than home. She lathers her breakfast roll with strawberry jam and lingers over coffee, talking with one of the thin women, the one with the wispy hair, whose fierce expression and fiery brown eyes belie an emaciated body. She introduces herself as Harriett Wagner.

"Call me Hallie," she says. She's from Philadelphia and has been here three months.

They continue their conversation during veranda rest. "I don't know how I can put up with this." Florence throws up her hands. "Just sitting here for hours at a time."

"You get used to it," Hallie says, echoing the woman in the waiting room. "Especially when you start to feel the benefits." Suddenly the pinched-looking face transforms into an almost voluptuous smile.

Florence thought Hallie was in her fifties; now she sees that Hallie is probably in her thirties, not much older than Florence. "Have you felt some benefits?"

"Yes. Not as much as I'd like, but I have gained a little weight."

Hallie's dress hangs loose on her bony frame, and lank hair hangs from a thinning scalp.

Florence shudders to think what Hallie must have looked like before she gained weight. "I'm hoping to be home for Easter," she says, a bit tentative. She knows she can't go back to New Mexico this year. Surely, she can manage at home for a while.

Hallie raises her eyebrows. "What does Dr. Black say?"

"Oh, he hasn't said. I just met him yesterday and will see him again today. I hope to ask that very question."

"Taking a walk, is it?"

"Yes. It seems much more humane, a less clinical way for him to get to know his patients."

"He is very progressive."

Fortified with food in her stomach, Florence skips happily down the stairs, away from the others who are adjourning to the veranda, and goes back to the cabin to choose her outfit. She'll meet him outside, so the coat and hat are most important for her look. She has only her small mirror here, though, not enough to see the whole effect, but no mind. She attaches the fur collar to her tailored wool coat and chooses the felt-brimmed hat with the tall peacock feather.

Boots creaking in the crusty snow, she walks the path between cabins, and when she turns the corner to the main building, she stops short. From the corner of her eye, a shadow, no, a large animal, appears, as if from a dream or a memory. And a sudden recognition, as if she's been in this dream space before. Looming in front of the main building, a large creature covered in fur. Is it a bear? No time to shriek and run, because from out of the fur comes the face of the doctor.

It's Dr. Black, smiling, with gleaming eyes and a tawny mustache, in an enormous beaver coat. He's like an animal in these cold mountains, where the primitive lurks just below the surface.

Florence shakes off the apparition and smiles back as she approaches. There's nothing sinister about this man. He's a doctor who will take care of her. He holds out his arm for her, more like a suitor than a doctor with a patient, but she plays along. This could be much more fun than the usual doctor-patient relationship.

"We'll go this way." He points toward the pine woods behind the building, where there's a gap leading onto a path. "It's a little early for you. This is one of our exercise routes for the almost-well patients, so you'll get a preview."

"A little early?" A sudden, dark dread, like a storm cloud, comes over her. "Am I not almost well?"

"Oh, certainly, once we get you rested and nourished." He winks. "A charming young lady like you is bound to spring back."

She smiles and the storm cloud passes as quickly as it came. Now she's on familiar ground. Maybe she'll add him to her conquests. She glances at his hands, encased in sleek wool gloves so she can't see a wedding ring. *Now Florence*, she scolds herself, *you are an engaged woman*. Well, this is just harmless flirtation. Of course, Mama and Papa wouldn't understand—they're from a different generation.

The path ascends, and from the undergrowth just ahead comes a two-note bird call. "Oh, look!" Florence lets go of the doctor's arm and starts to run. "Bobwhite!" she chirps, imitating the plump, black-and-white bird that scurries away at her approach.

Dr. Black laughs with such merriment that Florence giggles and breaks out into a short-lived belly laugh. Short-lived because immediately the laugh brings up a cough, and another one, until she is bent over in utter embarrassment, holding her raw chest.

The doctor stands tall and takes her arm again. "My dear," he says, all apologetic. "I shouldn't have allowed it. I should have known it was too early for this."

He holds her steady as her coughing slows and stops. Now she sees a red splotch of blood on the snow. She quickly covers it with her boot.

Of course he's seen it, too, and he shakes his head as he leads her back down the path. "I didn't mention this before, but your right lung is quite compromised. Strictly veranda rest for now, I'm afraid."

No. Florence stomps her foot on the hard-packed snow. "I feel like a condemned prisoner!"

As she trudges back to the cabin, the chills begin, and by the time she gets there, she's freezing and her skin is burning up. She wraps up in all the blankets available but is still shivering.

When Ruth comes in, she takes one look at Florence and shouts, "I'll get the doctor."

Dr. Black takes her temperature and prescribes hot tea and fresh air. Florence moans. She's had enough fresh air. Give her a nice little coal stove in the parlor at home, and Mama fussing and bringing her tea and *kuchen*. She's no better here than she would be if she stayed home.

Despite her feeble protests, Dr. Black and Nurse Maude help her move and resettle to the women's pavilion, where she sinks onto the lounge chair wrapped up in a buffalo blanket. The chills make her shiver, and she snuggles farther under the blanket.

"Just stay here and rest," Maude says. "The cold air will help bring your fever down." Then she and Dr. Black, without so much as a "by your leave," march briskly back down the little road, strong and carefree, while Florence sits here, shivering. She reaches out of the blanket and picks up her hot chocolate. At least they left her that.

chapter 24

TWILIGHT

Mont Alto, Pennsylvania, 1911

Why did I come here? It's only been a month, but it feels like years. Surrounded by sick people, gasping and coughing, thin and emaciated. Florence lies on her chair, gazing out at the mountain behind the cottages, snow-covered and stark against the cold sky. Once again, she's in the cocoon of blankets—as well as her coat, boots, gloves, and the big fur hat. *I look like a raccoon.*

Well, she knows why she came; she tried to comply with the "most up-to-date medical knowledge." And now she's worse, and they won't let her go. Now she's a prisoner in a gilded cage.

A light snow begins to fall. Silent flakes like feathers gather into a diaphanous curtain. The people walking by have become a blur of floating shapes outside of Florence's cocoon.

Her appetite has grown with the help of the delicious food and elegant atmosphere of the dining hall. And her health has improved. *But now this! Lying here, doing nothing. Is this helping?* Every time she thinks her illness is gone, it starts up again. And now, if it's not her imagination, she can feel something in her right lung tugging her down and draining her energy, leaving her laboring to breathe.

People stroll and stumble on the path. That woman she met at the infirmary, Mrs. Weingartner—there she goes with her trunk, free as a bird. She's leaving today. Tall and voluptuous, she looks healthy compared to the rest of the poor specimens. Florence was astounded when Mrs. Weingarten mentioned being here for a year. A year! If Florence stayed for a year, she'd be twenty-three, an old woman.

Why me? She sinks farther into her nest. *Why can't I be strong and healthy like Mrs. Weingartner? I'm younger than she is, and this is supposed to be my carefree youth.*

Her youth. A feather of snow on her nose, the smell of childhood, the sleigh rides on Doe Hill. An adventure. Sue, who was ten, led the little pack—Bert, six, and Florence, five—as they trekked along Main Street through soft pillows of white. All the way to Doe Hill, where, at the top, sat an enormous mansion, the home of the richest lady in town, Miss Mahaffey. Miss Mahaffey had a stable full of horses. Not work horses like most people's—hers were show horses. A slender woman with a narrow face, she was quiet, mysterious. She would ride through town, accompanied by her dog, Bell Echo, big as a pony and gentle as a lamb. Once a year Miss Mahaffey invited the children to come up Doe Hill for a sleigh ride.

The children tramped through the snow and up the steep driveway all the way to the top, where Miss Mahaffey waited with Bell Echo and a little sleigh. Florence reached up to pat the gigantic dog, his curly, black hair soft and springy, and he nuzzled her shoulder. Miss Mahaffey situated the children on the sleigh, and they were off.

Shrieking and laughing, snow in their faces, they flew, the sled like a comet, down the long drive, Bell Echo running behind. When they reached the bottom, another grown-up hitched the dog to the sled, and Bell Echo pulled them back up the hill.

Florence inhales the smell of snow, the smell of childhood and that magical, fairy-tale day. Is there still some of that magic in her life, despite the illness?

She sinks lower in her seat. No, the magic is gone, and she is living—just barely—in a land of despair, a white hell.

All around the campus, the snow-capped mountains rise, a rim of silence.

She picks up her pen and paper, not so easy with these gloves. There's one person she can confide in, one person who cares about her feelings, whatever they are.

Dear Ernest,

I have been very sick again. Am just able to navigate and that is all. I might just as well tell you. My right lung is in pretty bad shape and I am just existing. I have not enough energy to even eat, so you may know how few letters I write.

I sit and think most of the time, and I am not at all the same girl who left you last fall.

The slightest effort exhausts me. I am tired now from just writing this much.

Sometimes I think I'll get well and sometimes I think I won't.

I could if I would, I know, but sometimes I am tired of it all and don't care. How I wish I could see you once more. I care for you just in the same old way only, dear comrade, all physical strength and energy is gone. If you will just forgive this poor little note and believe that my heart is alright, it will make me glad.

Lovingly, your comrade,

Florence

Ruth appears, climbing up the stairs, dark eyes and dark, curly hair framing an expressive face that squeezes into a frown when she sees Florence. Ruth takes a chair beside her and touches her sleeve. "Sorry," she says.

Florence throws up a hand. "I don't know if I'll ever get out of here. I'll just be one of those who disappears. One day I'll be here, and then you'll see an empty bed. Erased, like this new spring erased by the snow."

"Oh, such gloom!" Ruth exclaims. "Didn't Dr. Black call this a little setback? I'm sure you'll rally. In fact, I brought something to read to you. It's by Ella Wheeler Wilcox." She rummages in her bag, pulls out a piece of notebook paper, and reads:

> *Let the old snow be covered with the new:*
> *The trampled snow, so soiled, and stained, and sodden.*
> *Let it be hidden wholly from our view*
> *By pure white flakes, all trackless and untrodden.*
> *When Winter dies, low at the sweet Spring's feet*
> *Let him be mantled in a clean, white sheet.*

Let the old life be covered by the new:
The old past life so full of sad mistakes,
Let it be wholly hidden from the view
By deeds as white and silent as snow-flakes.

Ere this earth life melts in the eternal Spring
Let the white mantle of repentance fling
Soft drapery about it, fold on fold,
Even as the new snow covers up the old.

Florence wipes a tear from her eye. "That is lovely." She sighs. "Perhaps there is hope for me."

"Absolutely, there is hope!" Ruth smiles. She is an interesting blend of progressive ideas and sentimentality. Does she know about Florence's dark side, the flippant side, the side of her that likes to play and trifle with men?

"Do you think I need to repent of my 'old past life full of sad mistakes?'"

"Oh no, no, that was just a metaphor for the coming of spring and something new."

"For hope."

"Yes."

The wind picks up and blows the snow sideways with a roar. They lie huddled under the buffalo blankets in silence.

When the wind dies down, Ruth speaks. "Are you still planning to marry your fancy Chicago lawyer?"

"I don't know."

Florence's shoulders deflate. She has had time here, lots of time, to struggle with "the question of Phillip," as Ruth calls it. The question. She didn't know it was a question until Ruth voiced it that way, and then she wasn't sure of the question itself. Phillip has seemed so distant lately, his letters coming fewer and farther between. It is worrisome. Maybe she's not entirely committed, but she doesn't want to lose him. It's comforting to know there could be financial security. His letters are either perfunctory, detailing some construction project in Seattle that he's litigating, or gushingly romantic, declaring his undying love. He doesn't respond to her witty descriptions and critiques of the people and regimens at Mont Alto. Not like Ernest, who responds with funny stories about the Pittsburgh crowd and detailed descriptions of the plays he's seen.

In his last letter Ernest wrote about a chipmunk. He described the chipmunk hiding under his mother's rocker, her discomposure (and Ernest's mother *never* gets flustered—Florence met her once and was intimidated by the tall, stern-looking matriarch), the cat chasing it into the kitchen, and his father, who had been drinking, trying to reason with the chipmunk. Ernest is a good writer, and his story made her laugh.

Would she really give up her friendship with Ernest, leave Pennsylvania and her family and friends, to marry someone who doesn't know how to tell a joke?

♪

When the day of the "ball" comes, Florence is still ensconced in her chair in the women's pavilion, so she can't have that dance with the doctor after all.

To keep herself from sinking into self-pity, she reads a pamphlet Ruth lent her about Alice Paul and Emmeline Pankhurst. The two suffragettes led a group of women to storm the House of Commons in London, insisting on women's right to vote. The women were arrested and put in prison and then staged a hunger strike. Not wanting to make them martyrs, the government force-fed them, and Alice fell sick from the force-feeding.

"Despicable!" Florence shouts in a weak voice that diverts her from self-pity. Now she is angry. As soon as she gets out of here, she will join the fight for women's suffrage. In the meantime, she will follow doctor's orders.

Dr. Black is attentive and makes extra appointments for her. He's still quite attractive to her, but Florence has lost interest in smart repartee. Despite the anger that bubbles up at times, there's a murky cloud surrounding her, a gray fog she can't find her way out of.

At one of the appointments, Dr. Black talks about a new treatment discovered by Dr. Dixon, the founder of the Mont Alto sanatorium. "He was able to isolate the tubercle bacillus and found that if he injected it into animals, it provided some immunization. Thus, a small amount of the toxic bacteria can fight the disease."

"Isn't immunization for people who don't have the disease?"

"Yes, and we are finding that some patients who have the disease are also responding. It's still experimental, of course, but I can get you in on the trial if you like."

Florence clutches her chest. "I don't know. Wouldn't there be a risk of getting worse?"

"There might be."

♪

When Florence steps into the cabin, Gertrude's bed is empty. Bare. No bedclothes, no clothes, no shoes, no books. Gertrude's trunk and all her possessions are gone. Well, Gertrude has not been very present lately. She barely answered questions, and Florence gave up trying to engage her. A silent presence, almost invisible in the cabin. Now, it seems, Gertrude really *is* invisible, and it looks like she's moved out. Or worse.

As fast as she can, Florence walks back to the main building, arriving out of breath at the nurse's office, where Maude sits at a desk writing in a ledger.

"Where is Gertrude?" Florence cries.

Maude sighs. "Please sit down, Miss Rodkey."

Florence sits, trying to slow her breathing, but she is too anxious to rest. "Did she get worse? Is she on the second floor, the hospital?"

"I'm afraid it's worse than that."

"Oh, no!" Florence bends over, clutching her face in her hands.

"Yes. Another nurse, Betty, found her body."

♪

What can you do at veranda rest except think about death and this disease? And about Gertrude. Florence hadn't done anything to help Gertrude, to draw her out, to at least entertain her a little. How thoughtless she's been. She doesn't actually know anything *about* Gertrude. Did she have family? Will there be some kind of memorial service, or does the sanatorium just let people disappear?

Florence puts her hand over her heart and that raw pain in her chest. *And what about me? Will I become thinner and thinner and disappear while I'm still alive, like Gertrude? Will my bed be empty one day? I'll be dead, and everyone else will just go on living?*

Back at the cabin, when Ruth comes in, the two women stare at each other in mutual shock, Gertrude's empty bed like a void, a barren abyss.

They sit on their beds in silence.

"Life is short," says Ruth.

"Yes. And why would I spend it with someone I really don't love?"

Florence has been jolted into a deeper place in her heart, as if a secret door opened to reveal a treasure, something that doesn't glitter or sparkle but has been sitting there all along, like a star that emerges from behind a cloud. The star shines with a presence. The presence of Ernest.

chapter 25

DOWN IN THE VALLEY

Mont Alto, Pennsylvania, 1911

At the post office, finally, a letter from Phillip. Florence snatches it up and rushes out the door, splattering slush on her boots and coat. She can't wait to get back to her cabin. Inside, she plops onto her bed and tears open the letter.

What's this? She stops cold. Phillip!

Dear Florence,

I have secured a church in Chicago for the wedding and my country club for the reception. The date is June 25, and I'll send you a train ticket—from Mont Alto, if you're still there, and from Pittsburgh, if not.

No flowery language, no hearts and flowers, just a blunt statement. Florence slumps over as a tear rolls down her cheek. How could he do this?

"Florence!" Ruth comes up behind her. "What is it?"

"He set a date for the wedding and reserved a church in *Chicago* without consulting me, and now he is *ordering* me to show up. In less than two months!"

"Oh my." Ruth pulls down the hood of her black cape, and her deep brown eyes radiate warmth and comfort as she sits on the bed beside Florence.

A section of Florence's pompadour has come out, and she pushes aside the chestnut lock spilling across her breast. "As if I am his servant. How dare he!"

"You are overly agitated, my dear. You'll work yourself into a fever. Let's go get some tea."

Ruth leads Florence back to the main building to the "tearoom." It's a little closet off the main hallway, though it has a window, and they've done it up with fancy wallpaper and little marble tables with Tiffany lamps. Florence and Ruth sit, and Ruth orders tea with lemon and lots of sugar.

Florence takes a sip of tea, then slumps in the chair with her head down.

Still holding the letter, she scrunches it into a little ball.

"What else does he say?" Ruth asks as she drops two lumps of sugar into Florence's tea.

"Oh," Florence straightens and smooths out the letter. "And, by the way," she reads, "I'll expect we'll be in agreement that a respectable wife does not dally with other men, nor does she make a spectacle of herself marching around the streets with placards."

"It sounds like going to finishing school."

"Exactly! And I won't agree to any of that."

"Of course not."

"I'll go to every suffragist march I can find!"

Ruth leans over and takes her hand. "Are you still in love with him?"

Florence stares out the window. "I don't think," she says in a quiet voice, almost a whisper, "that I was ever in love with him." She opens her eyes wide at this revelation, startling herself.

"No, I don't think so either. You want a husband, not a prison warden."

"Yes. I won't be a bird in a gilded cage. When I marry—*if* I marry— I'll have someone who will treat me as an equal, someone who'll respect me and be my friend."

"This man sounds familiar." Ruth smiles.

♪

But it's not so easy to forget about Phillip. Florence should write him immediately and break it off. She lies in her bed, sleepless. Suddenly, unbidden, the image of the Chicago house comes to mind, a picture of that future life she's carried for months. The sparkling chandeliers, the massive fireplace, Turkish rugs, and a grand piano—a Steinway, of course—and Florence playing Mozart for an adoring audience. Servants all around and not having to lift a finger. And, of course, Phillip, himself, like when he walked her down the aisle at the theater, nodding to acquaintances, smiling and proud of this beautiful woman beside him. And when they sat down, that radiant smile just for her.

All those months of struggling to work, struggling to get better, not feeling secure in her income, envisioning a future of luxury and ease . . . Florence gulps, and a sob erupts, then another. She holds her breath to stifle the cries, but then her whole body shakes with weeping and coughing.

♪

The next day Florence and Ruth lie in chairs in the women's pavilion, and Florence continues the discussion. "How could he do this to me? He can't take a little teasing? He can't abide a suffragist? I know. Good riddance, you say. Phillip can marry his rich Chicago girl, who will agree with everything he says and not mention women's votes."

Ruth sits up in her chair. "I didn't say good riddance. But weren't you unsure about him anyway?"

"I wouldn't have him back now if he lay prostrate at my feet begging!"

"Though just last week you were marveling at his good looks, his sophistication, the gifts he sent."

"I know. In some ways he was the perfect match." She pauses, gazing up at the dark clouds. "But in truth, when he came to El Yeso, I was almost afraid of him."

"Afraid?"

"He can get irate, and he has such definite opinions about everything, including women's suffrage."

"Oh." Ruth shakes her head.

"Ernest is the only young man who has cared for me and has not attempted to overpower me—or even kiss me or grow familiar in some way."

"Ernest sounds like a real gentleman. Isn't he a better prospect for you?"

"Well, he's not wealthy. And I always thought he was too young. But he has been devoted and faithful, and I haven't seen him in so long, he's probably become a grown-up man now." She sighs. "At this point, though, I don't know if I'll ever see him again."

"Oh, posh." Ruth bats at Florence's arm. "No more self-pity."

The wind has died down, and still the clouds drift across the mountaintop, hiding then revealing the stark sunlight. Has Ernest grown disgusted with her dilly-dallying? No, he's still there for her, shining like the sun behind the mists of melancholy she has been blinded by. And will she recover, or will she succumb to this awfulness? Gertrude's death, then letting go of Phillip, gray February skies, rain and slush . . .

♪

April comes, and with it another snowstorm. Florence decides to "pull herself together." To *hope against hope*, as she read somewhere. She will not participate in Dr. Black's "experiment," as she thinks of the tuberculin trial, but she will buckle down to a renewed regimen for recovery. She dutifully takes a glass of milk every four hours, eats her full three meals a day, and takes short walks. She needs to keep exercising, Dr. Black says, even when the weather is bad, and Florence, intending to leave this place, adheres to the strict schedule.

After breakfast one day, she steps out of the main building and onto the path, and with sudden insight, she understands, in her body and her mind, that she *is* better, stronger.

Florence walks on the newly fallen snow, past the little cabins, row upon row, white, identical, propped up on stilt-like pilings. Except for an occasional clearing of a throat, a cough, and sometimes a series of coughs and gags, there is silence. This place would be serene without all of these human noises, reminders of where she is and of her own malady. Even so, it is a peaceful place. Behind her, at the end of the row, rises the grand building, large and white, like a resort hotel, and above it the ridge line of the mountain. The ridge line encircling her, the hills surrounding this place, this valley like a basin, the rims of the mountains in every direction defining a secret place, cut off from the rest of the world, a cozy refuge.

Or a prison.

The mountain rim, shrouded in ashen gray or bursting in a radiant dazzle, is the backdrop, the symbol of this drama she's living. Either one way or the other, either hopeless or dazzling with promise. Today the dazzle. There is light, there is hope. Florence will mend, she will arise from the pit of this gloomy place, the spectral depths of her mind, where the future is blank, a future without her. But now, a glimmer, a streak of light, and a future of joy and music and love.

Hope is fragile, sometimes hidden, sometimes lost behind the clouds, sometimes sinking below the horizon in a precipitous fall. And then, emerging from where it was all along, the light. The light behind, the light within.

chapter 26

APPLE BLOSSOM TIME

Pensacola, Florida, 1943

"I'll be with you in Apple Blossom time, I'll be with you to change your name to mine," Flossie hums as she fastens a button on her jacket. Of course it's September, not apple blossom time, and do they even grow apples in Florida? But this is her song, a song of longing and romance and love ever after. Sometimes it's unclear if the feeling evokes the song or if the song creates the feeling. Maybe it's soupy and sentimental, but Flossie loves it that way. This is her wedding day.

She stands in the yellow bedroom surrounded by women: Elizabeth, in pastel blue linen, her salt-and-pepper hair pulled into a soft bun. Dotty, Flossie's new friend and matron of honor, in pink satin. Aunt Mary in lavender, her peaceful smile a balm for Flossie's anxiety. Sallie stands quietly in the corner so as not to muss up her pink flower girl dress. Nannie couldn't come—she no longer travels—but she sent several presents, including a cookbook. The Rodkey grandparents sent a gold locket inscribed with "FLR" and a turquoise ring set in gold, both of which belonged to Florence.

Nannie called on the phone, too, a real challenge for her. She loves Flossie dearly, she said, as she broke down in sobs. A rare display of emotion for Nannie, and with it came a sudden knowledge. Nannie has always loved her. Behind her gruff manner and strict rules, she has always been a loving and protective grandmother; a mother to Flossie in everything but name.

Flossie inspects her hair in the mirror. She emerged from the hairdresser's this morning with a new hairstyle—a head full of curls swept up and back. Everybody's been complimenting her on it, and, hopefully, George will like it, too.

This is a navy wedding, she thinks, a real adventure, in this harbor town, with battleships coming and going and fighter planes roaring overhead. The aircraft have names like F6 or F4 or TB-something-or-other. George has pointed them out and named them, but Flossie can't tell them apart. Maybe she doesn't want to know. Maybe she doesn't want any of this—the planes, the ships, this navy town, the constant threat of war and all the unknowns that go with it.

But in the midst of it there is George.

Of course there's always been Hammie, dancing to the beat with a charming smile, but George is an anchor, a refuge of comfort and security.

Flossie takes a deep breath. She would not have chosen this situation, this time and place, for her wedding, but she has chosen the right man.

For the rest of her life.

Can she imagine the rest of her life? It hovers, an empty vessel waiting to be filled, a crowd of people and events, vague outlines and shadows, a line of unknowns stretching into the future.

She begins to peel off her clothes—linen slacks, embroidered blouse with the bodice tucks, bobby socks—and takes her wedding outfit from the hanger.

Flossie's cousin Helen would have been the matron of honor, but she just got married, too, to Jiggs, her George, and they couldn't get here from Pittsburgh. Even though Jiggs has enlisted, the government won't let "non-essential" people travel to military bases. After the war, Helen and Jiggs will live with her parents and fix up an old farmhouse in the Laurel Mountains, turning it into an inn. *And,* Helen wrote, *we're building a ski resort, like the ones in Colorado!* Flossie wrote back: *I'll bring the gang!* Something to look forward to after the war.

With a tinge of grief for the beautiful white dress she had initially imagined, Flossie puts on the sleek new suit Aunt Mary made from a *Vogue* pattern: a stylish peplum jacket and loose skirt in a fine blue wool. It's somber but chic, "appropriate for a wartime wedding," according to Aunt Mary and Elizabeth. To dress it up, Flossie wears a wreath of gardenias and roses and carries a bouquet of the same. Sallie, the flower girl, holds a bunch of gardenias. The room shimmers with a blissful fragrance for Flossie's wedding day.

In the navy chapel, they are a small gathering. Elizabeth and Aunt Mary sit in the front pew on the right, the bride's side, and a few of George's new medic buddies on the left.

When the organ starts, Flossie, at the back of the chapel, swats away another tear and takes her father's arm. Ernest, beaming and teary-eyed in a dark gray suit, walks her up the aisle, and George, with a blushing smile, reaches for her hand. They step in front of the chaplain, a beefy fellow with a shaved head and a red-faced smile.

The rest of the ceremony goes by both too fast and too slowly. The chaplain drones on and on about the duties of marriage, seeming to direct most of them to Flossie, and then it's time for the vows.

Flossie hands her bouquet to Sallie, who stands frozen, open-mouthed, before remembering to take the flowers. Then, the bride and groom repeat the vows, George in a clear voice, Flossie gulping back tears.

The organ pounds out the wedding march, and the bride and groom walk down the aisle through the tiny cheering crowd.

As they step onto the portico, Flossie gasps. At the foot of the stairs, two lines of sailors in dress whites hold swords aloft, forming a passageway, a corridor. "What—" She looks at George.

George laughs. "Yes, we walk through it."

As they make their way through the sword arch, humid air, laced with the smells of salt water, gardenia, and roses, flutters the wreath in Flossie's hair. She laughs. "I feel like a queen."

When they emerge at the other end, Sallie jumps up and down, her pink ruffles flapping, and throws rice over the couple. Soon a storm of rice fills the air.

At the reception dinner, in another room in the chapel, the navy band plays lively dance tunes—Glen Miller and Nat King Cole—and, at Flossie's request, Duke Ellington's "Take the A Train." As it starts up, though, Flossie stops mid-dance, with the sudden memory of Roddy. He sang this song with such high spirits. She glances at her father. Ernest's head is bowed over, resting in his hands. Roddy—brother, son, stepson—is somewhere in Europe with the troops.

Flossie looks around the room. *This is the most important day of my* life, *and that awful war is ruining it.* She grimaces. *But how can I be so selfish? People are dying and my brother is risking his life for his country.* Her shoulders droop.

"What is it?" George asks. He puts an arm around her as they go to sit.

Flossie shakes her head as she sinks onto her seat. "The war."

"Perk up, dear." He smiles. "This is a day of celebration!"

The music flows into another lively jazz tune, and she springs up, jumping and twisting in the Lindy Hop, holding out her hand to George, who surprises her by grinning and following her, matching her steps, though at a slightly less vigorous pace. He must have practiced.

The toasts begin with a heartfelt and tearful speech by Ernest, who can't resist starting with a quip: "Well, that went off without a hitch." He looks at Flossie and George. "Except for the hitch." Everyone laughs or rolls their eyes.

Bobby DeLuca, a young doctor like George, has taken Roddy's place as the best man. With his oiled hair slicked back and his face radiating cheer, Bobby stands and raises his glass. "To George and Flossie! In this time of uncertainty, as you embark on the matrimonial seas, may your love be a strong battleship to carry you through the storms of life."

Hearty cheers rise and echo, "Hear! Hear!" Elizabeth and Aunt Mary wipe their eyes.

A lean soldier with a buzz cut stands. "And may George find all the body parts before he sews another one up!" The sailors laugh hilariously as the jokes veer away from the wedding and toward botched surgeries and missing organs until one young man stands, raises his glass, and gives a graphic description of an amputated finger sewn onto the wrong hand.

A gasp arises from the congregation, and then silence. Aunt Mary shakes her head. "These are *doctors*," she says, her voice carrying through the room. "They're supposed to be saving lives, not joking about dismembering people."

"Yes." Ernest throws down his napkin and stands to go.

"Sit down, Ernest," Elizabeth says. "Don't embarrass Flossie." Flossie, watching from the bride and groom's table, suppresses a laugh and makes a helpless face at her father, who sits down with a scowl.

After the wedding, at the new bungalow, Flossie unpacks the remaining things from her big suitcase. From the top, carefully wrapped in tissue paper, she takes out the framed portrait of her mother. Daddy looked pained when she asked if she could take it with her. Finally he agreed that maybe the picture would help her, to have her mother watching over her in her new life.

She knows exactly where she wants to hang it—on the side wall in the little dining room. A family portrait, in its sepia tone and dreamy quality, an heirloom. How appropriate for her new house, her first house as a married woman.

Flossie goes back to the open suitcase and plucks out two new housedresses, both of them made by her: a gingham check with a full skirt, and the other in robin's egg blue, her best color, to match her eyes. She hangs them in the closet along with the new apron Nannie made for her—pink and white with a ruffle at the hem. And, of course, the ivory satin negligee with matching robe, an important item in the trousseau. She folds it carefully and puts it in the small suitcase. The honeymoon will be a weekend in St. Augustine.

She picks out the nightgown, and there lies the letter, the envelope thin with age, the writing faded. The letter Daddy gave her. Why hasn't she opened it yet? What if her mother is too different from the way Flossie's pictured her? After all these years of imagining the perfect mother, would Flossie be let down by the reality?

Well, this is not the right moment. She's going on her honeymoon. She'll save the letter for when she's alone. She tucks it under the slips and bras in her drawer and finishes packing the small suitcase.

♪

In St. Augustine, tall trees draped with Spanish moss overhang the roads, hibiscus bloom over every fence and wall, and soldiers and sailors crowd the streets. Many of the hotels, they learn, are being used to house the military. Flossie gets a bit of a shock and some pain on the first night—*is this supposed to be pleasure?* she thinks—but George is a gentle and caring lover, and she easily drops back into her honeymoon bubble where everything is a delight. They stroll under the canopy of oaks on Magnolia Avenue, admire the villas, visit "Old Senator," the five-hundred-year-old live oak tree, and eat some fabulous seafood. And then, too soon, the weekend is over.

♪

It suits Flossie just right, this navy life. There's so much to discover in Pensacola. On the base there's tennis and a brand-new golf course George has been going to with his buddies, but tennis is Flossie's game. And she loves the tropical environment—walking beneath the palms and magnolias and hollies and exploring the beach. She and Dotty have gone swimming almost every day, and George and Marsh, Dotty's husband, join them on weekends.

When George is in training, though, which is most of the time, Flossie gets lonely. And the planes are beginning to rattle her. Their constant and intermittent noise seems to make everybody more anxious, causing them to speed up and walk faster, get busier, and scurry back and forth to prepare for war, even if they, like Flossie, are just wives out shopping for fish and oranges.

One day, when George is out on a plane, the now-familiar roar shatters the quiet air, and she looks up, holding her breath. No one can forget there's a war on. *But at least, since George is a medic, he won't go into battle. It's fine. He's fine.*

♪

Flossie revels in her new role as housewife: sewing curtains for the windows, shopping at the commissary, and trying out new recipes from the *Woman's Home Companion Cookbook* that Nannie gave her as a wedding present. Her favorite is a strawberry and whipped cream pie with a graham cracker crust. Such a luxury to get strawberries in winter. Maybe she'll try a more ambitious sewing project later, but for now she's happy wallowing in her newfound domesticity.

George is passionate about photography, his new hobby, and has set up a dark room in the basement. Some Saturdays he's down there most of the day.

Of course, they both know that eventually George will have to go out on a ship. And though he won't be actively fighting in the battles, he'll be on a ship that could be hit. The two newlyweds keep an unspoken pact: no discussion of war. Flossie is good at keeping a stiff upper lip, something she learned from Nannie, and now her ability to ignore the harsh reality comes in handy. When the fear comes up, she can push it back down by planning a new recipe or working on a gorgeous dress.

For two glorious months, she revels in this newlywed idyll.

♪

Today, George and Flossie are playing tennis on the secluded court at the end of the wooded path. Usually there are no other people here, but now a shadowy figure moves in and out of the shade of the towering magnolias lining the path. Probably a sailor out for a walk.

Flossie lobs the ball over the net to George, and he smiles and hits it back. *Her husband.* She's still not used to this new status. Everything is new and different here, the bungalow so full of light, the warm weather, the other navy couples passing by on the street. She'll go to the Officers' Wives Club tomorrow, where she'll see Dotty. They've gone to the beach together several times, and she seems to have so much in common with Dotty, who has been married to Marsh for a year already. There is so much to talk about in this new life.

George is as graceful and coordinated as a dancer, playing tennis with ease and rhythm. Of course, he played on his college team, so he's a more experienced player than Flossie. She has always been a good athlete, too; she even won the volleyball award at Carnegie Tech. And everyone says she's a beautiful skier. She runs back and forth on the court, hitting the ball with a loud "oof."

Spanish moss sways and flows from the live oak trees, and even with the gentle breeze, Flossie sweats profusely in the tropical heat. How undignified. She stops and wipes her brow with a handkerchief, then starts to laugh, giddy with the heat and happiness.

"Are you okay, honey?" George comes up to the net. *Honey.* Isn't this marvelous? For someone to call her honey. She giggles some more, and he breaks out into a smile. "Well, it's pretty darn hot. Let's take a break."

"Hello, George and pretty wife!" a voice booms from the path. A young officer, spiffy in his navy whites, emerges from the trees and lopes up to them. It's Bobby DeLuca, with his slicked-back hair and jaunty grin. He touches his cap to Flossie. "You're an old married couple now."

Flossie laughs and George smiles. "Say, Bobby," he says, "will you take a picture of us?" George, who is inordinately proud of his new Rolleiflex, takes the big box camera out of its bag. He's been taking lots of pictures, mostly of Flossie in sexy poses with her hair spread out.

"Sure," says Bobby as he takes the camera. He turns it up and down, looking at it from all angles. "How do you operate this thing?"

George steps up to show him.

Bobby holds the camera and looks down into the lens. "Say 'Victory!'"

Flossie gulps at this reference to the war she'd rather not think about, but then manages a smile.

When he hands the camera back to George, Bobby stands quiet, frowning, then clearing his throat.

"What is it, Bobby?" George asks.

"I have some news." Bobby is a handsome guy, almost like a movie star, but now his shoulders slump as he looks at the ground.

George and Flossie exchange a look, and her muscles tense. "What—"

Bobby stands up straight, as if he's just remembered that he's a brave sailor, and looks at George. "We're being deployed."

chapter 27

HOME SWEET HOME

Mahaffey, Pennsylvania, 1911

"Why don't you wear gloves?" Ida lugs a burlap bag filled with broccoli, while Florence kneels on the ground beside a row of potato plants. Ida is home from her teaching job in Arizona, and all the sisters are here except Edith, who is now sailing with a friend to France on a majestic ocean liner. Florence gets twinges of jealousy—oh, to live the life of luxury on a sea cruise—but at the moment she is glad to be right here.

"Maybe I'll make mud pies." Florence grins and waves her dirty hand. After the long winter at the sanatorium, her senses are awake—the smell and feel of the soft earth, the touch of breeze off the mountain, the sounds of the horse and plow in the field, the old elm trees that bend and sigh. "I'm so happy to be home."

"Until you get bored again with 'old Mahaffey,'" Ida says, making quotation marks with her fingers. "Then you'll be off on some new adventure."

"I certainly hope so," Florence laughs, bending back over the row. She digs her hand deep and wiggles her fingers in the earth until she feels a nice plump potato and pulls it out.

Once home, she basked in the presence of her family—Mama and Papa, her sisters and brother—helping out in the garden and entertaining friends again. All of those things she thought of as deadly boring just a year ago.

It wasn't smart, Florence realizes now, to leave the ranch and come home in the middle of winter. But how could she miss Christmas at home? At the sanatorium, Gertrude had disappeared, and then Florence realized she might not have much time left. *And I want to have every minute I can with the people I love.* Florence loved New Mexico, and after Christmas, she had planned to go back and continue as the schoolmarm. And then she'd made herself sick again. That torturous train ride. The blood in the cough, the grim reality of the disease. Saying the word "tuberculosis." And then the sanatorium, the mountains, the cold, clear air.

At Mont Alto all she wanted was to come home. Especially on the day Gertrude didn't come back. Her absence left an enormous hole in their little home. And there wasn't even a memorial service. Maude explained that it wasn't done at Mont Alto, since people were supposed to focus on health and the future. To Florence's mind this further highlighted the cruelty of death.

She brushes the dirt off a potato and holds it up. "Look at this one!"

She hadn't thought it possible that any place could be more boring than Mahaffey. Then Mont Alto, bleak and cold, had become an uphill battle. A battle that, after much mooning and self-pity, she decided to fight. When Gertrude was gone, something coalesced within Florence, like a honing or a centering, a sharpening of focus. Florence sought exercise, exercise, more exercise, and rest, rest, and more rest. Strict hours for going to bed and waking up. Attending every meal, cleaning her plate, and drinking milk. She even increased exercise time on her own and made use of veranda rest with more reading. She read the Mary MacLane book three times and adopted Mary MacLane's philosophy. That young girl of nineteen, living on a desolate farm in Montana, described her life as misery, but felt *"She had the strength of will to take what she wanted, to do as she chose to do, to live as she wanted to live."*

Florence fortified herself with those words and told herself, *I am strong, I can work hard, and I will be cured.* She kept up the correspondence with Ernest, gradually recognizing how much his friendship had sustained her. She still enjoyed teasing him, but now it was good-natured and affectionate. And, to his evident delight, she told him how much he meant to her. When she came home, she told him, they could resume their comradeship.

She wrote to Phillip, controlling her impulse to write angry invectives. She politely declined his offer of marriage and enclosed the ring.

Dirt. That's what she's been missing. This good-old Pennsylvania dirt. Even though she *had* to come back to old Mahaffey, she missed the family, the farm, the earth, the Pennsylvania dirt. Just being here, kneeling in the garden at the potato patch, Mama and sister Sue over at the strawberries, feeling the earth with its soft crumbles, smooth and moist.

She digs up another potato, wipes off the dirt, and plops it into the bag. Behind her the parsley and mint spring out of the soil, the aroma of mint bringing her full circle, from home, to Mont Alto, and back to home. She plucks some leaves of the herbs, laughing to herself and imagining the next meal—mint tea, potato soup with dill and parsley.

A putt-putting sound comes from the street and jogs into the drive. And here is the red Model T, a beaming Ernest in the driver's seat. "Good morning, ladies!" Ernest doffs his touring cap and jumps out.

"Oh!" She wipes her forehead to push aside a lock of hair that's fallen out of her bun. Dirt coats her hands, and her face must be smeared with it. It's been months and months since she last saw Ernest, and now she looks like a street urchin. A blush grows on her face beneath her mess of hair.

Ernest rushes to the motor car and pulls something off the seat. He runs back to her with a big smile and a huge package in his arms. He doesn't seem to notice the dirt.

Ernest stands still, gazing at Florence as she regards him, dumbstruck. There's something different about him. He seems to have grown taller since last year, and his shoulders are broader. And there is something different in *her*. Something warm and joyful, a new reaction. Ernest is no longer Mary's little brother. He's a full-grown man, and handsome to boot.

Since she's been home, the realization has been growing in her. Ernest is funny and fun, and he doesn't criticize her or judge. He really cares about her, not as an ornament to enhance his social standing, but with depth and integrity. Of course, she knew this all along, though she took him for granted.

"Welcome home," he says, beaming as he holds up the package.

"Wait!" she calls, turning to run into the house. She washes her hands, changes her dress, and sits at the dressing table to brush and pin up her hair. When she goes back downstairs, Ernest is sitting in the living room with Ida, the big box on the floor between them.

Ernest has always been there, as familiar as her morning oatmeal, as essential as the family she was born into. Ernest is a part of her, past, present, and future. Hasn't she known that her best friend, though not rich and successful, is the one she loves?

"A welcome home present for you," he says and gestures for her to open it.

Ida's eyes open wide, and Mama walks into the room. "Oh my!"

"So big!" Florence kneels and carefully opens the lid. Inside, wrapped in newspaper, she feels a thin piece of wood, like a sculpture, smooth and delicate. She carefully removes the newspaper that nestles a delicate fan-shaped horn. "A gramophone! They had one at the sanatorium, but I never imagined having one at home! How extravagant."

Marge, the youngest, comes into the room, red hair stringy and loose, hands and apron smudged with dirt. Her jaw drops open. Marge has a boisterous personality, almost as lively as Florence's, and the sisters sometimes call her "little Flossie." "What is it?" she says.

"Can you believe it? A gramophone!" Florence proclaims. Awed by this generous gift, everyone stays silent as Ernest sets up the new contraption.

"I brought two phonograph records, too," he says, as he takes them out of the box and hands them to Florence.

"Oh, Elgar! I love Elgar. And 'Alexander's Ragtime Band!' Which one shall I play first?"

"Alexander's!" shouts Marge. "'Alexander's Ragtime Band!'" She claps her hands, spraying garden dirt onto her dress and the floor.

Mama raises an eyebrow and smiles indulgently at her "littlest" girl.

Ernest adjusts the gramophone horn, winds the handle, and sets the record on the machine.

An *oompah oompah* sounds and a horn toots as the band starts up and voices sing: "*Come on along, Come on along . . .*" Ernest holds a hand out to Florence and they do a two-step around the room. She warms from the inside out, and she can't stop smiling. Ernest's arm around her, his hand on her back, his gleeful smile, the dimple on his chin—this is her center, her home. Soon Marge, Ida, and even Mama are bouncing and singing along.

Afterward, they sit, and Mama serves lemonade and shortbread while Florence and Ernest almost trip over each other to talk—what the Pittsburgh crowd is up to, Ernest's sister, Mary. She tells him about Ruth, the friend she made at the sanatorium, and the feeling of ecstasy when the doctor proclaimed that Florence was cured.

When Ernest gets ready to leave, the two walk out to the motorcar together. He climbs back into the Model T, and Florence comes forward to take his hand. "Will you come again soon?"

Ernest's face breaks into several different expressions at once, ending with a timid smile. "Do you mean as a suitor?"

She blushes and looks at her feet. "Well . . ." She rubs her toe in the dirt. Suddenly that sense of completeness, that wholeness and shelter, is transformed and broken up, like a simple melody that has broken into a million tinkling notes all going in different directions.

Is that what I meant? Do I not know my own mind? Maybe she should just run back into the house. And then she remembers: *I am strong, and I can be bold, like Mary MacLane. I can admit the truth to myself and say what I want.* She takes a deep breath. "I know I've been a flibbertigibbet," she says, "but yes. If you want to."

Ernest leaps over the car door and enfolds her in a hug. "If I want to! What else do I want?" They stand in a quiet embrace, two loquacious people now silenced.

chapter 28

COURTSHIP

Pittsburgh, Pennsylvania, 1911–1914

Over the next two years Florence and Ernest plunge into a flurry of social life. At first, Ernest seemed disoriented, as though finding it hard to move from the role of the laughing little brother who accepted her teasing as a sign of affection, to her number one suitor. But he soon rallied and gained energy and confidence as he realized that she truly accepted him as her beau.

Florence revels in her newfound energy and health and the belief that she is *cured*. Of course, Dr. Miller is less enthusiastic, warning her to be cautious, keep up with the rest and exercise and nutrition. And she still has "bad" days, when her breathing becomes labored and the humidity feels oppressive. She can ignore these little things when she recalls the exact moment at the sanatorium that Dr. Black said the word: *cured*.

She and Ernest go to the fancy new movie theater on Regent Square and watch a moving picture for the first time—Mary Pickford and Douglas Fairbanks, walking and talking on the screen. They take a picnic to Schenley Park, visit the zoo at Highland Park, and they dance. At a party in a grand house on Shady Avenue, an orchestra plays ragtime tunes, while they dance the turkey trot and the bunny hop. Much more fun, Florence reflects, than the stuffy gathering in Chicago where she met Phillip. At Westview Amusement Park, she and Ernest laugh and howl on the roller coaster. Phillip would never have lowered himself to go to an amusement park.

It's a most glorious time, marred only by Florence's brother, Bert's, dire reports about a war looming in Europe. Florence closes her ears to it. This is her time for fun, her emancipation from a dreaded disease, and she won't let anyone put a damper on it.

Florence has moved into an apartment on Coal Street with Mary, Ernest's sister, just a short trolley ride to her school, and she and Ernest include Mary in the fun whenever possible.

♪

One hot July day in 1914, Florence and Ernest embark on an outing in the Model T, with Mary and little Marge, who insists on coming, squeezed into the back seat. Following behind in Papa's rattly old farm truck comes Florence's brother, Bert. They shout and laugh and wave to Bert as they caravan to the mountains in Ligonier.

Ernest, with Bert behind, pulls into a little dirt road and stops. They tumble out of the cars, breathing in the cool mountain air under the trees.

"I have a surprise for you." Ernest smiles, a mischievous glint in his eyes, as he points to an opening in the trees. A woodland path.

Marge claps her hands as Florence and Mary exchange a puzzled glance.

Ernest gestures for them to follow and leads them through the woods. The earth smells fresh, a woodpecker drums, and rays of sun peek through the leaves. Ernest turns to face them, winking at Marge, and suddenly the path opens up.

"Whoop-de-do!" Marge exclaims. Before them, a waterfall! Ten feet high, the majestic waterfall extends the width of the creek and spills into a clear, deep pool. Large boulders, warmed by the sun, provide handy seats, and they all sit.

"It's gorgeous!" Florence starts to take off her shoes and stockings.

"No, the gorge is back there." Ernest grins.

The others roll their eyes as Florence and Marge divest themselves of their footwear and step gingerly across the pebbles. Laughing, they wade into the cool creek, and Florence scoops up a handful of water, tossing it with a splash toward Ernest.

Ernest throws a pebble into the water beside her. "But this isn't our destination," he calls, pointing to a continuation of the path on the other side of the narrow beach. The sisters put their shoes back on and follow the group as Ernest leads them along the path curving round and round and deeper into the woods. Again, he stops and turns to face them. "Behold." He gestures behind him to an opening, a giant hole in the rock face. "Dulany's Cave!" Ernest takes an enormous flashlight out of his rucksack and starts into the cave. "Come on along!"

Bert, who has been quiet up until now, shouts and follows Ernest.

Mary shakes her head and turns away from the cave, while Florence hesitates, then steps in behind the men, followed by Marge.

"Good heavens!" Florence exclaims. They are standing in an enormous room, perhaps twenty feet high and wide. Ernest directs the flashlight up and around, where layers of rock overlap and jut out in ridges and outcroppings, water dripping from the walls and ceiling. The uneven floor is pocked and pitted, with smaller rocks and crumbled shards strewn about. A musty smell permeates the damp air.

"This cave is mostly sandstone," says Ernest. "That's why it's tan, and it has no stalactites or stalagmites." He rotates the flashlight to focus on one end of the cave, an opening into a narrower passage. Like this room, the passageway has high walls and a lofty ceiling, but the path slopes downward on a steep, crumbly floor that looks even more dangerous.

"Follow me," Ernest says without looking back, and he speeds up his pace as he starts down the tunnel.

"Not me!" Marge cries and turns back.

Mary, wringing her hands, peers from outside into the entrance. "Don't go far!" she calls.

Bert starts to follow Ernest.

Florence shrugs and steps in behind. "It does look perilous," she says as she takes a few steps down the steep decline.

"Oh, I've done this before," Ernest calls as he disappears down the slope.

Florence hesitates. *Don't be silly. I am a brave, adventurous soul!* She shrugs and takes a big step. Suddenly the gravel rolls out beneath her feet, and she falls onto her seat.

"Are you hurt?" Bert climbs back up the slope, an expression of concern on his face, the older-brother protectiveness he's always shown.

Florence brushes off her skirt and stands. "Just my pride."

"I told you to wear boots. Those are the wrong kind of shoes for a hike."

Florence examines her shoes. She chose high heels today. And the truth is, her ankle is throbbing. "I guess you're right," she says, suppressing a cough. "I'll go sit with Mary."

The cough comes back in fits and spurts as she joins Mary to sit on a moss-covered boulder while Marge wanders around, picking up pebbles.

Mary gives her a worried look. "Are you all right?"

"Oh, it's nothing." Florence waves a hand in the air, dismissing the topic. "Just the damp air in the cave." Maybe it's not nothing, but she won't think about that.

They sit and wait, sunlight dappling their faces and the forest floor as treetops high above sway in a gentle breeze. Marge examines the pebbles she's found and puts some in a bag while Florence clears her throat, trying to dislodge the phlegm that has built up since she was in the cave.

Florence and Mary chat about the coming school year, which teachers are coming back, and the new French teacher. "I heard that she's a suffragist," Florence says. "I can't wait to meet her."

Mary shakes her head.

"What? Don't you believe in women's right to vote?"

"I do, but not with all that marching and shouting."

"Well, if we don't make them pay attention, how else is it supposed to happen?"

Mary shrugs, and Florence drops the subject. They've had this disagreement before. Mary is her good friend, but in this she is like Florence's sister Vance. Too conservative.

They fall silent and wait.

And wait.

Florence stands. "What is taking them so long?"

"I hope they're okay," Mary whispers.

"Maybe they're lost!" shouts Marge.

Florence sits back down again. "No, no, Ernest knows this cave." *At least I hope he does.*

The three remain silent, afraid to talk of anything else, as if keeping their thoughts concentrated on the expedition will keep the men safe.

Finally, Ernest and Bert emerge from the cave, their faces wet and their clothes damp. Ernest is laughing, exultant, and Bert smiles.

"What was it like?" Mary asks.

"Well, that was extraordinary," Bert says.

Ernest reaches into his rucksack and pulls out a large, muddy-looking stone with a section broken out into a wedge-shaped cut, its interior glistening and milky white.

"Ooh, diamonds!" Marge shouts.

"No," Ernest says, turning the stone round and round. "This is calcite. The walls of the cave are sandstone, and there are a lot of these lying around, too."

"And look at this!" Bert exclaims, holding up an old horseshoe, the iron corroded and peeling.

"How did that get in there?" Mary asks.

"I don't know," Ernest muses. "Maybe from the Civil War."

"And we had some live visitors, too," Bert says. "They flew right past us."

"What? Ghosts?" Marge shouts.

"No," Ernest says. "Bats."

♪

Back in Pittsburgh, a pink sky hovers over the mills on the Monongahela River, reflecting silver and mauve in the water. The group drives through the city to Florence and Mary's apartment at the house on Coal Street. When the two cars splutter to a stop, a tall, thin woman with gray-streaked black hair is standing outside the door. Mrs. McKinnon, Florence and Mary's landlady, flaps her arms in distress.

Florence steps down from the Model T. "What is it, Mrs. McKinnon?"

"They've started a war in Europe!" cries the older woman, wringing her apron.

They all stand in stunned silence, and Florence glances at Bert, who raises his eyebrows. He told them this was coming, and Florence chose not to believe it.

♪

The war, and the question of whether America will join, triggers an atmosphere of uneasiness and foreboding in Pittsburgh. Florence and Ernest bemoan the idiocy of the Europeans for starting a war over the death of one man, and Florence applauds the pacifists. In defiance the two do their best to ignore the war news and continue dancing and singing and going to parties.

As the summer comes to an end, though, Ernest's brother, Gordy, is drafted and sent overseas. Now it's hard to ignore the new reality, even harder to maintain their pacifist convictions.

Especially when Ernest is called up for the National Guard, with service in the 18th Regiment, and will be sent to camp for two weeks at Fort Indiantown Gap. Then he'll be on weekend duty. Thankfully, he will not be sent overseas like Gordy, since, as the eldest male, he is considered the sole support for his mother.

As the atmosphere grows more ominous with news of the war in Europe, Ernest's mother becomes more anxious and critical. She hovers over Ernest, complains about the government, the president, the dearth of letters from Gordy, and pronounces Florence "a flirt." Seemingly repudiating this, Ernest laughs and informs Florence of his mother's judgment. Florence recalls, though, that *he* made similar comments in his early letters to her. Jealousy, she'd thought. And not too different from Phillip's or even her sister Vance's reproaches. Well, maybe she is a flirt. But she's alive and well compared to some of the people at Mont Alto, so why not have fun while you can?

She and Ernest have grown closer over the summer, in their fun as well as their mutual convictions about the war, and Florence is now surer than ever of her feelings. Ernest has a serious, even a judgmental, side, but he's also smart and witty, and they have endless conversations, kindred spirits bantering back and forth. Ernest is no longer just her comrade. He is her soulmate.

In Mahaffey, on their last night before Ernest leaves for camp, the two walk out to a little grove of birch trees behind the house. Ernest stops and turns to Florence, looking at her in silence, then reaches into his pocket. He takes out a little box covered in black velvet and hands it to her. She smiles at him and then down at the box. Then opens it. A diamond ring.

This is the second time she's been given a diamond ring. It's not a surprise, as it was with Phillip, but Florence is overcome with emotion. She feels a sense of deep joy and peace. She chokes back a sob as Ernest smiles through a tear in his eye. "Will you marry me?"

"Of course!" she exclaims and steps up to embrace him.

chapter 29

ANCHORS AWEIGH

Pensacola, Florida, 1944

Flossie pushes back her bushy hair and sticks a bobby pin in to hold it back. It's another beautiful Florida day: sunny, blue skies, blue ocean all the way to the horizon, pelicans flying in formation. A picture-perfect, postcard kind of day.

Except that nothing is perfect today. Flossie stands on the dock in front of the USS *Lexington*, a massive gray-black battleship, its sinister presence assaulting her world, a blight on this tropical paradise.

Sudden heavy clouds move across the sky, and the ocean rages below. The sky, the ocean—even they know it's a bad day. Between the dock and the ship, a basket dangles from a long connecting cable. A man is in that basket.

Now the basket sways and dips even lower, the zipline wobbles, and she screams.

A sailor standing nearby laughs. "We all have to do it," he says. "This is just a practice run."

"Will it hold?"

"Never broken yet."

"My husband was put on one of those, a ship-to-ship cable." Despite this discouraging subject, she feels a surge of pride in saying, "my husband."

The sailor shakes his head. "Why was that?"

"He had to perform an emergency appendectomy on someone on the other ship." She pulls the well-worn letter out of her pocket and smooths it down. "Thank goodness, he got back safely. I hope he doesn't have to do that again."

The man in the bucket wobbles again as the zipline sways.

Flossie holds her mouth, stifling another scream.

The sailor smirks. "This is a piece of cake compared to that ship-to-ship line out in the open sea."

"Oh!" If this was meant to reassure her, it did the opposite. *What if George has to do it again? What will happen if the ship is attacked when George is on it? What if the Germans sink it? Or if he's in one of those fighter planes? What will happen to George?* Flossie wrings her hands and hops from foot to foot. *I just married him. I can't lose him now!*

Flossie has been coming to the boat basin every day for two weeks.

♪

Two weeks ago, a massive aircraft carrier came into dock, and George was one of five young doctors, the new flight surgeons, conscripted for medical duty. All week, sailors scurried around the ship, polishing and sweeping and lugging barrels and boxes up and down the ladders from the tugboats.

"Where will you go?" Flossie asked George.

"They haven't told us."

"Good heavens, not to Europe, I hope!"

He shrugged. "Probably not. Probably to the Pacific again."

"Oh." Her shoulders sank. That could be even worse. Even though the Americans made considerable gains in the Pacific, it was still dangerous. *Will a Japanese submarine sink George's ship? Will this be my last sight of my beloved? The gentle healer who calms and protects me? The one who smells of wool and tobacco and touches me with such tenderness?*

They lingered in a long embrace as the beastly roar of the ship's horn sounded from the harbor and filled the air.

♪

Now, Flossie clutches her hands, trying to keep them still, while this new ship creaks and clangs, coasting slowly away from the dock, and disappears into the distance.

She trudges back from the busy dock, through the town and its one grocery store. No dress shops or department stores here for window shopping. Just the one drug store with the soda fountain, and today even that doesn't tempt her. Here she is in a strange new place, all by herself, going home alone to an alien house, without George's sweet smile and gentle cuddles. It's the first time she's lived in a house by herself, with no clue how long it will be for.

Flossie, head down and shoulders hunched, walks alongside the bayou, the marsh grass beside her softly rippling. She stops and digs the toe of her shoe into the sand. How will she endure?

On her left, a gurgling sound, and there, beyond the grass, three huge manatees, as big as baby elephants, loll in the water. Just the other day she learned of these gentle giants from Dotty, and here they are now, lounging and flopping around like people taking a bath. As she watches, Flossie feels herself letting go of the fear, her breath slowing down.

She lifts her head high. She will make a plan. How to get through the days without thinking about the war every minute. She'll focus on other things: finishing the dress she's been working on, hemming the curtains, getting more involved in the wives' club. And to relax, swimming in the warm ocean with Dotty, lolling in the water like the manatees.

Flossie turns around and heads back to the base and the chapel where the wives' club meets. She'll talk to someone, one of the women who has been here longer and has lived through a husband's deployment.

She steps onto the path toward the chapel. This is the first time she's been here since the wedding. After the procession through the sword arch, Flossie and George stood on the porch between the tall columns and looked at Daddy below, grinning and taking a picture with his old box camera, and Bobby saluting and laughing. Everyone else—Elizabeth, Sallie, Aunt Mary, the sailors in their crisp whites, Flossie's new women friends—were standing in a half circle, everyone beaming at George and her, everyone shouting congratulations and throwing rice. That was a *truly* perfect Florida day, with bright September sunshine and a dazzling blue sky.

Now the sky has darkened and the air has thickened into a gray mist, as if to rub in this overwhelming loneliness. Ahead, the lovely brick chapel looms stark and bare. Flossie walks up the steps.

"Flossie!" The heavy door opens, and Dotty rushes up to her. Dotty, with her bright eyes and floppy pageboy haircut, usually lively like Flossie, today is more subdued. "I know," she says, with an understanding smile. "Marsh is on that ship, too." She takes Flossie's arm. "Let's go somewhere and talk."

Flossie's shoulders drop and the tears begin. Tears she didn't know she was holding, tears of sadness, of grief, and of relief. Her husband is gone.

chapter 30

THE MARCH OF THE WOMEN

Pittsburgh, Pennsylvania, 1914

Florence stands in front of the mirror and adjusts the armband. VOTES FOR WOMEN, it reads, the script in purple on a yellow felt background. The colors of the women's suffrage movement, as Emmeline Pankhurst said. Yellow for sunflowers and light, "the color of light and life, is as the torch that guides our purpose, pure and unswerving." Purple for "the royal blood that flows in the veins of every suffragette, the instinct of freedom and dignity." Florence pairs the armband with a white dress to "show the purity and femininity of the movement and to counteract the voices trying to tarnish this noble cause." She pulls the armband around so the words rest on the outside of her arm.

Was it only two months ago that she stood at another mirror like this in a white dress?

♪

With all the sisters dressed in beautiful pastel satin gowns Edith found for a bargain at Marshall Fields, Florence stood in their midst and laughed nervously. Then she broke into tears. "What am I doing?" she cried. What would Ruth think of her now? Was Florence caving to a subservient role?

Edith patted her on the shoulder. "You're getting married, little Flossie."

"But will I still . . . can I still be a suffragist?" Florence whispered. This was completely irrational, she knew. She had been attending meetings at the Pittsburgh Suffrage Headquarters, lobbying for universal suffrage in Pennsylvania, and joining leaders like Hannah Patterson in barnstorming and educating people throughout Pittsburgh. Florence had even given a few speeches herself. And Ernest actually seemed proud of her.

"Of course you can," Edith said.

"And you are lucky Ernest supports you," added Sue. Enormous in a maternity gown, Sue was Florence's matron of honor. It remained unspoken that Sue's husband, Harry, was lukewarm, if anything, about women's rights.

Florence had been thankful to be back in Mahaffey after the sanatorium, but she remained adamant that she didn't want her wedding in that little outpost where people were so narrow-minded. Especially at the Lutheran church she'd grown up in, where the pompous new minister preached against the women's vote.

The wedding was held in the Edgewood Presbyterian Church, Ernest's family church.

As she and Papa strolled arm in arm up the aisle, everyone smiled: Mama, Bert, Nannie, Mary, and Florence's six sisters, all in their glimmering satin gowns. Ernest, with a dimpled grin, stepped forward, and Papa laid Florence's arm on his. Suddenly Florence burst into tears again. All the feelings from the previous three years mounted like a cloud around her: the fears of the disease, the agony of the train ride, the infatuation with Phillip, her subsequent disillusionment and anger, the despair at the sanatorium, and then the breakthrough, when she saw Ernest at the heart of everything. She'd made so many mistakes and wrong turns along the way, it was a miracle to be here, to be marrying a good man, to know that she loved and was loved by him.

The officiating minister, a quiet, studious man with a craggy face, stood at the altar holding his Bible and smiling at them as she and Papa walked down the aisle. When Papa took her hand and gave it to Ernest, Florence felt a rush of tears. Ernest's eyes filled with tears, too, his dimples softening his dear face. Till death do us part. To love, honor, and obey. Well, the obey part was conditional, in her opinion, but she would fulfill these vows. Ernest was still her trusty comrade, and she'd be the worthiest wife there was. At this moment, Florence, whose faith was, at best, inter-mittent, felt the angels hovering and blessing her union.

After the wedding Florence and Ernest took a weekend honeymoon in Niagara Falls, and then they set up house in an apartment on Hawthorne Street near the insurance company where Ernest had a new job. Florence found she enjoyed keeping house, making everything tidy and handling the budget. And she could also work with the suffragists. Ernest, who seemed to think she could do no wrong, was her best supporter at her speeches and rallies. Florence would enjoy it while it lasted, she thought, until she came down from that pedestal he'd put her on.

♪

Florence straightens the sash again and lifts her chest. Today is the biggest event of 1914—the Pittsburgh suffrage parade. Will Alice Paul be there? Alice Paul, a Quaker who *always* believed that men and women are equal, who marched for women's votes in England before she came here. Who was sent to jail numerous times and even went on a hunger strike. Florence has read everything by and about Alice Paul. She pulls her shoulders back and stands straighter, a proud suffragist.

Like Alice, Florence will persevere in the battle for women's right to vote. It's infuriating that many people don't understand how important this is. Mostly men, but lots of women, too, speak out *against* women's suffrage.

Florence will never return to that church Ernest took her to last Sunday. Not the family church, but another Presbyterian church in Pittsburgh, the city with a Presbyterian church on every corner. The minister proclaimed, "Women are not educated; they are not intelligent enough to cast a thoughtful vote" and "are too busy with their work in the home to vote."

Well, Florence gave him a calling out after the service. Then how can *men* vote, she said, with all the work they have? And how can they make educated decisions any better than women? She and her sisters, she said, are more educated than three-quarters of the men in this country.

In her room Florence puts on her wide-brimmed hat with the upright feather, and pinches her cheeks for a little color. A dignified woman, a serious woman, a suffragist. She goes out to the living room, where

Ernest has been waiting, he and Mary sitting in the two old wing chairs Florence brought from Mahaffey. She's tried to convince Mary to come with her to the parade, but Mary is reluctant.

When she enters the room, Ernest stands and holds up the camera.

"Not here, Ernest," she says with a wave. "Save your film for the parade."

Mary places her teacup on the carved wooden table and smiles. "You look lovely, Florence."

"Are you sure you won't come, too, Mary?"

"You know I don't agree with all the rough shouting and making a spectacle of yourself."

"It's just marching in a parade!"

"Well, who knows what will happen down there? Remember how the women were jeered and heckled at the Washington march last year?"

Ernest steps forward and takes Florence's arm. "I'll be there, too," he says.

"But you can't march," Mary says. "It's only for the women."

"We'll see," he says.

♪

They step off the trolley into a mass of more people than Florence has ever seen in one place. Ernest secures his straw boater and takes her arm.

"There must be thousands of people here," she says. "How will we find the starting point?"

"This way!" A tall woman holding a placard marches past. "Women only," she shouts, looking at Ernest.

Ernest secures Florence's arm even tighter, and they follow the tall woman. Around the corner stands a group of at least two hundred women in front of an enormous building with leaded glass windows and sculpted cornices. The building encompasses a whole city block, enough for all of the women to stand in front of while a photographer sets up his equipment.

Florence stares. "How can he take a photograph of all of those people at once?"

Ernest smiles. "The photographer opens the shutter, then runs from one end to the other."

"Well, here I go." Florence marches up and squeezes her way into the group.

The photograph takes at least thirty minutes, with the photographer shouting at everyone to hold still while he races in front of them with his big camera and tripod. After the photo, Florence waves Ernest over and they follow the crowd around the corner, a crowd that includes men and colored women. Of course, the overwhelming majority are women, and as they begin to walk, a sound swells into the air with women's voices. They are singing "The March of the Women," the banner song of the suffrage movement.

Florence knows all the words and joins in, lifting her voice in a resounding soprano and raising her arm to conduct and encourage everyone around her. It's natural to move into her music teacher mode.

"*Shout, shout, up with your song! Cry with the wind for the dawn is breaking: March, march, swing you along, Wide blows our banner and hope is waking,*" and so on, all four verses. They sing the whole song at least three times, and Ernest, ever the good sport, steps into a vigorous march, singing along with all the wrong words, laughing along with Florence.

When the singing ends, the talking and shouting resumes. Everyone is energized now, infused with elation and hope.

Florence, who sees not Alice Paul but another famous suffragist, tugs on Ernest's arm. "That's Daisy Lampkin," she shouts above the noise. "She organizes the Negro women." She smiles and waves, and Mrs. Lampkin waves back. Of course, Mrs. Lampkin doesn't know Florence, who's just a cog in this great wheel, but it's all part of the festive spirit.

When Florence told Papa she would march with both Black and white women in the parade, she thought he'd be proud, but he didn't react the way she thought he would. "I don't approve at all," he said. "Marching through the city in a rough crowd . . . you could get hurt."

"But Papa," she protested. "You fought in the Civil War and lost your ear fighting for equality for the Negro! Now we are fighting for women's equality, too!"

"No, this is not the way." He shook his head at Mama standing nearby. "If there's any mischief to be made, this girl has to be in the middle of it."

Mama harumphed and smiled a kind smile at her second-youngest daughter. "Well, this time I agree with her," she said. "In fact, I'm proud of her and Edith." Edith would be marching on the same day in the Chicago parade.

"Huzzah!" Florence lifted her arms and laughed.

Thousands more people line both sides of the street, cheering and jeering.

On the sidewalk, other women, also dressed in white, smile and wave, and some of them, along with some men, clap and cheer.

Two angry-faced men in pork pie hats look at Florence and shout, "Dirty whores!" and then, incongruously, "Hey, darlin', come home with me!"

At that, Ernest, with fire in his eyes, grips his camera and starts toward the men, but Florence pulls him back. "They're not worth a second thought." She puts on a brave front, but underneath she is shaken. To be so viciously attacked—not what she could have imagined. Thank goodness Ernest is here with her. She tightens her hold on his arm.

As they turn the corner, the fear subsides, and in Schenley Park, bright yellow forsythia and purple and white azaleas bloom on the hillside. "Look," Florence smiles, "the suffragist colors!" An uplifting feeling warms her very core, a sense of delight. To be here on this historic occasion, and to think that Ernest is championing her.

Ernest hasn't changed much, but the way Florence sees him has changed. He's grown up. And maybe she, too, has grown up. From wanting the glitz and glamorous life with Phillip to seeing the truth of a man who really cares about her. Dashing old Phillip is probably at this moment lining up with the anti-suffragists in Chicago.

Florence holds out her left hand and gazes at her finger. She now has another diamond ring, more modest and smaller than Phillip's, but so much more precious, and a wedding ring as well.

chapter 31

THE SUNNY SIDE OF THE STREET

Pensacola, Florida, 1944

Rain spits from the sky and drips from the roof gutter as if God is wringing out a rag over Pensacola. On the lawn and the street, broken coconuts, palm fronds, and tree branches are strewn pell-mell, and on the washing machine behind Flossie, a pile of wet laundry waits for the rain to stop.

She leans her elbows on the dining room table and stares out the window. The envelope in front of her is postmarked 1910, and the handwriting is familiar. The rounded letters and loops and the way it flows, as if the person whose hand formed these words is just around the corner. She's finally ready to read the letter.

When the hurricane hit last week, Flossie was playing the piano at the officers' wives club. She and Dotty, with about five other young women, were singing "The Sunny Side of the Street" and laughing.

Suddenly a fierce roaring sound came from outside the window. Tree branches and palm fronds flew about like a scene from *The Wizard of Oz*. The women ran to the middle of the chapel and huddled there, while tree limbs and palm leaves banged and slapped at the windows. The women looked at each other in shock. One of the wives suggested they pray, and she led them in saying Psalm 23, which most of them knew from Sunday or Hebrew school.

The women stayed in the chapel until the storm died down. As Flossie and Dotty left, though, the rain was still bombarding everything outside and they were soaked when they got back to their respective bungalows.

Everyone said the storm was milder here than on Florida's East Coast, but Flossie and Dotty were shaken. Pittsburgh never had a hurricane like this, with high winds, wild lashings of branches, and trees falling.

Flossie took a shower and dried off well, and now the wind has abated and the rain has petered out into a drizzle. In the yard, the street, and the beach, everything is a mess, except, amazingly, the potted lilies on the front porch that she saved from the wedding. They're blooming again. It's a sign of hope, a sign that George will come back safe and sound.

Flossie picks up the letter. An ordinary envelope, not the thin airmail paper used now. Of course, they didn't have airmail in 1910. The paper crackles in her hand and gives off a slight musty smell. And a scent—is that Lily of the Valley? It conjures up a memory from the deep recesses of her brain, a memory of something she can't quite grasp. This is paper Flossie's mother held in her hands, and that familiar handwriting, in its casual looping style, is so much like her own. It's like Flossie has something of her mother in her, something of her spirit living in Flossie's body. She takes a deep breath and lets out a sigh. After all these years, a mother to hold her and comfort her.

Flossie gazes at the old sepia photograph that was always on the landing at home. When he gave her this one letter, Daddy said that something from home, something familiar, her own mother's picture, would be comforting in her new space.

What were you like, Mother? Would Flossie have called her Mother? Mama? Mommy?

And why did Daddy give her *this* letter out of the huge stack he kept in the cedar box? Is there something important here, or did he pick one at random? Had he plucked it out of the box without looking? It seemed an odd action for someone who jealously guarded those letters for so long. Maybe it was more of a surrender.

And why have I waited so long to open it? At home she was too wrapped up in wedding plans and packing to give the letter her attention. And maybe a bit scared. In the past few days, she's looked at it so many times, reaching for it and almost tearing it open, then hesitating and putting it back. The same thoughts that have been in her mind for weeks arise: *Am I afraid to see more of my mother's handwriting, to hear her voice from across the years? What if she is different than the mother I've imagined?*

She brushes her fingers over the envelope. In a way, this is scarier than the hurricane. It's an opening into some new but old part of herself, this mother she never knew. Who might be less of the goddess she was in Flossie's mind and all too human.

Not that Nannie Craighead was lacking in her mothering. Flossie always knew Nannie loved her. But Nannie was a strict disciplinarian—eat every last bite of dinner, don't stay out after nine, wear the old-fashioned clothes.

When Elizabeth entered the family, Flossie was almost a teenager, and Nannie was not about to relinquish her position as head of the family. When Flossie went off to college, though, Elizabeth stood up for her, and Nannie had to cede her authority, at least when it came to clothes, to a granddaughter studying costume design.

Flossie looks around. This bungalow is compact, efficient. No old Victorian woodwork to dust or high windows with wavy old glass to wash. She's a housewife now. Isn't there something else she should be doing? Sweeping the floor or making cookies for the wives' club rummage sale or preparing another casserole to put in the icebox for when George comes home? *If* he comes home.

She straightens in the chair. *Pack up your troubles, Flossie.* No more gloom and doom. Stiff upper lip. George *will* come home, and she will tackle this letter. She can do it.

Flossie picks up the letter. *Dear Ernest,* she reads, and suddenly her stomach starts roiling like the stormy ocean. She runs to the bathroom and leans over the toilet. She didn't have much of an appetite this morning, and now the breakfast she did have—one small bowl of cereal—comes heaving out. She stands and it's gone. All of these unknowns and worries must be affecting her body more than she thought.

She returns to the table. Her latest sewing project, a chic pair of wide-leg pants in beige linen, sits sprawled behind her on the credenza, the letter on the table in front of her.

She takes a deep breath and opens the letter.

♪

Three hours later Flossie walks barefoot on what is left of the beach. The rain has stopped, though the air feels like a steam bath, and the ocean, gray and churning, has encroached so high that the beach is just a narrow strip. The sand dunes have rearranged themselves into random hills and depressions. The letter is in her pocket.

This beach is like her life, stirred up, roiled over, rearranged. Her husband at sea, her father with his secrets, and her mother—not who Flossie thought she was.

She sits on a dune and wiggles her toes in the sand. For the third time she slides the letter from the envelope. Her mother, at twenty-two, was younger than Flossie is now. This is a letter to Daddy, but it sounds like he's only a friend. Florence brags about her social life and her suitors as if Ernest is a girlfriend she shares secrets with. And then, at the end of the letter, comes the shocker:

El Yeso Ranch, 1910
> *One piece of news I have reserved to the last.*
> *Last night I promised to become the wife of a man who loves me. I cannot talk of this to you as I would like to do or could have formerly, but let it suffice to say that I told him about you, and he is perfectly willing we shall always be friends.*
> *This, of course, is to remain a secret . . .*

Her mother was engaged—to another man? Who was this, and what happened?

The year was 1910, and she and Daddy got married in 1914, so something had changed in those four years.

"Hi-de-ho!" Dotty skips across the beach, spraying sand around her bare feet, and plops down beside Flossie. She and Flossie discovered that they both love the Cab Calloway movie, *Hi-De-Ho*, and now they use the phrase as a greeting. Usually Flossie says *hi-de-ho* back, but this time, she has to force a smile.

"What's up, buttercup?" Dotty pushes back her blond curls, leans over, and studies Flossie's face. "You look a bit peaked."

Flossie tries to keep her face from scrunching up, but a tear sneaks out. "I'm just a little under the weather right now."

Dotty laughs. "Well, here we are in the tropics and practically under water! I think we're *all* under the weather!"

Flossie attempts another half-smile.

"Oh, no, it's something else, isn't it?"

Flossie sighs. Who else can she talk to right now? "It's everything, really. I've been reading this letter from my mother to my father, from before they were married. And it turns out she was engaged to another man."

Dotty frowns. "But she ended up with your dad, I presume?"

"Yes, but what happened in the meantime? You see, I never knew my mother. She died when I was born."

"Ah. Well, why don't you ask your father?"

Flossie pauses. "Oh, of course. I could do that. He ended up with her after all." She hugs her knees and bows her head over them. "I'm just not thinking straight, with George out at sea who-knows-where, and I was sick this morning."

"Sick?"

"Yes, I was so worried I threw up. Now I feel fine. It just feels like everything is topsy-turvy."

Dotty leans over again and studies Flossie's face. "There might be another reason for feeling sick," she says, looking at Flossie's stomach with a grin.

"Oh! I hadn't thought of that!" *Could I be pregnant? When was my last period? I've forgotten to keep track.* She touches her stomach. A baby? *Could I be a mother? It's what I've always wanted, but not now, not in the middle of a war with George out at sea!* They did use condoms, but was there a time they forgot?

Dotty pats her arm. "I'll come with you to the clinic tomorrow."

"The clinic? I don't know, Dotty. I want children, but being pregnant is one of the scariest things I can imagine. Knowing what happened to my mother . . ."

♪

The test is positive. Flossie is pregnant. She sits at the dining room table with her sewing machine and the beautiful green silk she's chosen for her new design—a cocktail dress. She examines the drawing again and rearranges the pattern pieces she has measured and cut.

She stares out the window. Palm trees sway in a light breeze, and the sky is a vivid blue again, as if the storm never happened and the universe is conspiring to pretend it's just another ordinary day in Florida.

This is not an ordinary day. It's the most extraordinary day in her life. *I'm having a baby.* What does it mean? Elizabeth had a miscarriage before she got pregnant with Sallie. Will that happen to Flossie? Or worse? If only George were here.

Flossie can't focus on the dress. *Should I be designing maternity dresses instead?* She gets up and steps out the door. Maybe a walk will help. The soft breeze caresses her skin as she heads to the beach, then a bomber roars overhead and shatters what sliver of peacefulness she felt. She wants a baby, but not during this awful war. And what if George won't even be here for the birth? She lifts a fist into the sky and shouts, "Damn you, Hitler!" Swearing is not done in her family at all, and Flossie never swears, but this felt good. She shouts it out again. "Damn you, Hitler!"

They're saying in the news that the Allies are winning, and the war will be over soon. But what do they know? It's been years now, and Flossie keeps hearing Nannie's voice, "*That's what they said the last time.*"

And what about this man her mother was engaged to? She straightens, resolute, and walks back to the house.

Flossie picks up the heavy black Bakelite phone receiver and turns the dial with her finger to 110.

"Number, please," comes the voice.

"Pittsburgh, Pennsylvania. Churchill 1-9036."

Daddy picks up after one ring.

"Hi, Daddy!" Flossie exclaims.

"Hello, Flossie. How's the weather down there? We heard there was a hurricane."

"Yes, it was pretty scary, but we're fine now. George is still out at sea." She hesitates. "I have some news!" She can't wait for him to respond and blurts out, "I'm going to have a baby!"

Silence.

"Well, shiver me tinders," he says. "I'm going to be a grandfather! That's wonderful, honey. Wait, here's Elizabeth."

"Flossie, what good news! When is the due date?"

"Sometime in February." She clears her throat. "I wish we weren't in the middle of a war, though, and naturally it would be better if George were here. Hopefully he's coming back soon." A scrap of green silk lies in front of her on the table. She picks it up and squeezes it.

"And I'm sure you'll be fine. You're right there beside the navy hospital."

"Yes, I guess."

"Well, we have some news for you, too," says Elizabeth. "Hammie's mother called, and she's heard from him."

"Oh." Flossie squeezes the silk harder, twisting and turning it in her hand. "Is he okay?"

"Yes, he's okay. He's still somewhere near Pearl Harbor with the army."

Pearl Harbor. How dreadful. Flossie sighs. "Did she tell him I got married?"

"I think so."

Flossie lays her head on the table. Thank God Hammie survived. But how awful she was. Getting married when Hammie was so far away, and then he was in a terrible bomb attack. Will they ever be friends again?

After they end the call, Flossie runs her fingers over the green silk fabric for the cocktail dress. She'll start on the bodice, and when she finishes this, she can make some maternity clothes. *Oh, I forgot to ask Daddy about the letter.* Well, so much is happening in her life right now that the past doesn't seem so important. But that thought evokes the familiar ache that comes when thinking of her mother.

A mother to help with the pregnancy and the birth, a mother's love . . . Flossie sighs, and a song comes unbidden into her mind, a sad song, "Lili Marleen," and as she hums, the lyrics form on her lips. Dotty told her that this song is about a prostitute, but, still, it's about missing someone, of feeling the absence of someone you love. Flossie's face is wet with tears. She is missing the mother she never knew, the mother who would have loved her.

♪

In the next week Flossie finishes the cocktail dress and designs a sundress, like one she saw in the Neiman Marcus catalogue, with a halter top and loose, flowing skirt in a print with huge yellow lemons and green leaves. It was gorgeous and expensive, of course. Flossie could, she thought, design and make one like that for half the price, and she just happens to have some fabric in a similar print.

Every day Flossie walks to the post office, hoping for letters from George. The base doctor said walking was good exercise when pregnant, so this counts as part of her pregnancy regimen, though she doesn't actually have a regimen, except for all the citrus fruit she eats—oranges, grapefruits, and lemons for lemonade—everything fresh off the trees. And she takes naps, something she's never done before.

He writes often, but George's letters come intermittently, sometimes a month late.

The air is gray with clouds today as Flossie walks through town. Past the old brick buildings with balconies and colonnades in the Spanish style, under palm trees and tall magnolias, and to the post office. She steps up to the window, but there is no letter from George. She turns to leave.

"Just a moment, ma'am!" the postmaster, a balding middle-aged man with a Florida twang, calls her back. He places a package on the counter. "This just came for you."

"What is it?" Flossie picks up the package, the size of a shoebox. The return address is 159 Lacrosse Street, Pittsburgh, PA. The handwriting is her father's. What is Daddy sending her? It's so heavy. A meat grinder?

She walks back through town and to the bungalow.

Inside, Flossie shoves aside the pattern paper and puts the box on the dining room table.

She peels off the packing paper. It *is* a shoebox. How strange. She lifts the lid, and now she sees why the box is so heavy. It's stuffed with letters. All dated between 1910 and 1914, all from Florence Rodkey to Ernest Craighead.

A note on top of the pile from Daddy: *Now that you are becoming a mother, I think it's time for you to see these words from your own mother. Perhaps they will bring her love to you as they do to me.*

Flossie's eyes fill with tears, and she collapses over the table, her shoulders heaving with sobs. The love of her mother. She will see it, she will feel it, the presence of her mother, in the words and in the handwriting, in her mother's love for her father.

And she will also find out about this other man, this Phillip, the man before Daddy.

Flossie dries her eyes and opens the first letter. The paper is thin and frail, but the writing is clear, and the letters well preserved, as if written yesterday.

In the next few weeks, she puts aside her pattern pieces and fabrics and reads the letters, all fifty-seven of them.

The picture emerges of a young woman, younger than Flossie is now. Sprightly and smart, mostly enthusiastic but sometimes sad and scared, and teasing Flossie's father as if he were a little brother. Florence writes about her travels to New Mexico and her other suitor, Phillip. He sounds quite dashing and rich, but not as nice as Daddy.

Flossie's emotions swing up and down as she reads; she feels alternately proud, admiring, compassionate, and embarrassed. Almost angry. Florence obviously cared about Daddy, but why was she so cavalier with him? And why did he stick with her through all of that—her other boyfriends, her fickleness? Flossie recalls the tremor in his voice and Daddy's tears when he mentions Florence. He really did love her. And in the later letters, her love for him shines through.

Flossie pauses from her reading and gazes through the window at the sky. This is not the mother she imagined, that beautiful musician on a pedestal. This is a young woman who loved adventure, liked attention from young men, was worried about money, was sometimes arrogant, sometimes despairing in her illness. This knowledge is a deep well, a mystery partially revealed, and Flossie is just beginning to fathom its depths.

She sits at the table, silent and still, gazing at the portrait. The beautiful young woman with her head bowed, looking modest and contemplative, not at all like the picture emerging from the letters.

And all of these letters are from before Florence and Ernest were married.

What was their life like *after* they were married—when they had their first baby, Roddy, and then were expecting her, Flossie?

chapter 32

LULLABY AND GOOD NIGHT

Pittsburgh, Pennsylvania, 1918

Florence burrows her nose in her child's hair and sniffs as she walks, humming and singing Brahms's "Lullaby." Little Roddy is fifteen months now, the star of her life. A beautiful boy with soft blond curls and chubby legs and a divine smell, but he's fussy at the moment. She switches to the German that Mama used to sing. *"Guten Abend, Gut' Nacht, mit Rosen bedakt . . ."* That version feels more soothing somehow. Soon the crying stops and Roddy goes back to sleep. She lays him in his baby buggy.

Florence sits at the dining room table and picks up her list. Ernest finally gave up on his dream of going to journalism school, and then he realized insurance was not for him either. He quit the insurance company and started a real estate business, which suits him and his love of history and old houses. Of course, it's early days for his company and still a bit of a struggle. It's essential to economize. Florence enjoys being the household accountant, and she checks her list again.

March 8
2 loaves bread   *.10*
6 cans cream   *.25*
2 cakes soap   *.10*
Starch   *.05*
Cabbage   *.05*

5 lamb chops	.34
Tomatoes	.10
Apples	.10
	1.14

She folds the list and tucks it into an envelope, congratulating herself on her careful money management. *I hope they haven't raised the prices since last week.*

Florence puts the letter into her purse and stands. She is pregnant again and hoping for an easier delivery this time. Hopefully Dr. Miller, who has been recommended, will comply with her request. She spent a long time composing a letter to him.

Should she take the trolley or walk down to the Braddock Avenue grocery store? With a fifteen-month-old and a seven-month pregnancy, the streetcar would be easier, but then she couldn't use the baby buggy. Walking is good for her anyway, that's what the doctor said.

As they stroll along Hawthorne Street, toddler Roddy, who has awakened, sits like a little prince in the fancy wicker carriage, a gift from Ernest's mother, who is almost as excited as Florence about having her second grandchild. Florence was intimidated by her new mother-in-law's stern visage, but when Roddy came along, Nannie Craighead glowed with happiness, cooing and fawning over the baby.

Roddy giggles and gurgles as the carriage bounces over cracks in the sidewalk. With his birth, Florence had an endless labor. He was a big baby, and for five hours that felt like an eternity, she screamed in agony, trying to push that baby out. When she held him in her arms, though, this perfect little being, her mood changed immediately, and she was ecstatic.

No one had told her about colic. For weeks the baby fussed and screamed, and Florence was exhausted. She vowed that next time she would convince the doctor to do a Caesarian.

After his first birthday in July, the baby calmed down a bit, but the amount of energy he took from her was astounding.

Little Roddy, her beautiful boy with the blond curls, loves being outside and riding in the buggy, and now he coos at squirrels and birds, then falls asleep again.

Today is warm for March, and breezy, with white and fuchsia azalea buds popping out on the hillside yards. Florence is feeling bright and alive despite the heavy load she's carrying in her belly. She stops to sit on a bench and feel the breeze and the sun's warmth. She hasn't sealed the letter to the doctor yet. She takes it out of her purse.

> *My Dear Dr. Miller,*
>
> *Could you give me an idea as to your rates for a maternity case? Of course, I suppose that would depend on and be influenced largely by the number of examinations previous to, and the amount of attention needed at the birth; but supposing it to be an average case.*
>
> *I would very much like to have you, but, knowing your reputation, I have a righteous fear of your price.*
>
> *This will be my second child and I want a Caesarian section. The first baby was born at the Presbyterian Hospital under the auspices of our esteemed Dr. Ziegler.* ~~And as I consider him less of a human and more of a, well, let me say, "German," I have decided to let a local Swissvale practitioner murder me rather than go to him again.~~ *[Really, Florence, that is offensive, she thinks.] but I would prefer a local practitioner this time.*
>
> *Money that one possessed and was able to retain at such a time would interest me very little, because I consider no amount in reason too great to pay for skillful service of this nature. But can you imagine a situation wherein the perhaps necessary sum was so elusive that one would never quite place a finger upon it.*
>
> *May I hear from you concerning this matter.*
> *Yours Sincerely,*
> *Florence R. Craighead*

Florence winces. Is she too hasty in dismissing Dr. Ziegler? Well, his countrymen are murdering her countrymen in Europe, and just the other day, Ernest's mother received a grim letter from Gordy, who was trapped in a muddy trench in France as the bombs fell. Luckily, Ernest is in the National Guard and goes to Fort Indiantown Gap only for weekends.

She takes out a pen and another piece of paper and rewrites the letter without the offending sentences.

She pauses. Does she sound like a fishmonger in the letter? Later she writes in her journal: *This, dear reader, might by a coarser mind be called but skillfully begging for a cheap rate. But who knows indeed that in the next existence I may be the doc and he the patient and what retributive justice I may then shower upon* <u>*her*</u> *head. So let us call it the giving* <u>*him*</u> *a chance to lay up treasure.*

She rolls her eyes at her preposterous reasoning, but, who knows, this might get her a better rate. Maybe she *is* a fishmonger. Well, she and Ernest are saving up to buy a house, and every penny counts.

Life keeps turning corners and coming into new territories. It never turns out the way you thought it would. For instance, her tuberculosis. She can finally use that word, even with herself, because she is finally free of it. Well, almost. They told her that her lungs are still weak and always will be, and it was quite a struggle to give birth the last time. When the memory comes up, the pain, the gasping for breath, the long hours in labor, Florence pushes it back down. *Think of something else, anything else.*

Now, though, she feels fine, only a little tired due to the pregnancy and a caring for a toddler.

A woman with frizzy gray hair stops to admire Roddy, smiles at Florence, and continues along the sidewalk.

Florence turns her face to the sky, absorbing the brightness of the day.

Another surprise was Ernest. When he rallied and became a responsible husband, working in the insurance company and then starting his own business, she felt a new kind of pleasure, a warmth that radiated from the inside out.

♪

In April she goes into labor, and, after they take Roddy to Ernest's parents' house on Lacrosse Street, she and Ernest rush to Magee Women's Hospital.

Florence has persuaded Dr. Miller to do the Caesarian, despite his reservations. She is confident it will make this birth easier than last time.

chapter 33

WE'LL MEET AGAIN

Pensacola, Florida, 1945

Flossie and Dotty shade their eyes with their hands as they look out toward the horizon. They're sitting on the beach, watching for the ship that will bring their husbands home.

Two weeks ago, Flossie was finishing a hem on a new sundress when a sudden uproar sounded just outside her window. A crowd of people, mostly women, shouted and cheered, jumping up and down in the street, hugging one another, dancing and waving American flags. She opened the door as Dotty skipped toward her. "The war is over!" Dotty exclaimed. She held out her hand for Flossie, and they joined the celebration.

"Yes! I see it!" Dotty points to the horizon, and Flossie peers harder. A tiny dot on the vast ocean, the USS *John Jay*. They pick up their towels and Dotty runs to the boat basin, a distance of a mile, while Flossie, almost nine months pregnant, hobbles behind as fast as she can.

It's January in Pensacola, cool and overcast. Of course, at home in Pittsburgh it would be freezing, whereas here they need only a light jacket. They hug their arms in the cool salt breeze as the ship grows bigger and bigger.

Back in June, Dotty had rightly guessed Flossie was pregnant. When George's ship returned to port for repairs, she gave him the news, and his reaction surprised her. Unlike his normal quiet and composed nature, George gleefully shouted the news to all his buddies at the clinic. Then he had to go right back out on the ship.

Thank goodness he'd be home now that she was due in a few weeks. Because he was a doctor, he was allowed in the delivery room with her, and that knowledge helped assuage some of her many fears. Could she give birth normally? Would she be safe? Would the baby? Her mother died giving birth to her. Did Flossie inherit the weakness that would lead to her own death?

George had assured her that she and the baby would be fine. Her mother, he said, had weakened lungs from tuberculosis, and in 1918, a Caesarian section was new and risky. As was the use of ether. Her doctor should have known not to give ether to someone with such low lung capacity.

It all made sense, but while George was out at sea in who knew what kind of danger and Flossie sat alone in the bungalow at night, the dread and panic would rear its head. She slept with the light on.

Flossie and Dotty fall silent as the giant ship comes closer. The horn emits a deafening blast as it pulls into the dock, and then sailors in dark blue uniforms and dixie cup caps bounce down the gangplank, lifting their arms in victory signs. Next come the officers, more sober-looking in khaki, and sporting big grins.

"There he is!" shouts Dotty, and she runs to greet Marsh.

And there, squinting into the sun as he searches the dock with his eyes, tall and handsome, is George. Flossie lets out a breath along with the tears that have been building, and she hurries to him. Enfolded in his arms, she cries in relief.

George pats her hair. "Aw, now, don't cry, honey."

"I was just so worried," she sobs.

"Well, we didn't end up going to Japan this time. We were in Alaska when the announcement came, so our ship didn't enter the battle. The battle was over."

"Thank goodness. Now you're here, and I hope you won't have to go out again before the baby comes."

"No, I think they're gonna let me stay for a while now." He pats her stomach. "And look at this big boy!" He beams. "Or girl!"

In the bungalow Flossie leads George around the small house to see the baby shower gifts from the other women and the folks at home in Pittsburgh—a crib in the baby's room, a bassinet, a pile of baby clothes. She picks up each cute little outfit and oohs and aahs, while George smiles indulgently. Then they sit down to a hearty meal of steak and potatoes with stewed tomatoes, Nannie's special recipe.

"And what's over there?" George asks, pointing to a pile of fabric on the credenza.

"Oh!" Flossie stands, maneuvering around her enormous bump. "I've been busy since you've been away," she says, and holds up a sun dress in a cheerful green and yellow print—gigantic lemons and lemon leaves. "I made this. I copied the pattern from the Neiman Marcus catalogue, and guess what!"

"What?"

"Dotty and I took a trip to Mobile—"

"Mobile? That's a long way from here. How did you get there?"

"Dotty had Marsh's car, and we managed to cover the gas. It only took a couple of hours. Anyway, there's a fabulous little dress shop there, and we went in. I had Dotty wear this, since I'm obviously a different size now, and the woman in the shop asked Dotty where she got it. Dotty said *I* designed and made it." Flossie smiles with pride. "The woman asked if I could make some more, and she would sell them!"

George gives a little laugh. "Now, didn't I tell you—you *are* an entrepreneur. Will you do it?"

"Of course, George! And I'm working on some more designs as well. I want to finish them before the baby comes, since I probably won't have much time after that." Eventually, she thinks, she can really do it. She can be a dress designer.

♪

As it turns out, Flossie doesn't have much time before she goes into labor. The next day it starts. "Ooh," she screams with the first few pains. "Help!"

"I'm right here," George says, and when they get to the hospital, he comes with her into the delivery room.

The pains keep coming. And the baby doesn't come. Flossie sobs and screams. "I'm going to die!"

"No, you're not, Flossie," says Al Jankowitz, the attending doctor. "This is normal labor, and soon you'll have a baby."

The attending nurse, whose nametag reads "Vivian," nods and pats her on the shoulder. "You'll be fine, Flossie."

Between labor pains, Flossie looks around for George. What is he doing over there in the corner? He looks a little green in the gills.

"George?"

"I'm here."

"Aagh!" she screams again.

Still, the baby doesn't come.

After five more hours, Flossie screams, "This is *not* normal labor!"

"Just a little longer than usual," says Dr. Jankowitz, but she notices he exchanges worried glances with the nurse and George. George looks worried, too. He's a new doctor, after all, and probably hasn't had a lot of experience with childbirth.

The labor goes on all night, without a respite for her, although George nods off in his chair in the corner. In the morning, Flossie, exhausted, keeps trying to push—this is harder than playing six sets of tennis in a row.

Then something falls on the floor with a loud plonk, and George is no longer visible.

Nurse Vivian disappears from Flossie's vision, too, and Dr. Jankowitz frowns.

"What is it?" Flossie gasps.

"Your husband fainted," he says.

"Oh, no!"

"But he's fine. Starting to revive now, just in time to meet his new baby! It's almost here!"

Flossie gives a final push, and the baby arrives.

"It's a boy!" George says in a feeble shout.

chapter 34

AULD LANG SYNE

Edgeworth, Pennsylvania, 1946

Flossie pushes the baby carriage along the sunny sidewalk under the maple trees. A few yellowed leaves drift and fall around her and the carriage, like blessings surrounding the mother and baby. Little Andy, now eighteen months, is finally sleeping.

On September 2, 1945, almost a year ago, Japan surrendered, and President Truman announced the war was over. After George came back from his battleship duty, Andy was born, and then George was transferred. They moved to the naval base in Oklahoma City, and after six months in Oklahoma, he was discharged. They came back to Pittsburgh.

This old-fashioned wicker contraption Nannie gave her is so conspicuous that it makes Flossie feel self-conscious. Originally the buggy was used for baby Roddy, a gift from the Mahaffey grandparents. Nannie used it again for Flossie and then lent it to Elizabeth for Sallie. Since then, it has been sitting in the barn in Edgewood gathering dust, and Nannie, reminiscing about the days as Flossie's substitute mother, insisted she take it.

Now Flossie and George have an apartment in Edge*worth*, a woodsy suburb of Pittsburgh on the flat plain of the Ohio River Valley. On the second floor of a brick duplex, the apartment overlooks a quiet street and is near George's new office in Ambridge, the steel mill town.

Thank heavens George wasn't sent out on a ship again after the baby came. Now they have a home and can start their new life and family.

Flossie pats her belly. She hopes it's a girl this time, and she prays for an easier labor than the two-day ordeal with Andy. Across the street, Flossie's new friend Mary-Ott waves as she wheels her two little ones in a double stroller. Mary-Ott assured her that the second birth is usually easier.

Flossie was not reassured. She herself was a second baby, and her mother died having her. Fear shoots through her chest, and her shoulders tense. Maple trees wave in the breeze, dappling the sunlight around her, and she remembers George will be assisting with the delivery. She lets out a breath. This gives her a safe feeling, despite George's fainting episode at Andy's birth. That became a joke with the other doctors on the base, who teased him. He was good-natured about it, though, and laughed along with them.

Flossie can't wait to start looking for a house, a real house. She's already talked to a real estate agent who found a few houses to show her in neighboring Sewickley, a pretty town, not too far from Ambridge. She and George can't afford to live in Sewickley Heights, of course, where the rich Pittsburgh bigwigs lives, but they will be comfortable on a doctor's income. Living in a small town will be a new experience, a new community. Flossie looks forward to making new friends like Mary-Ott.

George went to the office for a few hours this morning, and then they will drive to Edgewood to see the family. Nannie has been ill, but Elizabeth didn't say what the illness is. It couldn't be the arthritis, Flossie thinks; it sounded more serious than that. Whatever it is, hopefully Nannie will feel better when she hears about the new baby.

♪

The car bumps along over potholes as they drive past Schenley Park, through Squirrel Hill, and finally into Edgewood. Flossie breathes in the smell of home—shady avenues lined with stately houses, the Edgewood Country Club, where she learned to swim and play tennis with Hammie, and the gleaming old bricks of Lacrosse Street as they jolt and climb up the hill.

She winces. Should she have written to Hammie again, telling him about her marriage and baby Andy? But where was he? Was he even still alive? She winces again. She hadn't wanted to think about that, so she buried her guilt and didn't try to write.

♪

The day has turned cloudy, and as they walk to the door, a breeze carries a faint whiff of smoke. There's been talk in Pittsburgh of switching the coal-burning train engines to diesel to clean up the air, but that seems a long way off. Thank goodness Flossie and George live outside the city now, where the smoke won't affect the baby. At least the Pittsburgh smoke. There is smoke from the Ambridge mills, and Flossie is determined to buy a house far away from it, up in the hills.

Daddy steps out the door, his face glowing with a crinkly-eyed grin, and Elizabeth follows behind, rushing to pick up the toddler. Andy squirms and thrashes until Elizabeth puts him down, then squeals and runs when he sees Sallie's dog. Apollo, who is getting on in years, limps and barks but seems to take the toddler's frenetic energy in stride.

In the kitchen Nannie sits at the table with a plate of shortbread cookies in front of her. Flossie picks up the fidgeting child and takes a chair beside her grandmother. She breathes in the warmth and smell of the kitchen—the old wood of the green cabinets, the seasoned oak table, a whiff of pot roast from last night's dinner, and the feel of family, Nannie, Elizabeth, and Daddy sitting in their usual places, George standing behind them. Flossie hands a cookie to Andy, who smashes his face into it, and crumbs cascade over his mouth and shirt.

"Nannie, how are you feeling?"

Nannie's face is pale and dry, with more wrinkles than Flossie remembers. Nannie usually radiates energy. Now she really does look old, and her breathing sounds labored. She's always been thin, but now she looks even thinner, almost emaciated. And there's a grayish tint to her pale skin. "I'm fine," Nannie murmurs in a rasping whisper. No trace of her usual forthright delivery.

Behind Nannie, Elizabeth shakes her head and waves her hand, gesturing for Flossie not to talk about it.

She screws up her eyebrows. Why doesn't Elizabeth want her to ask? Flossie slumps in her seat. Nannie looks terrible.

Despite the rasping breaths, Nannie's face suddenly transforms into an ecstatic smile. Of course, Nannie has always been strict, but Flossie knows she has always loved her granddaughter. Sometimes that love breaks through the austere countenance like sun shining beneath a cloud, a bright surprise on a gloomy day. How could Flossie bear it if Nannie died? Life without the mother she has always known, the mother who has always been there.

Flossie sits up straight. *She* is a wife and mother now and has her own life to live. But this place, this point on the map, 159 Lacrosse Street—with Daddy, Nannie, Elizabeth, Roddy, and Sallie—this is still home.

Home is this kitchen, with the moss green cabinets, the color Elizabeth picked out and Daddy painted. Home is the worn linoleum floor, the trap door that goes down to the basement, the old refrigerator in the corner that Elizabeth still calls the "icebox," the kitchen table, so much homier than the formal table in the dining room. This is where Elizabeth announced she was pregnant with Sallie, where Roddy staggered in drunk one night and said he'd dropped out of school, but where, despite these life-changing upheavals, comfort and stability still prevail.

This whole house—the dining room with its tall windows and lace tablecloths, the living room with the horsehair sofa and high bay windows looking out on the line of poplars, the upstairs with Nannie's hulking old Victorian beds and wardrobes—this whole house resonates with the lives lived here.

Flossie loves her new life, her burgeoning new family, and can't wait to decorate a new house. The war made everything unstable; although, she admits to herself, she loved the excitement—living in Florida's cute little bungalow and then in Oklahoma City—but this house, this place, with its history and stability, this is her foundation, the root of her tree.

Elizabeth scurries around the kitchen, beaming at Flossie and Andy, her first grandchild. Elizabeth has always been her rock, backing her up when Nannie got too bossy and Daddy became unreasonable. Elizabeth brought both her dry humor and the note of compassion so needed in this family.

Flossie smiles as her eyes tear up. Really, she's had the love of two mothers.

The most important thing, now, is that she herself is a mother. And she has a new family. This new bond, the connection with George and Andy and the coming baby will always be there, another root in her tree.

Flossie soon learned that motherhood is not all cuddling and cooing and lullabies. She never imagined the work it takes to keep up with a child who is constantly running, jumping, grabbing, shouting, and being oppositional when she tries to stop him. With toddler Andy, she is tired most of the time.

Andy's first word was "no," and he employs it constantly. "No" to vegetables, "no" to being picked up, "no" to bedtime and to almost anything she suggests. Then he runs away, and she has to catch him before he pulls down whatever is in reach. Flossie is almost always worried and wonders if it's her worry that causes Andy's frantic pace or if it was the difficult birth. But when he's sleeping, he is so angelic, she falls in love with him again. And when he laughs, she laughs with delight.

In the doorway appears an awkward twelve-year-old with large brown eyes and a new perm in her long golden-brown hair. Sallie, a skinny girl in a green plaid dress that's already too short for her long legs, stares open-mouthed at the toddler. She clasps and unclasps her hands. "Can I hold him?" she whispers. Little Andy races around the kitchen, opening and closing cabinet doors with loud bangs.

"I don't know if he'll let you," says Flossie. "Here, try this." She reaches into her bag and hands Sallie a stuffed rabbit with long floppy ears. Sallie squats down and makes the bunny jump and hop while Andy laughs with delight.

Elizabeth walks around the table pouring coffee into cups. Her light brown hair, pulled back in a soft, immaculate bun, is now streaked with gray. When she puts down the coffee pot, she straightens and grins, smoothing down the front of her calico apron. "We have a surprise for you."

"Oh, what—"

A loud knock sounds on the door, and George goes to open it. In the doorway stands a young man, straight and tall, with blond hair in a crewcut and wearing a broad smile.

"Hammie!"

Flossie begins to jump up to greet him, then hesitates. A shot of fear runs through her chest. Or is it shame? She stopped writing to Hammie when she didn't hear from him after Pearl Harbor; she didn't even know if he received the ring she returned. She hadn't known whether he was dead or alive. What would he think about her marrying George? And what would George think of Hammie's presence? The guilt Flossie buried under the excitement about her new life now rises in her chest like a bolt of fear. She feels her whole body turn red.

Hammie brushes his hand over his stiff buzz cut and smiles that charming smile. "Hello there!" he exclaims, greeting the whole group.

"Y-you're home," Flossie stutters.

Elizabeth, sensing Flossie's distress, stands from her chair and limps to Hammie. "Come on in. And here, have a cup of coffee and a short-bread cookie." She pulls out a chair, and Hammie sits at the table.

Flossie notices his left hand and a wedding ring. She lets out a breath. "You're married?"

"Yes," he beams, "for a couple of months."

Sallie, still on the floor, shouts over a happy litany of loud no's from Andy. "What's your wife's name?"

"Her name is Ann, and we met in Pearl Harbor, where she was a nurse."

"Ooh," Nannie shudders. "That must have been horrible."

"Yes, it was," he says, "but it also brought out the best in some of us." He turns to Flossie. "And look at you, a new mommy, and"—he points to her stomach and gives a salute to George—"congratulations! On several counts."

George blushes and smiles sweetly as Flossie chokes back a sob and wipes her eyes. Her whole family is here, with George and Andy and even Hammie, and things are okay.

More than okay. She is home.

AUTHOR'S NOTE

Most of the characters and stories in this book are based on real people and events, although all are re-imagined, rearranged, and fictionalized.

Florence Rodkey was indeed a talented musician and was engaged to Ernest Landers (Phillip) before she married my grandfather, Ernest Craighead. She had tuberculosis and spent time at El Yeso Ranch as well as the Mont Alto Sanatorium. She died of ether pneumonia a day after my mother, Flossie, was born, when her first child, Rodkey (Roddy), was almost two.

The characters of Florence Rodkey's parents, brother, and sisters are based on family stories as well as my imagination. It is true that Florence's father, Robert Rodkey, lost part of an ear in the Civil War and spent time as a prisoner of war in a Confederate prison.

Florence was a suffragist and marched in the 1914 women's suffrage parade in Pittsburgh. Edith was a school principal in Oregon, Illinois, outside of Chicago; Ida was a teacher in Arizona; and Vance was a nurse. Bert, whom I met once or twice and fondly knew as Uncle Bert, became an economics professor at the University of Michigan and was a mentor to his nephew, my Uncle Roddy.

Florence's sister Sue was married to Harry Milligan and had four children. But with her fifth child, she, too, died in childbirth, and Vance then married Harry to care for the children (there's another story).

George Hayes, my father, was a naval flight surgeon stationed in Pensacola during World War II. I don't know the names of the ships he served on, nor their movements, so these are fictionalized (with apologies to military historians). After the war, he established a practice as a family physician, known as a general practitioner in the twentieth century.

My mother, Flossie, majored in costume design at Carnegie Institute of Technology (Carnegie Tech), now Carnegie Mellon University.

Though she never worked professionally as a dress designer, Flossie was a talented seamstress. She made clothes for herself and me and created some spectacular Halloween costumes for my brothers and me.

Elizabeth Whitmarsh Craighead was Flossie's stepmother and also my father's cousin. Her daughter, Sallie, has been my favorite aunt and role model.

Mary Craighead Brinton (Aunt Mary), Ernest's sister, was an important mother figure for the young Flossie throughout her life. She was my great aunt and a part of my childhood, too.

Nancy/Nannie Craighead was Ernest and Mary's mother and my great-grandmother. She died a month before I was born, and I was named after her.

El Yeso Ranch was and still is a ranch in New Mexico. In the early 1900s the DeGraftenreid family owned it and ranched there. I have used their real names here, though my account is completely fictional. I drew on delightful descriptions of the ranch life in my grandmother's letters as well as an account of the adventures by a young minister, Coe Haynes, who visited El Yeso in 1904. Haynes writes of a Mexican man named Manuel who worked on the ranch, but I don't know if he would still have been there in 1910.

Roddy, Flossie's brother, was originally an "America Firster," as was Nannie. He served in the Second World War with the 462nd Antiaircraft Artillery Automatic Weapons Battalion, 2nd Infantry Unit, which was part of the unit that liberated the Buchenwald Concentration Camp. This was a traumatic experience for Roddy that impacted the rest of his life. But he did "make something of himself," despite his father's dire warnings. Uncle Roddy finished his career in banking as the president and then chairman of the board of Detroit Bank and Trust. He and his wife, Carol, had three children close in age to my brothers and me, and we spent many happy vacations together.

Hammie Hamilton was a real person and a good friend of Flossie's from high school, but I knew nothing more about him, including whether he was ever a suitor. His character is completely fictional.

Helen Craighead was Flossie's cousin. She and her husband, George ("Jiggs") Park, founded and ran Hidden Valley, an inn and ski resort in Somerset, Pennsylvania. My brothers and I learned to ski at Hidden Valley along with Helen's children, our second cousins, and Flossie and

Helen both continued as enthusiastic skiers until they were in their eighties.

Helen's father, Gordy/Gordon Craighead served in World War I and sent letters home from the trenches. He married Gladys McKinnon, Aunt Gladys to me, and they had three children: Sonny, Helen, and Nancy.

Mrs. Doak was a real person and was Flossie's boss at her first job in a hospital gift shop. One of her granddaughters, Amy, was a friend of mine in high school, and I was in the creative writing club with her other granddaughter, Ann, who later became Annie Dillard.

SOURCES

The letters of Florence Rodkey, 1910–1915
An account of El Yeso Ranch in 1904, by Coe Hayne, NM GenWeb
    Project, Ethel Stears, 2005
The Fulton Family of Westmoreland County, Ernest Craighead, 1940
Ancestry.com
Family stories and memories

ACKNOWLEDGMENTS

My gratitude extends to my late grandfather, Ernest Craighead, who kept and treasured every letter he received from my grandmother Florence and researched, preserved, and annotated the Craighead family history in a time before the internet was invented. His scrapbooks, souvenir collections, and book, *The Fulton Family of Westmoreland County, Pennsylvania*, have been valuable sources for my research. If there are genes for writing style, I think I've inherited some, because I see a resemblance to my writing in the letters of Florence and the books of Ernest Craighead, my grandparents. With this book, I've enjoyed getting to know the grandmother I never knew, and my grandfather in a way I never did in his lifetime.

Many thanks to my scrupulous editor, Sarah Peachey, and to colleagues and writer friends who have cheered me on and also given great feedback through the years of this project: Tracey Enerson Wood, Sarah Angleton, Mary Chaffee, Carolyn Kleinman, Ruth Linnaea Whitney, Laura Delaplain, Ron Baard, John Karl, Mary Fillmore, Mary Harwood, Joan Zipko, Zoe Fowler, and my brother and fellow writer, K.C. Hayes. Thanks also to colleagues in many workshops and conferences and at the Burlington Writers' Workshop. Thanks to my talented cover designer, Lynn Andreozzi. And gratitude to the excellent and supportive crew at Sunbury Press: Lawrence Knorr, Katie Cressman, Nicole Browne, and John Jordan.

DISCUSSION QUESTIONS FOR
PENNSYLVANIA LOVE SONG

1. You were introduced to two women in the story, Florence and Flossie. They are mother and daughter. Do they accurately reflect the times they live in? Why?

2. Which of the two women, Florence or Flossie, did you relate to most? Why?

3. Does one or both of the two women resemble a female relative in your family? Would you have chosen one or both of these women to be a friend of yours? Why?

4. What personality qualities do Florence and Flossie have that you feel are admirable?

5. Was Flossie's father right or selfish to not share Florence's letters with Flossie when she was a young girl?

6. Which is better—to have an idealized vision of a dead parent or to know the full truth, including the flaws, about a dead parent?

7. Does a marriage based on romantic love have a better chance of succeeding than a marriage chosen for economic security? Is this more or less true now than in the past?

8. Do you believe in love at first sight? Do you believe a good marriage starts with a solid friendship? Why?

9. Flossie's father remarries after Florence dies. Compare Florence and Elizabeth. How are they and Ernest's two marriages similar or different?

10. How much should children know about their parents' courtship and their parents' previous loves before their parents married? Does this type of knowledge hurt or help the children find appropriate marriage partners of their own?

11. The title of the novel includes the word "love song." Of the couples in the book, who had the most romantic love story? Why?

12. Do you know the "love stories" in your family? Do you think it is important to share these and pass them on? Why?

ABOUT THE AUTHOR

Nancy Hayes Kilgore, a Pennsylvania native, is the author of three other novels, *Bitter Magic* (Milford House Press, 2021), *Wild Mountain* (Green Writers Press, 2017), and *Sea Level* (RCWMS, 2011). Her writing has won the Vermont Writers Prize and a Pushcart Prize nomination. She has published in literary magazines and on Vermont Public Radio. Nancy is a graduate of the Radcliffe Writing Seminars; she holds a master of divinity degree and a doctorate in pastoral psychotherapy. Dr. Kilgore is a psychotherapist, former parish pastor, and leads workshops on creative writing and spirituality. She lives with her husband, the artist Jess Kilgore, in Vermont.